This book is a work of fiction. All characters, names, locations, and events portrayed in this book are fictional or used in an imaginary manner to entertain, and any resemblance to any real people, situations, or incidents is purely coincidental.

LACE AND BLADE 2

Edited by Deborah J. Ross

Copyright © 2009 by Norilana Books and Deborah J. Ross

All Rights Reserved.

Cover Paintings:

"The Accolade," [detail] by Edmund Blair Leighton (1853-1922).
"Landscapes with Wild Beasts" [detail] by Roelandt Jacobsz Savery, 1629.

Cover Design Copyright © 2009 by Vera Nazarian

ISBN-13: 978-1-934648-99-5
ISBN-10: 1-934648-99-X

FIRST EDITION
Trade Paperback Edition

February 14, 2009

A Publication of
Norilana Books
P. O. Box 2188
Winnetka, CA 91396
www.norilana.com

Printed in the United States of America

ACKNOWLEDGMENTS

Introduction © 2008 by Deborah J. Ross
"More in Sorrow" © 2009 by Rosemary Hawley Jarman
"Dragon Wind" © 2009 by Mary Rosenblum
"The Crow" © 2009 by Diana L. Paxson
"The Biwa and the Water Koto" © 2009 by Francesca Forrest
"Trial by Moonlight" © 2009 by Robin Wayne Bailey
"The Pillow Boy of General Chu" © 2009 by Daniel Fox
"Miss Austen's Castle Tour" © 2009 by Sherwood Smith
"Rent Girl" © 2009 by Traci N. Castleberry
"The Baroness' Ball" © 2009 by Pauline Zed
"The Sixth String" © 2009 by Elisabeth Waters
"Comfort and Despair" © 2009 by Tanith Lee
"Writ of Exception" © 2009 by Madeleine E. Robins

Original Anthologies from Norilana Books

Clockwork Phoenix

Clockwork Phoenix 2 *(forthcoming)*

Lace and Blade

Marion Zimmer Bradley's Sword and Sorceress XXII

Marion Zimmer Bradley's Sword and Sorceress XXIII

Warrior Wisewoman

Warrior Wisewoman 2 *(forthcoming)*

Sky Whales and Other Wonders *(forthcoming)*

Clothesline World *(forthcoming)*

Lace and Blade 2

Leda
an imprint of
Norilana Books

www.norilana.com

Lace and Blade 2

Edited by
Deborah J. Ross

CONTENTS

INTRODUCTION   11
   by Deborah J. Ross

MORE IN SORROW   13
   by Rosemary Hawley Jarman

DRAGON WIND   37
   by Mary Rosenblum

THE CROW   61
   by Diana L. Paxson

THE BIWA AND THE WATER KOTO   85
   by Francesca Forrest

TRIAL BY MOONLIGHT   100
   by Robin Wayne Bailey

THE PILLOW BOY OF GENERAL SHU   124
   by Daniel Fox

MISS AUSTEN'S CASTLE TOUR   146
   by Sherwood Smith

RENT GIRL 175
    by Traci N. Castleberry

THE BARONESS' BALL 213
    by Pauline Zed

THE SIXTH STRING 229
    by Elisabeth Waters

COMFORT AND DESPAIR 237
    by Tanith Lee

WRIT OF EXCEPTION 261
    by Madeleine E. Robins

INTRODUCTION

by Deborah J. Ross

It was a joy and a privilege to put together the first *Lace and Blade*, and this second volume has brought me additional, unexpected delights. I am grateful to those authors who trusted me with yet another of their creations, and am thrilled to present newer voices as well.

But more than the specifics of the contributors, editing this second volume allowed me to experience the richness of possibility in the type of elegant romantic fantasy. What I had not realized was the sense of tidal current or musical theme and variation, in both concept and incarnation.

For the first volume, I had received not one but two stories featuring Spanish highwaymen, each so different and compelling that I included both of them.

This time, the spirit moved to the East: two Chinese general stories! Two Asian musical instrument stories! At the same time, I present here splendid tales of imaginary kingdoms, of Brazilian magic alive in Paris, of the Chinese Treasure Fleet, of a ball in Latvia and a castle in Transylvania, of love conventional and transcendent, of dragons and werewolves, romantic trysts, villainy and sacrifice, fulfillment and redemption.

Our hearts tremble with yearning for connection, for enchantment. We open ourselves to the beloved, the other, the known, the impossible, and become more fully human. The universe deepens, resonant with the music of endless varieties of love. . . .

Deborah J. Ross
Boulder Creek CA
September 2008

MORE IN SORROW

by Rosemary Hawley Jarman

(for John Kaiine)

Rosemary Hawley Jarman was born in Worcester, England and came to fame in 1971 with her novel, *We Speak No Treason*. Reprinted many times, the book's hero is the much maligned King Richard III. It sold 30,000 copies in its first week of publication, and gained her the prestigious Author's Club Silver Quill for best first novel, while in the US she was nominated as a Daughter of Mark Twain. Further equally successful novels followed, also an illustrated account of the Battle of Agincourt. She is the author of many short stories, and her first fantasy novel, *The Captain's Witch*—soon to be re-issued by Norilana Books—is set in the mythical realm of Taratamia, the Opal Kingdom. She lives in an antique stone cottage between sea and mountain in West Wales, where she is working on a sequel.

If unfulfilled love can sustain contentment, then I was as contented as any man could be. For yearning brings in its train a tormented ecstasy, and in dreams everything is possible.

I had nothing to grumble about, certainly. I was twenty-five, in superb health, surrounded by good friends, and I had lately been promoted in the élite guard of the royal house of Taratamia. Admiring my new uniform in my private quarters, I was, I confess, full of myself. I struck a pose and addressed the tall looking glass formally.

"Good evening, sir. Are you not *Captain* Rudek Palzani, of the seventh Rose detachment of the Red Royals cavaliers? What a splendid fellow! I approve the moustache."

I admit it was very lustrous, honey gold, its ends subtly tipped skyward. "Excellent eyes, too, sir," my *alter ego* fulsomely continued. "Richly blue, and you are tall and spare, and toned of muscle; that opal ring you wear for the royal house becomes the elegant, dangerous hand of a courtier, swordsman and warrior...."

You conceited, idiotic and shamelessly egotistic young man! thought I, *all these things you may be, but I only hope she still thinks so as well....*

There was pride in my clowning, and yet always a touch of the self who had been told often by father and brothers: "You will never amount to anything." My inexcusable bragging was rooted in the long past.

But the manner in which *she* had looked at me! She had found something in me to warm her, and far more than that. I swear it, in the name of the Lion.

I was stationed in Tam, the royal capital of glorious Taratamia, the Opal Kingdom. Tam was judged the loveliest city in the universe, with its marble streets and the river Milesa flowing under seven bridges west, to a millrace and Avatal Bay. The royal palace was pitched high among floral plateaux, overlooked by the gigantic Lion of Stone, effigy of our godhead.

I turned from the mirror and my image of scarlet coat, gold lacings and glassy boots. Respectfully I buckled on my captain's sword, a fine honed weapon decorated with lion-masks. All the while her face, her name, glowed in my mind. Incomparable Michalla, and, I feared, out of my reach. My first real love, a craving love from first glance. Yes, they all say that, but in my case it was true.

At first I thought she was a slim youth, for I saw her in the Great Court of Arms where only the élite swordsmen are allowed to practise. Michalla was nobly born, obliquely linked to the royal house; my family too had the right connections, but whatever my estate it could have altered nothing of how I felt.

The Great Court has a fresco of suns and the Lion round the walls, and a long chequered floor. Within this male preserve, Michalla was dueling with a fiery wiry man called Maxith with twenty years of bladework behind him. And by the gods! She was good. She was exceptionally—I might say supernaturally gifted: I saw her use her filigree-pommelled rapier like a hornet's sting, with a pirouette of a parry then a nasty thrust to Maxith's quilted breast which stumbled him toe over toe in his fighting slippers. The bout must have been nearing its end; he saluted her with his weapon then bowed deeply. "The final concession, Madame, once again. Congratulations."

My Michalla laughed, and flung back her head, and the silver net over her coal-black hair floated loose. A shining tumult unfurled. "Yes, enough for today," she said, removing her face guard. Maxith bowed again and left, handing their dainty lethal weapons to the sword cutler's servant.

She turned and looked straight at me. She was a small woman, the top of her head would come level with my collarbone. Her flawless face, shaped like an ivy leaf, had a pearl flush from the duel. Huge grey-green eyes she had, and a full mouth red as a battle-flag. She wore tight breeches, lilac silk over slender muscled thighs. Her jacket was shaped to a waist my hands could cup, and her small bold breasts were framed by a foam of lace.

My heart was pounding, my face was hot. Yet she liked what she saw, for she came forward smiling, pushing back a vagrant black tress from her cheek. And my voice burst out louder than intended.

"You were marvellous," I said, then hastily: "with the blade, I mean."

And she, teasing me: "Is that all? Am I, myself, not marvellous?"

My wits almost deserted me. "What?" I managed. "Madame, *you* are more than marvellous. Never in my life have I seen—"

She cut in quickly. "Why haven't we met? What is your name?" She was charmingly, innocently direct.

I told her my name. She came dizzyingly nearer, and her skin was as perfect as a baby's, her eyes as clear as green glass. And I found myself dumb, as she placed one hand like a white star, on my sleeve. And all at once I wanted to draw that small lithe body against me, arms crushing out her breath, take her—in fact, openly take her there and then on the lozenged floor of the Great Court, while another part of me longed to kneel and praise her feet with kisses.

I know she felt similarly moved. For she said "Rudek" softly, stood on tiptoe still holding my sleeve and raised her face to look deep into my eyes. There was more to this. She knew my past and perhaps my future. She knew me to my bones.

Then into this time of recognition a rude intrusion: a gruff, angry cough.

Ah. Here was Daddy, and he had a moustache to frighten children.

Father was not pleased. He had come to take her home, out of danger from such as I. The carriage waited outside, the horses clattered their hooves; the moment was lost and broken.

"Miclushka. Who is this young man?"

I bowed as humbly as possible, while she reassured him. The vast grey crescents about Father's mouth bristled, as I described my unblemished character (true), my abstemious nature (not quite so true) and the moustache finally settled into an unwilling serenity. We sparred in formal courteous phrases. Michalla gazed at me, dare I say tenderly, then back at her father almost as fondly, and finally the longed-for words came from the stern old man.

"This is my only daughter, sir. I suppose you wish, like many others, for permission to call."

"I should be deeply honoured, sir."

I noticed Michalla's little foot tapping impatiently, while she frowned. The frown made her more adorable. Father's next words were uncomforting.

"I shall have to give the matter my full consideration. I must consult the Almanac for your pedigree."

I was rather annoyed.

"I assure you it will not disappoint, sir. I am an honourable man. The Regiment would vouch for that."

He growled, and frowned. In his case, the frown did not improve him. He said, "We shall see. We shall be going to the lakes shortly for my wife's health. A month, or maybe longer. Your visit may not be possible before we leave. I promise nothing. Now we will bid you good day. Come, daughter."

And that was it. Unbelievably, eyes locked on mine, she was as bereft as I.

Now, however, I was going out with friends, one of whom was a prince of the blood. I would have traded it all for that entrée into my beloved's house.

I had to shelve my yearning. Prince Lepo always insisted we should be happy. I ran downstairs into the street, where the setting sun poured shadows on the barracks square.

As soon as I arrived I guessed it was to be a Girl Night. A whimsical game, a Prince Leporet diversion. Lord Carne unbolted the door of the princely apartment. No servants, no guard. Tonight we were the prince's security.

"You're a mite late, Rudek. Highness is about to robe."

In Lepo's chamber, the monumental bed wore silk and wolfskins, with a score of crested satin pillows. At least a hundred beauties had been between these sheets, and not one bore a grudge when her tour of duty was done, for everyone loved Lepo. He was ridiculously generous, kind, funny and wild. An older prince was the royal heir; Lepo was the royal clown.

On tables loaded with silver and crystal, fizz was overrunning the necks of slim jade bottles.

"Rudek!" he cried jubilantly. "Felicitations on your promotion. Well done, laddie." He waved his goblet in salute. Bare-chested, he sat before a glass, while one of his friends struggled to drape him in startling mustard silk trimmed with magenta feathers.

"Can you lift your butt, Highness? You're sitting on the top of the gown."

"I'll do his makeup," said Carne.

"No, Rudek does it best. You fix my hair."

Carne opened a coffer. A profusion of wigs in terrifying colours burst forth. They were built up like cumulus clouds, foaming like fountains. Ice blonde, purple, carnelian, and a glorious fall of ink-black hair, probably a peasant girl's one treasure, yet a poignant reminder of my love. And then my riotous imagination saw her naked. There would be a soft ebony heart between her slender thighs . . . now my body betrays me. Obviously!

The prince missed nothing. He let out a loud guffaw.

"By the Lion's holy tail, I've given Rudek a hard-on! And I haven't even got my bosoms up yet. Come on, Carne! Sort them out."

Carne began stuffing wads of swansdown inside the prince's bodice.

"That's not right," said a laconic voice. Captain Tallis— now *there* was a warrior—sat on a chest, swinging his booted legs. "The right one's higher than the left. And it's fatter."

He came off the chest and jabbed his hand inside the bodice, pushing Carne aside. "There."

"You're so rough, Tallis," complained Lepo. "Apologise."

Tallis shook his head, smiling. He was an austere, enigmatic man, a fabled leader. He owned a Lionsword, reputed to be so ancient it was imbued with enchantments. I was sceptical about such matters.

"Hairpiece now, Carne," ordered the prince.

He became a stunning redhead with a band of stars across his brow. His dilated eyes were rimmed with soot and pearl. I applied a subtle rouge. "Don't make me look like a whore," he murmured.

Jewelled, he swayed from the room between his escort, an overgrown lily in a field of mustard and valerian.

"The Old Town, first."

It was dangerous after dusk. Once leaving the marble precincts of the palace quarter, it was a chain of branched cobbled ways. The upper walls crouched inward, stifling light. A sharp corner plunged us into the main alley. There was only room for us to walk in line across the street, keeping Lepo in our midst. *We must be mad*, I thought, my hand on my sword-hilt. *We could be bringing him home on a hurdle.*

Yobs and yokels squeezed themselves against walls. Eyes bulged like poached eggs.

"Pardon, princess, pardon, my lords."

"Outta the way, Jack Tanner, quality comin' through." At the Thirsty Toad, an amphibian was displayed on the inn sign. Within, they were carousing on benches, setting terriers to fight for money, and drinking with dedication. In a sudden silence, Lepo gloriously came among them, and we arrayed him on a settle. Rough wine was sped to our table.

We raised smeary mugs. "Madame, your health."

He loved this charade. His ardour for women was undeviating, so there was only one explanation. Silk on the body, red lips, high heels. He was curious to know the mystery of women in the eyes of men.

The next tavern stood in an alley which forked right and left at its end. The roofs closed in on the blackness of oblivion.

The sight of this pit seemed to breed a small frenzy in Lepo, and Tallis and I restrained him. We were becoming edgy. In the inn, there were a few riotous songs, someone snored like a hog behind a sideboard, and a couple of Red Royals lieutenants saluted us. Whispers: "Who is she? What a peach, looks familiar."

We were all drinking sparingly. But our prince was throwing them back. We'd come upon good wine, an import from Karlinkis in the Pearl Realm down south. After a small measure, the world seemed slightly to shift. . . .

Men were gazing at Lepo. Bored, he turned with uninterest from their hunger. We moved on.

We were almost at the black junction of the ways. Lepo drew away from us.

"You're not going down there, Highness."

"Nothing's happening," said the prince petulantly. "Last time I had six proposals, one was of marriage. Just stay right behind me."

Next instant he'd gone, into the pitchy way where not even a star shone.

There were sounds, Lepo's wild laughter, then a man's deep voice, cursing vilely, and silence. We brought the man out in short order, his lust pathetically quelled. More stunned than angry, now.

"A man," he said. "A great big man in a frock."

Lepo howled, happy tears ruining his maquillage.

The man wrenched free of us and fled up towards the lighted tavern. Lepo, still laughing, sat down on the cobbles. "I'm tired now. Dear friends, take me home."

As we left the alley behind, something—I know not what—caught my attention and I glanced back into the black maw. A figure was there, motionless. A slim man, even taller than the prince, with long hair and a sheathed sword at his waist. The pommel gave off one sparkle, like a turned gem. And the man stood within his own light. He had come from darkness. He was a piece of lit silence.

His gaze was unerringly fixed on me, with a deep and determined concentration. In that impossible light, I could even see his eyes. Ripe, olivine, but with red in the depths as if a torch burned at the bottom of a pure well.

I turned to Carne. "Who's that?' I said.

We both looked back at the empty spot where the figure had been.

రుఇఎఏ

There had always been bandits in the High Tiranian mountains south of the city. For generations, they had come down over Knife Pass to raid the villages on the yellow plain. They rode rough ponies and stole good horses and young women. It had become a part of military training to hunt them, but the mountains made them elusive. Their sporadic forays were looked on as something as inevitable as the weather.

Lord Carne and I had seen the prince to bed. We walked back to the barracks under a blazing white moon floating among the giant lilac and linderella trees and shimmering on pale stone walls. We crossed the seventh bridge. Below, the river sparkled with points of light as it rushed down to the millrace.

Carne, leaning to look over the parapet, said, "Some news came in today. They're becoming ambitious. They've a big leader called Bearfoot, fancies himself bandit king. The General thinks retribution is due. There's to be a nice serious scrap. They'll need a useful captain." His eyes gleamed at me. I thought suddenly of those other eyes, that turned out not to be there at all.

"Well, it won't be me," I said. "I've only been out there twice."

"You never know," said Carne. "Damned good warrior, you are."

We walked on. The moon was nearly day-bright, and on the blossom-hung walls, black shadows danced. To my left, one suddenly loomed tall, flickered and sprang. Up above something bent the frail branches. The shadow slid down the wall, steadying into a cruciform shape, as if a sword had been plunged point first into the ground. Without warning, the misery of wanting Michalla gripped me.

"I'm in love," I said. "As never before."

Carne said: "The Great Court's free most evenings. Will you practise tomorrow?"

"With pleasure. At the seventh hour."

"Don't be late."

I dreamed of her. She led me smiling to her bedchamber. I was making love to her, yet some sadness halted the act before it had begun. I dreamed of lying between her thighs, kissing the soft black heart of fur that she had threaded with diamonds, but it changed into a cluster of dark dead leaves blown away by the wind.

I had the foul taste of hopelessness in my mouth. I knew now I should never have her, the dream had told me. Lord Moustache would never let me near her. My father's words came again: "The boy will never amount to anything."

I looked forward to crossing blades with Carne, sweating out my melancholy in the Great Court.

After the seventh hour, Carne had not arrived. The evening had turned to the purplish warning of storm. I walked the length of the Court, marking the lozenges on the floor. I leaned my brow against the far wall. A sharp thunder split my nerves like a knife. That was the moment when I turned and saw him again.

Beautiful he was.

The radiance seen in the pitch black alley was muted, yet it still lifted the thunderous gloom and limned every feature, so that I saw him in his sublime perfection. Very tall, slender, almost fragile, with rich gold hair, the red gold seen in the most ancient coin of the East; it dressed his shoulders, covering his neck and back like folded wings.

Slowly he began to come to me, treading the tiles on his long light feet, and again I saw the eyes of dark olive with the tiny warming fire in the deep cold well. Eyes of a saint, a lover, a victim of love.

I stood against the wall, where his eyes had nailed me.

His voice seemed to come from someplace apart, although his lips moved gracefully. He came walking on, deliberate, almost soundless, and stopped.

"My name is Luce," the lips said, though the voice was thrown back from whence he had come.

And now I could smell him. Fresh, hot, musk-sweet man smell, and even semen, as evanescent as a blown feather . . . yes. I sniffed, and the faint, bitterly exciting odour was in my nostrils, my brain. His eyes endured on mine.

My bones became wax, under that gaze.

"How I love you," he said.

His hand, long delicate lily, moved to his groin.

Fear of the foreign grabbed me. He was unbuckling; his eyes shone dark red, they left mine and I could look down. He had freed his sword from its belt; that was all.

It was a fair weapon indeed, not like the sabre or the rapier or even the epée, but something perhaps hammered in an angelic forge, so frail and clever was its character. There was a fine diamond set into the hilt.

"Show me your sword, Captain," he said, softly and tenderly. "Let us compare."

His scent grew stronger; it was now like the almond scent of the gorse blossom. My eyes closed as if a hand pressed on the lids. I saw blackness.

He had made us naked together. I felt his slim taut body, his hard silky member risen against me, and my essence burst forth like a haemorrhage.

I opened my eyes. He had not moved. He stood, still clothed, a fair distance away. But inside my garment was the evidence: a slick of wasted seed, and I was trembling.

"Give yourself to me," he whispered.

I shook my head.

"I would never hurt you."

In all these moments I had been unable to utter a word. He said: "Believe me. It is not so different from what you know. Only far, far sweeter."

Oh, he was a seducer.

Tears in eyes, now. Beautiful eyes, wet olives, the fire unquenched.

He was also a phantasm, and I knew I must be ill.

Yet again, he was real. His burning flesh had been sweet as cream.

"Meet me," he said. "Meet me on the third bridge. I will take you to my home. It is not far. I will take you to paradise. I will fill you with honey. You will taste of my gold. You will weep with joy in my embrace. Tomorrow."

"No," I said. "Not tomorrow. Not ever."

"In three days then." The soft voice was fading away. "I will love you like no other could. I will be on the third bridge, at the tenth hour."

Oh, he was a seducer.

I did not even remember seeing him leave the Court, only some of the light went out of it, and a storm broke with great ferocity. Carne never came, which was as well.

On the third bridge, at the tenth hour. In three days' time, he had said.

I should never see Michalla again.

And what harm, from such beauty? He could not force me into any activity without my consent. And I wanted above all to examine the strange frail sword, the thin strong blade with the jewel.

Then came something terrible.

I was riding back to quarters at the head of my suite, in the rear of a mounted detachment from another of the Red companies. We had had much rainfall after the storm, and the river Milesa was in full spate. We were approaching the last of the seven bridges before turning for the barracks. Behind me, the cadets were on foot and the mounted detachment had gone ahead. No one else noticed what I saw in the water.

At first I thought it was an animal, then realised it was a struggling boy, about six years old. He was holding on desperately to a stone projection under one pier of the bridge. His hair was plastered to his face, his eyes forced shut by the water. Now and then, he sank and thrashed about and surfaced, each time a little weaker. The river roiled about him, but he continued doggedly to grip the stonework. Someone was leaning far over the parapet above, a long pole in hand, a saviour come to hook the child out like a fish. I recognised beautiful Luce, red-gold hair streaming down, slender fluent body hanging low in an effort to reach the child. Then, while our company trotted swiftly by, I saw the horrifying truth.

The tall man was using the point of the pole to strike at the boy's hand, prodding and jabbing until the water turned bloody, and the fingers began to weaken. The boy's face sank beneath the flood and rose with a noiseless cry. The point of the pole stabbed viciously; the hand let go at last. The current sucked at the child and spat him out. He whirled and vanished and the millrace had him.

Beautiful Luce stood up on the bridge. He was laughing without a sound, mouth stretched wide, as at the best joke in the world. He convulsed, clasping himself, bending double with mirth. Then our company turned the corner and he was lost to my sight.

I am certain he did not know I had witnessed this. He had been far too absorbed in a cruelty that was as casual as that of a man drowning kittens. I felt deep sorrow, and guilt, as if somehow I had been a party to his awful act.

I could tell no one about it. Even when Carne came, bright with a message, my joy was tempered. "I told you so," he said, helping himself from my decanter. "The General's sending word today. They're saying some damn good things about you. Just the man to whip Bearfoot, and so on."

There was to be a war council, and then a crack detachment of Red Rose Royals would hunt the bandit chieftain down. Under my command.

"You'll doubtless get a medal afterwards," said Carne. Eventually my spirits began to lift at the prospect of major action. I had seven days in which to bring my people up to peak performance. I knew just how to do it.

They were good men; the cavalry rode like demons and the foot soldiers would charge through flame on command. After three days of intensive training. I was so confident I dismissed the troops well before dusk. I intended to fulfill the assignation of the tenth hour.

It would have been easy to break the appointment, but I wanted to show my honour, to let Luce see that his ways were, in the most moral sense, not mine. This summer night, there was not a soul abroad. As I approached the third bridge, I thought for a moment he had not come. And then he morphed out of the fading sunset, enhancing it with his own radiance. He seemed to be on fire. When he saw me coming his face flamed with joy. He held out his arms.

I halted at what I hoped was a safe distance.

"My beloved," he said, in the soft voice like an echo. The sweet man-smell of him came again to permeate my skin.

"Let us not delay, not a moment longer," he said. "There is so much I want to teach you, my beloved."

He came nearer, and I stepped back off the bridge on to the road. He towered above me on the curve of the bridge, one long pale hand on his sword-hilt, which I now saw was hung with tassels like braids of filamented gold.

I was a professional warrior, an officer, yet he made me tremble.

I said: "I am afraid I cannot see you again. Ever."

I was looking down at the road. Above my head, I heard him laugh gently. He said: "Of course you can. Why else are you here?"

"I was curious to see your sword. That is all."

He laughed again. A darker, knowing laugh.

"Oh, you shall see my sword. I promise you. You shall see everything. Now, let us go to my home before night comes." His smile glittered.

I could command men. I could command this.

"No, I have told you. I shall not meet you again. That is all."

His smile vanished. Large tears began to gather in his eyes, the fiery little spark in their darkness moved, flames under dark water.

"You are angry with me, beloved."

His tears threw me into chaos. And even now I was so shaken by his crime that I couldn't speak of it. The mere mention would defile me.

"It is," I said clearly, that he might understand, "more in sorrow than in anger."

He came down off the bridge and without even seeming to move, placed himself behind me, barring my path. I whirled to face him. He looked down at me musingly.

"My love," he said, hand caressing the sword's jewelled pommel. "My fine soldier. You look so pretty in your new uniform. Sweet boy."

This was mockery, experienced. I suddenly knew he was, awesomely, far older than I had thought him. I watched his hand, alert.

"No," he said. "I would not draw a weapon on you. You already know that I need only touch you with my mind."

Night was coming down, fast. I put up my hand at him and he stepped aside. I walked away quickly. I did not turn round, but I heard his voice, fading under the sound of the racing river.

"Little Rudek," he said. "My darling. Now you are dead."

ଓଃଊଃଋଊଃ

Once again, my mind was refreshed by the oath I had taken to fight for the Opal Kingdom. Even if the fight was to be against some inbred tribe with pretensions, it was a day to seize. I was excited by my first real command, proud of my turnout, and my horse, a swift fighting bay, was the best. A clear day for our shining, tough company: flowing Lion-banners, pennoncelles undulating as if they swam in air, mounts and men and archers in top order. Seasoned sergeants in charge of my flanks. And all as quiet as any disciplined army can move, coming down over Knife Pass on to the yellow plain.

I had sent out scouts and knew what Bearfoot was doing. They had recently despoiled a village and were celebrating. Drunk, they were dangerous, but off guard. They still had hideous weaponry; cutlasses, spiked maces, stone clubs and crossbows. For their revels they were using the old gold mine workings, but Bearfoot's main camp where he lived with his warriors was a little way west up the pass, and it was there he would be returning. I had a keen young lieutenant riding with me. After our stealthy descent to the plain I was certain Bearfoot had no inkling of our presence.

"When d'you think they'll move out, Captain?"

I said: "He'll want to get back to his manor before dusk. As soon as we see him appear we charge and cut him off before the pass. Any stragglers can be taken by our flanks in a pincer. All of you only have to wait for my signal."

MORE IN SORROW

I had spread us out among the rock outcrops and barrows of the ancient plateau. The archers had longbows, the spears were wielded by hill-men on fast ponies. There was my proud cavalry troop. I had assessed this manoeuvre with precision.

I nodded encouragingly to the boy bugler, who lobbed a preparatory wad of spit at the ground. My heart began to beat a fraction faster. Had I known that the General was following my campaign from one of the higher canyons I might have been more nervous, especially as with him, acting as an observer, was the legendary Captain Tallis, with a contingent of Red Royals.

I whispered to the lieutenant: "Pass the word. Nothing moves before my signal. Not one horse or man."

The orders went down the line. They looked so good, my men.

The sun was westering, building shadows under the big rocks but it was still quiet. The horses' jingling and snorting was muted on the little dry wind.

I might be killed. A hero!

I shared a drop of water from the lieutenant's canteen. The minutes went on. I had no idea how long this attrition was lasting, but it seemed now like a dream, where everything has been taken care of long ago. Within the next half hour, I thought, it will all be over. *Don't be too confident*, said a strange voice in my head, and then, alarmingly: *"The boy will never amount to anything."*

From the foot of the mountain arose a great jubilant roar, almost inhuman. Following came bursts of laughter, not like the merriment of Lepo and his friends, but so crude and raucous it could have carried its own smell—of bad drink and carcasses and blood and the wounded viscera of the raped. Bearfoot's people had had their party. This was confirmed when a scout, wriggling like a serpent through dry yellow grasses caught my stirrup and whispered.

"He's coming out. And others after him."

The lieutenant's leg nudged mine. "Soon now?" he whispered. The little bugler clenched his fist round silver. I had my men deployed, static as chess pieces. I gazed towards the cave and saw Bearfoot.

He's more a troll than anything. Enormous, his head grazes the cave roof. He fills the opening. He was roaring, belching some foulness at others of his kind who shoved past him to get to the air, and he lurched, cursing them as they emerged in droves. He wore a bearskin, totem of the tribe, and thongs on his massive legs. His filthy hair streamed to his waist, and in his hand the skull of some unfortunate foe served as a drinking cup.

Now. This for Taratamia. Bearfoot begins to waddle west where I know the pincer movement waits on my command. The sergeants will not stir without it.

This is my day.

The lieutenant was waiting. The bugler's eyes rolled, the horn an inch from his lips. Now. The moment has come.

I could not move. I could not speak.

I could not lift my sword.

I could not lift a finger.

My horse shifted under me, distressed.

The lieutenant began harshly, urgently whispering at my side.

Bearfoot grinned and pranced at the heel of the mountain.

"Sir! Will you give the order! Sir!"

I could not stir one molecule, one atom, one cell, one eyelash. My blood was stilled. I was without form, and void.

I was breathing, but only that. Dead, I breathed.

಄಄಄

From the high barred window, I could see the cadets drilling in the square below. I stood against the wall. At first, it had been difficult for me to lie down on the cot; I had forgotten how to bend my legs. My servant came in and out. He fussed around, changing my clothes, showing me how to wash when I had forgotten. Day had rolled over into night more than once.

"The adjutant will be visiting you soon, sir."

I could not answer. I dared not try.

I was in civilian clothes. The prison was very quiet; jackdaws rattled about on the windowsill outside, and distantly I heard prisoners shouting for their lawyers, or to be let out.

There were vast blanks in my recall. It was not like being drunk, the aftermath of which I had known and recovered from quickly. This was more like an amnesia of the soul.

Gradually I became able to speak and hear and almost understand.

I drank water, but did not touch the food they brought me. I was beginning to know that something terrible had occurred, something that would rebound not only on my own honour, but on the whole of my beloved homeland. When I closed my eyes, the hideous troll-face of Bearfoot came close, as if he were in the cell with me and with it a rush of garbled memory, and I began to talk. I did more than talk, I raved for hours and in the end they sent two of the medical corps, who said I could be heard in the square. Their potions gave me sleep—and awful dreams of being trapped in a cave with Bearfoot who was preparing a pot to roast me in, and I woke, in a state.

"You were shouting again, sir."

They brought sugar rolls, fruit and coffee. My clothes were hanging on me. I took a small piece of food. I cannot describe the disgusting taste—troll excrement might come close to it. I have seldom wept, but now the griefs of my life whirled out of me, like the drowning child in the river.

I wept because I had worked for my promotion; I wept for my arrogance, and for the men who had doubtless met death through my failed leadership. If I were to be court martialled and hanged, it would be just. Better that, than to be invalided out for some mental aberration. I was no coward, and yet I wept for the cowardice that was making me weep.

Was it treason?

Did they count it cowardice?

Did I have a seizure of some kind? Something not unknown in the field, even among great commanders?

The debates were going on, out of my knowledge, away from my sight.

I asked how long I had been imprisoned. There were more uncomfortable places in which to die. My cell was for officers and had comfort of a sort.

"How long?"

"Days, sir. You've been rather ill. The adjutant is on his way. He is busy with all the celebrations."

"Celebrations?"

"Why yes, sir. Bearfoot has been tried, and hanged. His tribe is finished. The General is very satisfied."

"I don't understand."

There was a step on the stair, and laughter. I knew that laugh. Next moment the servant was bowing, nose almost on the floor.

"Highness. Excuse me." In came a tall grinning man, coat sparkling with orders and ribbons, face full of fun. He hauled me up to embrace and slap me. It took me a moment to remember his name.

"Highness. Lepo."

"Young Rudek. Congratulations! You are recovered. You are reprieved. You are released. By the Lion! You look rough."

Behind him, Lord Carne, also grinning.

"Rudek, my friend. The top men only just realised. They weren't sure whether or not you'd pulled off the most cunning strategy. And of course," with a glance at Lepo, "the fact that you have some exalted friends helped them decide."

I said again: "I don't understand. Please explain."

"The enemy thought it was a trick! When he saw you and your troops lined up and you didn't advance, Bearfoot was completely wrong-footed. He and his mob just wandered up the slope, slap into the arms of Tallis's men. He wiped them out, and mopped them up."

The legendary Captain Tallis. Oh yes. Another medal?

"I'm not due for a court martial?"

Lepo guffawed, "You're a sort of hero. Clever ploy, I must say, but a bit dangerous to pull off. Let's get you out of here."

I was undeservingly grateful. Not joyful. Not relieved. I breathed, and I was dead. And still dead, even with that which should have delighted me beyond my dearest dreams.

In the visitors' antechamber, Michalla waited for me. She, who I had longed for with my soul. That, I did remember.

She was smiling, until she saw me. Then came that sweet, wise frown.

"You are very sick," she murmured. She touched my cheek with one finger.

Through cold lips, I said: "Why are you here, Michalla? Your father will be so angry with you."

She took my ice-cold hand in her warm one.

"My father is a human being. And you, sweet Rudek, give up too easily."

She smiled, her heart-face a diamond among the black hair. Then she did two things. She walked a complete circle round me, brushing me with her body. And I felt nothing. I had scarcely a heartbeat. She then stood tall, and taking my face between her hands, kissed my frozen lips with her rich scarlet mouth. I felt not a flicker. Her face grew thoughtful. She stared away as if searching for the invisible.

"Ah," she said at last. "You have no idea, my Rudek, what you have tangled with. I know *swords*. They are demons, who come and go, who pierce their way through into the world of humankind. They do harm and have their way with beautiful people like yourself. They come disguised in light, bright sun-of-the-morning, but they are raised and strengthened in darkness. One such fell from heaven long ago. One touch, and you are theirs, unless someone who has the knowledge comes to defend you. I was given this wisdom by the one who schooled me to fight. I know your pure heart, Rudek, and I love you. I am wise. In my ancestry there is also a sword, but one that was wielded by a saint—hence my name. Now, let me be sure how much damage has been done to you."

She opened four emerald clasps on her bodice and I saw the roundest, whitest breasts, sweeter than roses, sheer founts of desire. And I was utterly unmoved, and still.

I began to cry silently. Fastening her dress, she turned to leave. "It is not your fault," she said, and she was gone.

They brought me my clean uniform, and let me out. Dreary and bereft, I went to my quarters. Nothing was real, or ever would be. I sat on until late afternoon, then I went into the city. I would go to the place where I had been happiest, where I might recover my life, or perhaps end my troubles there. Or have them ended . . .

The whole city was in festival mood. I thrust through crowds, and someone shouted. "Hero!" at me, which I saw as irony. There was a small man in a smart livery who for a while I thought was following me.

The Great Court of Arms was empty. Through the high windows the day's light gleamed its last. I walked the length of the hall, counting out the lozenges.

On this spot had I first seen *her*. Beauty.

On that spot had I first seen *him*. Cruelty.

I reached the far wall and leaned my brow, and heard a voice like whispers from a tomb.

"So you have returned, little Rudek!"

I moved from the wall to look at Luce, and he started towards me, with his seducer's smile. The sunset shivered a glowing nimbus about him, and his eyes were flames.

I asked: "Do you come here to hurt me?"

"I have already hurt you." In falling dusk he seemed to shine brighter, as if he had himself drunk the sun. "Now, after all that, will you come to me?"

I answered, "Never. Not for the world." It seemed a great effort. I felt a blackness advance out of his red and gold, as if an entity detached itself. The tempest of his anger began to engulf me.

"I do not brook a second rebuff, little Captain. This time, you will not recover."

The soft voice had altered, had become a thunder of murderous rage. Its fury rolled around the vast hall. Soon, it would swallow the world.

The big door opened with violence, crashing back against the wall.

Michalla was here in the Great Court. She had sent her servant to tail me, for she knew, as my protector, that harm was due to befall me. She came in running, in her fighting suit with her black hair in a tight matador's pigtail, and with her rapier in her hand. She had heard the raging voice of Luce, and I knew from some buried instinct that they were ancient enemies.

She halted between us. Then with the tip of her sword she drew a complete circle around me where I stood. I heard her say:

"I have touched him, and he is mine."

Luce looked at her with unmistakable horror. Without haste, she aimed her blade at his breast.

He made no effort to draw on her his diamond-headed sword. Instead, his whole body began to grow upwards, taller and thinner each instant, and his shoulders to broaden and straighten out, quickly assuming the nature of gold, not flesh. His form continually elongated. He became the sword, shining bright as fire. The place around his heart was the very last to remain flesh, and to this Michalla set her weapon's point. Then smoothly, almost lovingly, she pushed it in.

The blade penetrated to its whole length. He did not bleed. He did not fall, but crumbled into a pollen-like gold, while all the light in him was extinguished, leaving only his essence. Slender, tall and beautiful. Fragile and deadly. Becoming dust, that dust lasting only instants, while from the disintegrating hilt the gilded tassels curled and blackened as if cast into a furnace. The diamond rolled down to hit the floor, swiftly carbonising back to its source. A brisk wind arose, and whirled the black and gold dust away.

Then it was that my heart began to pound. It thundered in my chest, as if suddenly woken from a deep sleep. It shook my whole body. It danced for joy.

I was more alive than I had ever been. More man, more warrior, more lover. Engorged with love, I stepped from the circle she had drawn, saying, "Thank you, my darling, dearest, my love," and took Michalla in my arms. She sighed a deep luxurious sigh, and wound her arms around me. I kissed her mouth, I tasted the honey of her lips, her eyes, her throat. I loosened her lovely hair and buried my face in it.

I bared her breasts so I could kiss and suckle their fair white goblets, while she shivered and held me closely. And then, clutching her to me, I kneeled to open her breeches and find what I had dreamed was there. The velvety black heart, its cleft sweeter than roses under my mouth, and already dewed with the diamonds of desire.

DRAGON WIND

by Mary Rosenblum

Mary Rosenblum has been writing science fiction and fantasy since 1990, with a mystery as Mary Freeman from time to time. The author of eight published novels and more than sixty short stories, she has been a Hugo finalist and a nominee for many major awards. Currently, her SF novel *Horizons* is available from Tor Books, and *Water Rites*, a compendium of a novel and three prequel novellas, from Fairwood Press. She taught at the Clarion West writers workshop in 2008 and when she's not writing, she lives sustainably on her small acreage. Find out more about her at: www.maryrosenblum.com.

About "Dragon Wind," Mary writes, "In early 1400s, the Ming emperor on China's Dragon Throne, Yongle, sent out his trusted admiral and close friend, Zeng He, at the head of a vast Treasure Fleet. This powerful armada explored much of the world, including Asia, India, the Persian Gulf, Arabia, Africa, and very possibly the Americas. But Yongle's health began to fail and he became obsessed with the Mongol threat on his northern border, calling home the Treasure Fleet. With the Yongle's death and the decline of the Ming Dynasty, China's mastery of the seas ended."

Zeng He leaned on the railing of the First Ship, watching the nervous fisherfolk gather along their shore. Frowning, he surveyed the shabby docks, lined with small fishing vessels, their sails furled, nets still tumbled on the deck. The fishermen had raced home like frightened birds as they caught sight of the Xiafan Guanjun, the sixty-three ships of the Foreign Expedition. Afraid. Zeng He shook his head, sighed. Rumor preceded them and flew with the wings of untruth.

"Your lordship, the boat is ready." An Hu, his First Commander bowed, resplendent in a jade green brocade surcoat over a blue underskirt. Court clothes. Zeng He smiled to himself as he followed Hu to the rope ladder. Court clothes with careful padding underneath. In case of ill-thought arrows. He swung his leg over the side of the ship and climbed quickly down. Already, the rest of the landing party waited in their boats, swords at their sides.

A few townsfolk had taken to the water in their paltry fishing boats although they kept a careful distance from the landing party, pointing and exclaiming at the Treasure Fleet. Well, Zeng He thought with a moment of fierce pride, it *was* impressive—sixty-three ships, over four hundred paces in length, nine masts soaring above each ship like tall pines. The horse boat had docked at the end of the largest pier and a man-at-arms held Zeng He's muscular black gelding, his eyes on the gathered townsfolk crowding the rise above the boats.

Ah, the local lord was arriving. If you could call the petty tyrant inhabiting a tumble down stone compound a *lord*. Zeng He swung onto his horse, paced it up the beach, his lieutenants flanking him, their formal robes (carefully padded against arrows and daggers) brilliant as gems in the sun. The lord waited for him, a handful of fearful men clustered in a ragged formation at his back, awkwardly clutching rusty spears. The lord's robes had been put on hastily and needed a good cleaning, Zeng He thought with distaste. You could read the menu of the last formal banquet on the faded silk.

"Greetings from the Emperor Yongle, the occupier of the Dragon Throne." Zeng He halted his gelding. Behind him, his soldiers would have spread out, alert, their weapons and padded armor without blemish, brilliant in the sun that was making him sweat. "I bring you offers of his friendship."

He nodded and his servant stepped from the ranks behind him, carrying a small box of red leather with a gilded clasp. He approached the ruler, who looked if possible even more frightened than before. "This is a gift from the Dragon Emperor, a token of his friendship and his protection for your people and your land."

The servant flipped back the lid of the casket and the ruler's eyes gleamed. He fumbled the gold and jade necklace from the red silk cushion, held it up to the sun.

"We are honored by your visit and this offer of friendship from the Dragon Throne." The chubby man spoke faltering Mandarin. "I, Tsong Qua, son of Tsong Bao, and ruler of all this land between the sea and the mountains, welcome you. Whatever we can do to fulfill the Dragon Throne's friendship we will do." He glanced again at the gold and jade in his hands.

The fat ruler's obvious greed soured Zeng He's stomach. The fishing fleet was decrepit and the people had the edged, bony look of hunger.

"We are a poor people, living by the generosity of the oceans." Tsong bowed, his expression oily now. "What can we offer the Dragon Throne that will cement his love for us?"

The power of the Dragon Throne was a valuable commodity, Zeng He thought. It meant your neighbors would not dare to attack you. It meant you might dare to attack your neighbors with that shadow behind you and they would capitulate. This petty tyrant squabbled with his neighbors for no reason and kept much of the tax money for himself, if the rumors were accurate.

It would serve him right, Zeng He thought, if we simply marched in here and took what we wanted. But Tsong would not stand on the front lines. This type of man always sent others to stand in danger's way for him. And *they* were innocent.

"The Emperor Yongle, the occupier of the Dragon Throne has one request of you." Zeng He touched his gelding with one toe and the animal tossed his head suddenly, snorting, so that the golden ornaments on his headstall rang with the sound of weapons being drawn. He did not smile as the ruler edged backward. "The Emperor Yongle has heard of the marvelous beauty of a woman who lives in your lands. He has sent me to ask for her hand in marriage. She will be an enduring symbol of the friendship between the Dragon Throne and your people."

A murmur like the wind that precedes a storm swept through the assembled people. Apparently, a few of them understood Mandarin. Zeng He felt his warriors tense and again he toed the gelding. This time, Tsong stepped back quickly as the horse pranced closer.

"A . . . an honor like this . . ." He licked his lips, his eyes darting from side to side, as the murmurs grew. "It would make any daughter prostrate herself with grateful delight. But our maidens are simple women." He spread his hands, his eyes fearful. "Surely none of them could interest an emperor with his choice of beauty from the ends of the earth."

Obviously, they all knew whom he meant. Interesting. "Ah, but the emperor has heard much about the dragon daughter living within your lands. He has sent a rich bride price, of course. Commensurate with her preciousness."

On cue, the servants stepped forward, four of them, bearing a carved teakwood chest inlaid with mother-of-pearl and ebony wood. A gasp replaced the murmur of disapproval rumbling through the crowd as one servant lifted the lid.

Carved jade, gold, and rubies from the Hindi lands lay atop folded silk brocades, and a breath of frankincense and myrrh wafted out. The treasures of the fleet, Zeng He thought and kept his lip from curling with an effort. He didn't need words to know Tsong's answer. It came in the rubbing of his hands, the light of greed in his eyes as he stepped toward the heavy chest, no longer, apparently, afraid of Zeng He's war horse.

"Don't take her!" A tall man with graying hair and straggling chin whiskers stepped forward, dressed in a frayed loin-wrap. "She is our healer," he said in fractured Mandarin. "She saved my son, when he burned with the bleeding fever."

He had the knotted muscles and scarred hands of a fisherman and his ribs showed under his sun-darkened skin. Zeng He met his eyes, pity knifing through him before he banished it. "It is a great honor to your people." He spoke slowly so that the fisherman could follow his words. "You will find another healer and the Emperor will be forever your friend."

"The emperor will be forever the friend of *him*. Not of us." The man spat on the sand, in Tsong's direction.

"Guards! Seize him!" Tsong straightened, his chubby hands full of gold, red-faced. "A hundred lashes with a knotted thong for his insolence."

"No." Zeng He urged his horse forward to block the four men who advanced on the fisherman. "Words have no power. They are not stones." He turned his stare on the ruler. "Damage to his man for his honest distress would tarnish the beauty of any woman." He forced Tsong to meet his gaze. "Do you understand?"

"He is too insignificant to waste my time on." The ruler waved a hand, but his eyes had slitted with anger. "I merely wished to punish his disrespect to the Dragon Throne."

"The Emperor Yongle felt no disrespect." Zeng He watched the petty ruler flush even more deeply. "Your generosity here will be reported to the Emperor and he will be impressed with that generosity." It was a threat, and he watched Tsong's flush fade to pallor.

The man who had spoken out said nothing, simply turned away, shuffling down the beach toward the patched boats. The others began to trickle away, murmuring among themselves, casting dark and doubtful glances back at the soldiers and horses, at the tall ships filling the mouth of the small harbor.

We are taking the only thing they have of value. Zeng He quieted the gelding as the animal shifted restlessly beneath him. *And they will receive nothing for it. Ah, my Zhu Di, my emperor, my . . . friend.* He closed his eyes briefly. *I would stoop to do this only for you, to save your life.*

"I will send my soldiers to bring her to you." Tsong stepped forward, greed like lust shining in his eyes.

"I will accompany them." Zeng He stared down and watched the ruler's eyes shift aside. "To make certain that no violence tarnishes this gift. Meanwhile, we beg your permission to replenish our water and trade for fresh food from your peoples' fields."

"Of course." The ruler straightened, waved his hand as if he sat the Dragon Throne himself. "You have my permission."

A fair trade for the healer with dragon blood, Zeng He thought staring down at Tsong, would be to cut this man's head off here and now and leave the treasure for the people. "I thank you for your permission," he said mildly. "Have your people guide us to the dragon daughter's home." He reined his gelding into a rearing pivot, so that the ruler had to leap back to avoid the animal's hooves.

☙❦❧

A rough gaggle of soldiers met Zeng He and his escort above the beach, armed with spears and short, curved swords. While their leather chest protectors and their clothes were far better than those of the fisherfolk, their eyes gleamed with envy as they eyed Zeng He's well-armed and well-clad soldiers. Ethiope slaves led a horse litter furnished with brocade cushions and hung with silken drapes. Only the best for the daughter of dragons. If the stories were true.

Zeng He closed his eyes as the gelding picked its way along a well-trodden track through the shade at the edge of the sand and said a small prayer deep in his soul. *May I find here the one to restore Zhu Di's health.* The emperor's dragon blood needed the love of dragon blood in order to survive, the oracle had said.

The Emperor's healers seemed to assume that sex would do, Zeng He thought bitterly. He hoped they were right.

The path turned away from the beach, upward through the green twilight beneath the trees, into the foothills of the mountains that fenced the beach. Although well traveled, it was narrow and the soldiers scanned the shadows, their short bows in their hands, an arrow already on each string. Birds shrieked and darted among trailing vines and the dense, heavy air hung like a damp curtain against Zeng He's skin. He pushed up alongside their guides. "How much farther?"

"Just ahead." The man jerked his narrow chin. "In the clearing."

A few moments later, they emerged from the humid embrace of the trees into a wide clearing backed by a gray rock face. Water spilled from a small crevice in the weathered stone, burbling into a shallow basin lined with pebbles and edged with green fern before disappearing into the lush grass that carpeted the clearing. Next to it stood a hut built of sticks, lashed together with grass and thatched with leaves. A garland of bright forest blossoms hung from the eaves of the hut above a sack of rice and a fat bunch of little red bananas. Three silver fish gleamed on a banana leaf beside a small cooking fire in a tiled hearth sheltered by a canopy built from saplings and roofed with more banana leaves.

Offerings, Zeng He thought as he spied a pile of small red fruits in a crude basket made of vines. Thanks for an act of healing, a life saved. A wizened old woman in an embroidered dress crouched in front of the fire, poking at something in a stoneware pot. She jumped to her feet as the entourage filed into the clearing, and hurried into the hut.

A moment later a woman emerged. Tall and slender, dressed in a simple white shift with a belt of knotted jade silk, long dark hair bound into a heavy plait at her neck, she stepped forward, hands raised. "You are seeking me."

She spoke perfect Mandarin and a shiver ran down Zeng He's spine. She had not asked a question. "I am indeed." He swung down from his gelding, handed the red leather reins to his lieutenant and bowed. "I bring you an invitation from the Emperor of the Dragon Throne, O dragon-daughter. To become the Emperor Yongle's wife."

"He has to send his fleet to find him a bed mate?" A sad amusement curved the woman's lips. "I would have thought he could find willing women closer to home." She lifted her hand."Enough. I know why you have sought me out." She looked at Tsong's nervous guards. "He has sold what he does not possess."

They looked away, tracing protective signs in the air with their left hands.

"I do not choose to be the Emperor Yongle's purchased amulet." She turned back to Zeng He. "And he is mistaken. Rumor counts and recounts value and embellishes it with imagined gems. I will disappoint your emperor," she said gently. "What dragon blood I posses is merely a thread, a trickle that allows me to heal the infant with a fever, an old man who has pulled too many heavy fish into his boat." She met Zeng He's eyes. "I cannot heal the Emperor. Without me, those infants may die, the old men put their nets aside."

He saw only the faintest flicker of dragon gold in her dark eyes. Less, even, than Zhu Di himself possessed. Zeng He bowed again, his heart a stone in his chest. "A delicate vein of gold on the surface may run deep." He spread his hands. "I am not here to make choices, Dragon Daughter." He bowed again. "I am here to carry out the orders of my emperor."

For the space of three heartbeats, she stared into the tree shadows beyond the clearing. "If I say no to you, people I have helped will defend me to their deaths. But they are no match for the Great Fleet of the Dragon Throne." She turned and spoke briefly to the woman, then turned back. Bowed her head. "I submit to the will of the Dragon Throne. Unjust will though it be."

The old woman began to wail in a high, keening voice.

Zeng He nodded to the Ethiopes and they led the horse litter forward. He stepped to her side, offered her his hand. "I am sorry," he said very softly. "I am merely the hand of my emperor."

She turned her face away from him and stepped up lightly into the litter, settled herself among the embroidered cushions. Zeng He jerked his chin at his warriors and they formed up ahead and behind the litter, with the ruler's guards out in front, where the warriors could all watch their backs.

This was too easy. Zeng He told himself that it was only easy because the people who loved her were the fishermen and the ruler loved the rubies more. But the back of his neck itched with premonition as they wended their way back down the mountainside toward the beach. As they reached a jutting promontory where the trail bent back on itself like a snake, a bird cried a shrill note. A moment later, with a grinding rumble, the hillside above them seemed to lift and move. Men shouted and scrambled as a foaming torrent of muddy water thundered down the steep hillside through the trees. The lead horse reared, squealing, as the water foamed about its feet and fell, tangling in the litter's traces. The rear horse panicked now, backed frantically, fighting the harness as the slave leading it tried to hold it.

Zeng He leaped from his gelding's back and dashed toward the litter just as a black rain of arrows fell through the green light. One of Tsong's guards fell shrieking, an arrow in his chest, while another arrow took the leader in the throat. One thudded into Zeng He's padded vest and he felt the bite of the arrow point in his shoulder as he grabbed for the reins of the panicking horse, searching the tangle of silk and harness for the dragon daughter.

She had leaped clear, stood ankle deep in the last of the flood, the hem of her dress brown with mud. Behind him, Zeng He heard his men shouting, heard the hiss of arrows leaving the bows. He reached for the dragon daughter's arm, but a slender figure leaped from the shadows.

A youth, his black hair bound back, warrior-style, blocked Zeng He, a curved blade in his hand. "My sister did not choose this path." His voice rang like a hammer on silver. "The village idiot sold what he does not own."

"He did that." Zeng He's own blade whispered from its scabbard and even before the syllables had left his mouth, it flickered like lightning toward the youth.

Faster than thought, he blocked Zeng He's thrust, beating the blade aside lightly. "Run now," he said in a conversational tone. The healer scooped her skirt up about her hips, and was gone like a deer, vanishing in a white flicker into the tree shadows.

Zeng He cursed and leaped forward, thrusting, parrying, pushing the youth back and back. The youth was fast and equally skillful and clad only in cotton overshirt and loose trousers, not hampered by heavy padded armor. In moments, both of them were running blood from minor cuts. Zeng He thrust, at the last instant changed target and sliced at his opponent's thigh. The youth slipped aside, but his heel caught on a patch of trampled greenery and he staggered, leaving himself for an instant open.

Zeng He drew the path that led to the youth's heart blood. For an instant, time stood still and a thick, moist silence filled the space beneath the tree canopy, heavy as a held breath. Their eyes met. Dragon gold shimmered like fire in the youth's eyes and Zeng He's breath caught in his throat.

Then time started again, his sword was leaping forward and with a wrenching effort, he diverted it at the last second. It sliced a shallow furrow across the youth's chest and Zeng He staggered with the force of his misdirection, his own foot slipping now, skin tightening with the expectation of the hot bite of a blow.

He fell hard to one knee, but the blow didn't come. The youth had spun, was racing lightly into the tree shadows in the direction his vanished sister had taken. The fight had ended. Zeng He's men were collecting the spent arrows, checking wounds.

"Looked like ten of them." Shin Gao, his lieutenant, approached, a thick worm of blood crawling down the side of his face from a gash where an arrow's blade had grazed him. "Zhin Ah took an arrow through the shoulder and Ma Huang got one across his thigh—just a gouge, he can still walk." The lieutenant jerked his chin. "Every one of those sorry guards is dead. This was a score getting settled, I guess."

"That, too." Zeng He sheathed his sword, shaded his eyes against the beams of midday sun lancing down through the tree canopy. "Let's see where our timely flood came from."

It was a clever trap, they found. A small stream had been dammed up and a diversion channel dug to send the water crashing down across the trail, once the dam had been removed. Zeng He examined the muddy boulders and sections of tree trunk scattered by the flood. "This had been prepared for some time." He stared thoughtfully into the tree shadows. "I do not think it was aimed at us, particularly."

"Smart, for a bunch of robbers." Shin Gao spat thoughtfully. "I wonder how they loosed the water. Took a lot of strength, eh?"

"Indeed." Zeng He looked at the massive boulders and the trunks thick as a man's waist. "A lot of strength, indeed. Perhaps the mountain shook it down on us." He headed down the slope to where the rest of his warriors waited with the horses.

※※※

"They are outlaws, filthy pariahs, who prey on all." Spittle gathered at the corners of Tsong's mouth as he strode back and forth in the audience chamber of his stone-walled complex. "You will destroy all of them when you retrieve the stolen bride."

Zeng He raised an eyebrow at this peremptory order, but the ruler was too preoccupied with his display of outrage to notice.

"How dare they insult the Dragon Throne?" With an effort, the small man got his emotion under control and a crafty look replaced the rage in his eyes. "Of course, you will send your warriors after them to wipe out this smirch on the honor of the Dragon Throne."

"I do not think that *your* inability to control robbers in *your* domain in any way tarnishes the Dragon Throne," Zeng He said mildly. He watched Tsong flush. "Tell me about this band of robbers."

"They are trash, evil men who live on the sweat of their betters." Tsong waved a servant bearing a tray forward. "They attack upstanding citizens on the road, stealing their clothes, their purses. Will you try some of these preserved fruits?" He gestured at the platter the servant had set out on a low wooden table. "They are rare, imported, and are said to give one long life and vigor and fertility in bed." His eyes widened suddenly and he went pale. "Of course, long life is the greatest benefit, and vigor in bed highly overr—"

"I am quite aware that I am a eunuch. Don't fall all over yourself trying to make amends. It makes you seem more stupid than you are." Zeng He looked down at the tray of glittering ruby fruits. "I am impressed with your wealth. I was mislead by the apparent poverty of your people."

"Those who work hard gain wealth. Those who are lazy do not." The ruler's teeth were clenched so hard that Zeng He imagined he could hear them grinding. "It is only right that I take my share. It is expensive to protect a realm."

"Or a poverty-stricken village." Zeng He turned his back and left the audience chamber without another word.

"It's an insurgent group." His lieutenant, An Hu, waited for him outside. "One of our men speaks the local dialect. He has been spending time in the local tavern." He made a face. "I tried the local rice brandy. Stay away."

"I'll take your advice." Zeng He smiled thinly as they walked along the shell-paved street toward the harbor and the docks. The small market still bustled, although the buying and selling was tapering off as the day heated up. He paused at a thatched stall where an old woman sat cross-legged on a grass mat surrounded by piles of mangos and small brown dragon's eye fruit. Zeng He scooped up a handful of the small fuzzy globes and dropped a bronze coin in the woman's outstretched hand. She grinned at him, nearly toothless, holding the coin up to study the marks.

"It'll be worth ten times its value here." An Hu rolled his eyes as the woman tucked it carefully down the neck of her shift, still grinning. "We're turning bronze into gold, eh?"

"Too bad that doesn't work at home." Zeng He offered the palmful of dragon's eye to An Hu as he peeled one crisp, sweet fruit with his teeth. "Our petty tyrant is correct. I need to retrieve Yongle's bride-to-be."

"I already have the squad ready," An Hu said crisply. "The robbers used arrows, but I've seen a few spears about, so we should expect spears, too. No matter whom we ask, nobody knows anything about our woodland robber."

"So he's popular." Zeng He bit into a second fruit.

"It wouldn't take much to be more popular than the posturing monkey." An Hu spat peels in the direction of the ruler's stone compound. "Do you really believe that this local witch, or healer, or whatever she is, has dragon blood?"

"A trace."

An Hu gave him a sharp look. "But you would know, I suppose. You having grown up with the Emperor the way you did, I mean."

Only years of facing death together on the bow of the foremost ship in the Xiafan Guanjun permitted his lieutenant the layers of implication in that simple statement. "You are correct." Zeng He drew a slow breath. "I did grow up with the Emperor of the Dragon Throne and yes, I can see dragon blood when it flows through the heart."

An Hu bowed his head, lifting a fist briefly in apology. "I'll go make sure the squadron is ready to leave."

"Not yet. I have preparations to make." Zeng He frowned. "Tell our smith to heat the forge. We'll go after our popular outlaw and his sister in the morning."

"They could be two kingdoms away by morning." An Hu sucked in his cheeks.

"I doubt they will be."

An Hu saluted smartly, spun on his heel and strode off.

Zeng He looked down at the crushed fruit in his palm. Dragon's eye. Supposedly the real ones could show the future and more.

Some futures he did not want to see.

Zeng He tossed the remains to the ground, wiped his palm on his surcoat and stared, unseeing, at the crudely fashioned wall of the ruler's compound. *We did grow up together, didn't we, Zhu Di?* The dragon's blood that burned like fire in the now-emperor's eyes had scorched Zeng He's heart and soul.

"You gave me my name," he whispered. "Ma He became Zeng He, but my heart belonged to you long before then. Even now, when you must be emperor and I must go voyaging." He blinked, realizing that he was the focus of curious stares.

Shrugged and followed An Hu's path to the harbor, to prepare for their foray.

☙❦☙

They left the horses at the ship. Forest trails were no place for horses and speed would not aid them. An Hu had finally found a local guide, although the squalid, stoop shouldered man with the shifty eyes did not impress either of them. If he wasn't leading them into a trap, Zeng He thought sourly, he probably didn't have any idea where the robbers hid and would merely lead them down random trails until they all got tired.

At first, the going was easy, the air cool in the early dawn. The trail, obviously well used, followed the contours of the land as it traversed the feet of the mountains on its way to the next village along the coast. Their guide turned off on a narrower path that led nearly straight upward into the thickly forested shoulders of the peaks.

The trail narrowed and the thick air cloaked them, humid and heavy in the lungs, muting even the shrill call of the birds. Like a held breath, Zeng He thought, and scanned the forest twilight for movement. His men walked silently, arrows nocked to the string, vigilant. They stopped when the sun was overhead, ate dried meat and fruit, drank sparingly. The trail curved back on itself, rose steeply through thinning trees and ancient gray boulders to emerge briefly onto a ridge of stone thrusting out through the trees like a huge, arthritic knee. Late afternoon sun scorched them and insects chirred as they scuffed through the thin, tough grass growing between the rocks.

Here, the trail ended.

"I thought you knew where the robbers hid." An Hu leaned over their cringing guide, backing him toward the weathered precipice. "Unless they have wings, they didn't come this way." He raised his meaty hand.

"I heard . . . I know . . . this is it." The guide scrambled backward, heel catching in a ridge of stone, falling hard onto his backside. "It has to be. . . ."

The stone beneath him *moved.* It rippled like a horse's flank and like a horse bothered by flies, flicked the guide from his rocky perch. He arced out into the void, clawing at the air, his thin scream trailing after him.

The entire ridge shivered now, rolling like the deck of a ship in a storm. An Hu fell, grabbing for the rock. One of the warriors clawed at stone, young face desperate, teeth bared with effort. A comrade grabbed for him but his hand closed on empty air and the warrior fell, silent. Zeng He clutched the stone beneath him as it bucked and heaved, like a young colt, trying to throw its first rider. An Hu grunted as his grip came loose and he rolled down the suddenly sharp slope toward the edge.

Zeng He let go, lunged for An Hu and grabbed the man's thick wrist. The stocky warrior slid over the brink as the stone shivered beneath them. Zeng He felt himself sliding, skin shredding from his elbows and arms as he struggled to hold An Hu back.

"Let go, fool!" An Hu's dark eyes burned into his. "We'll both go."

"I claim combat." Zeng He shouted into the grunts of his struggling men, the deep grind of the shifting stone. "I claim the right of one on one combat. My life for the lives of my men. *I have the right.*"

The mountain stilled. A haze of dust shimmered gold in the afternoon light. A bird trilled, tentatively. Another answered.

Two of the men scrambled over, grabbed An Hu by the arms, hauled him back onto the sun-heated stone. Hard stone. Still stone. Sweating, Zeng He rolled onto his back, his eyes on the empty blue sky.

"So who in the names of the nine demons were you talking to?" An Hu's voice grated as if he'd swallowed gravel.

"And just what in the name of those same demons did you promise it?"

"Who went over the edge?" Zeng He sat up, stood and counted quickly. "Shan Ji." He crossed to the edge of the precipice, waved An Hu away as his lieutenant stepped quickly forward. "We're safe." He looked down, but the dense tree canopy had swallowed any trace of Shan Ji. He had been young, had been saving a bride price, this trip, his last trip.

"Our guide did not lie," he said softly. "This is how they came. Give me what I prepared."

An Hu took the leather pouch from his belt, handed it over. "Waste of good coinage, if you ask me." He shrugged. "Good hemp rope would hold her."

"It probably would."

"You going to tell us who you spoke to?"

Zeng He became aware of his men's tension. They were afraid, nervously glancing at the gray ridges of stone like the mountain's muscles beneath their booted feet. "The dragons are the children of the mountains." He faced them, hands spread. "The mountain defended its offspring, even if the offspring is partly human. I spoke to the mountain. I invoked the dragons' right of combat. I . . . have the right." It was hard to say, they would all know the rumors. And rumor paled compared to the truth.

The men stared at him, their faces carved like stone, eyes fixed on him like men on a sinking ship watching a rescue boat. "You are safe to return to the ship. I will face our challenger."

"And if you lose?" An Hu's growl broke the thick silence.

"I die."

"I think we will stay here." He gave Zeng He a cold, dark look.

"No." Zeng He lifted a hand. "If I do not die, I will come down to the ships. If you stay . . ." He lifted an eyebrow. "Can you swear by the spirit of your father that you will not interfere?"

For a moment, An Hu held his stare, anger bright in his eyes. Then he lowered his head.

"If anyone interferes, you will all die and so will I." He paused to let An Hu feel the weight of this truth. "You must take the men back to the ship. I will come down. Or I will not." He looked at the men, some of them his own age, the ones who had found what they sought on the moon's bright path across the waters, unlike Shan Ji, who had come with them hoping only for a bright future at home. He sighed. "If I do not return, he is your leader." And he put his hand on An Hu's shoulder.

That bound An Hu with the chains of responsibility. Zeng He turned away from the flash of anger in his old friend and comrade in arms' eyes.

They left reluctantly, filing back down the trail to find Shan Ji's body and bring him back to the ship for burial in the arms of the sea. Zeng He walked to the center of the rocky spur, his shadow stretching ahead of him. He dropped the leather pouch into a crevice in the rocks. "It is time," he said.

The youth seemed to materialize from the gray stone and the tree shadows beyond. He stepped forward, and golden light ran down his slender blade. "You are an honorable man to trade your life for the lives of the men that followed you. Their reluctance to leave suggests you are a good leader." He bowed briefly, his dark eyes glittering. "I am sorry to have to kill you."

"You could choose not to kill me." Zeng He stood easily, but his muscles were ready and he watched the youth carefully without seeming to. "You could choose to come with me and I would have no need of your sister."

The youth frowned. "If you know enough to have invoked the ancient right of challenge, then you know enough to realize that this is not possible. All time stops until this challenge is decided, until one wins and one loses." He stepped forward, circling, light as a dancer on his feet, his blade weaving spells from the golden sunlight. "It is time to decide."

It was as if time had indeed stopped. No bird called, no cloud moved in the sky, no leaf shivered. The sun, frozen in the sky, gilded the spur of rock with golden light and the youth darted forward, swift as a stooping hawk.

Zeng He parried and their blades skirled. He feinted, thrust, but the youth leaped sideways and backward as if on wings, feinted, then darted in so suddenly that Zeng He's parry was late and the hot kiss of the blade stung his shoulder. He backed, blade up, as he tore a strip from his surcoat with his teeth, bound the bleeding wound tightly.

The youth gave him time, pressing his guard, not attacking. But the moment the knot was tight, he leaped. Steel clashed again and Zeng He dove and rolled, came to his feet in an instant, had a moment as the youth spun. Zeng He's blade leaped for blood and only with an effort did he turn it, so that it slashed the youth's shoulderblade in a shallow gash rather than piercing.

The youth danced away from him, crimson staining his white tunic, his frown thoughtful as he faced Zeng He once more. Then he attacked in earnest. Zeng He backed, parrying, beating the blade aside as it seemed to multiply into a dozen blades slashing at his face, probing for his heart. Sweat stung his eyes and his wounded arm throbbed as the youth drove him slowly across the mountain's shoulder beneath the frozen sun.

He could not keep this up much longer. He dashed his sleeve across his face to clear the sweat from his eyes, barely parried a flashing thrust from the youth, felt the blade gash his thigh. His heel struck stone and he looked back to find himself on the lip of stone that had shaken Shan Ji to his death.

Now.

Or never.

The youth crouched lightly in front of him, a golden flame of triumph in his eyes. Zeng He saw his death there. In a fluid motion almost too fast to see, the youth tossed his sword from right hand to left, lunged. Zeng He's parry was too slow, he had not expected this. The blade homed on his heart . . .

Zeng He spoke the words.

They sizzled from his lips, burning like lava, scorching throat and tongue. For one instant, all motion ceased and his opponent's eyes widened with shock. Then the youth spasmed, arms and legs flying outward, back arching. The blade nicked Zeng He's side as it flew past, pinwheeling out into the void beyond the cliff. He leaped forward as the youth fell, caught him and lowered him gently to the sun-heated stone.

Time began with a lurch. Insects buzzed and birds chirped. A thin cloud passed in front of the setting sun, sending a brief, welcome shade over Zeng He. He touched the youth's throat, reassured by the steady pulse of life there, and stood, his knees trembling, to fetch the leather pouch.

The smith had melted the gold treasure Zeng He had given him, had spent the night forging it into chains. Zeng He fastened the manacles to the youth's sinewy wrists, chained his ankles. Then he fetched his water bottle, drank to sooth his still-burning lips and tongue, and settled himself beside the youth where his shadow would shade his unconscious face.

"Dragons have a temper." He spoke softly, gently. "It flows in the blood, is never entirely controllable. One day, when we were youths ourselves, Zhu Di lost his temper with me. I had bested him at swordplay and I had cut him." He sighed, letting the distant hills thick with trees draw his gaze. "He beat me, nearly to death. It changed something in him. Made him understand what he really was. I think it helped make him the emperor he is, restrained in vengeance, generous with friendship. After I recovered, he told me the words, the ones his father had given him. The ones that dragons use. If one speaks them in a fight, all dragons are struck unconscious." He chuckled softly. "Zhu Di said that without those words, no dragons would exist. Or dragon kin."

"But you are not dragon."

Zeng He started, looked down to find the youth's dark eyes open. Dragon gold gleamed and shimmered in their depths. Zeng He sighed. "I am not dragon. He told me the words in case I ever needed them. Against him. I never did." He smiled, unable to banish sadness from that smile. "Before now."

The youth raised his manacled wrists, grimaced as the chains jingled. "Clever to use gold to bind my powers, too."

Zeng He nodded. "The challenge has been answered. I won. You lost. You and I are both free of that, now."

"You planned this." The youth sat up, the gold in his eyes bright as the sun's evening fire. "From the beginning. That's why you spared me on the trail? And just now, when you had a chance to wound deep?"

Zeng He lifted one shoulder in a shrug.

"You gambled your life on that dice throw and you nearly lost." The youth stared at him for a moment. "What is it that you want? Apart from my sister."

"Not your sister." Zeng He met the youth's eyes, although the gold there stabbed him to the depths of his soul. *He will look into your eyes, Zhu Di will, and find what he has forever searched for. Searched for and thought he had found in me.*

But had not.

"Your sister has little dragon blood in her veins."

The youth shrugged. "She has enough to help the people here. That is what makes her happy. You did not answer my question."

"I want you to come with me, back to the Dragon Court. I want to bring you to the Emperor Yongle who sits on the Dragon Throne."

"As a slave?" Gold fire flared in the youth's eyes.

Zeng He's smile hurt him. "Oh, no. Not as a slave. As a guest." *One look. That is all it will take.* "The Emperor Yongle will . . . value you. As a guest."

"You have been touched by dragon blood." The youth's eyes pierced him. "I felt that from the first."

"I have." He had to look away, this time. "Your dragon blood will heal Yongle. I felt the truth of it from the moment we faced each other. And Yongle will reward you well. With his eternal friendship. That is no small thing."

Silence stretched between them and the sun began to slide behind the distant mountain peaks, its light turning to rich gold, the shadows swelling, stretching, strengthening. Below, twilight already filled the narrow valleys leading down to the beach, the harbor, and the ships. An Hu would be on deck, his eyes on the mountainside. Waiting.

"I will go with you." The youth's tone was thoughtful, but the dragon gold in his eyes pulsed in the fading light. "As you say, the friendship of the Emperor of the Dragon Throne is no small thing. If you leave my sister here to be happy, I will go in her stead. My name is Xinyi." A shimmer of anticipation flickered in those eyes. "I am curious to meet this Emperor with dragon blood. His reputation has preceded you here."

"He will be honored, Xinyi." Zeng He winced as his stiffened wounds pulled at him. He unlocked the manacles, removed the chains.

Xinyi leaped lightly to his feet and offered a hand to Zeng He. As Zen He took it, new strength coursed through his weary frame and a brief sting told him that his cuts were healing. Ah, yes, he carried much more dragon blood than Zhu Di. Zeng He closed his eyes briefly. It would be enough to heal the emperor. More than enough.

They made their way down the mountain in the night. The stones themselves glowed beneath their feet, lighting their way. Dragon blood indeed. It was An Hu who spied them as they emerged from the trees in the gray hour before dawn. He took the leather pouch with its jangling chains and asked no questions, hurried to rouse the men so that they could catch the turning tide.

It was time to go home.

That night, out on the open sea, after they had sent Shan Ji to his grave in the sea's arms, Xinyi sought him out where he stood at the bow of his ship, watching ghosts move among the thousand thousand lamps of heaven.

"You did not tell me everything." Xinji's eyes glowed like the sun's last light in the darkness. "I have read your heart and I know the price you yourself pay for your Emperor's health. I have a gift for you." Xinji held out his closed fists. "These are Dragon's Eyes. This one shows the future that would have been, if you had not stopped here or if you had taken my sister and left."

He opened his hand, palm up. A golden sphere flashed with light and suddenly, Zeng He was seeing the Xiafan Guanjun tied up in the imperial harbor, himself trudging up the stone paved highway away from the docks, his shoulders slumped.

"This would have been the last voyage," Xinyi said softly. "The emperor's failing health would have made him fearful and he would have withdrawn from the wider world. The Dragon Throne would have shrunk, become the seat of mere mortals, of petty chieftains, for many many years to come, the wide seas abandoned to strangers." The golden sphere popped and vanished from his palm and he opened the other fist. "This eye looks at the future that will be now."

This time, Zeng He saw his ships on strange seas, anchored off strange lands where bronze-skinned peoples dressed in robes embroidered with brilliant feathers offered him gold and welcome. He saw more ships, on more seas, on and on forever into the horizon.

"The Dragon Throne will flourish and become strong, it will stretch its shadow over all the lands between the sea and the sky," Xinyi murmured. "You did not trade your heart away for nothing and your heritage will be entire nations."

Zeng He watched the second Eye vanish from Xinyi's palm. "I did not think I traded it for nothing," he said softly, and turned away to watch the night-foam gleam with light as the bow of his ship cut through the dark waves.

THE CROW

by Diana L. Paxson

Diana L. Paxson is the author of twenty-eight novels, including the *Westria* series and the recent *Sword of Avalon*, featuring history and magic. She has contributed to many anthologies including *Thieves' World* and *Sword and Sorceress*, and has served as a judge for the Pagan Fiction contest. She lives in Berkeley, California. Read about her Westria books and more at http://www.westria.org/

In "The Crow," the protagonist of "Crossroads" from the first *Lace and Blade*, returns home, to the beginning of his journey, but like any hero he brings with him surprising gifts—not only the magic of Brazil, but courage and hard-won insight.

As Claude's carriage rolled toward the wrought iron gates, a gentleman costumed as a crow emerged from the barouche that had halted in front of the mansion. Claude took a deep breath. It had been three years since he had moved among the glittering throng he glimpsed beyond. The scents of straw and forest-tanned leather from his own costume reminded him abruptly of Brazil. He found himself wishing he had stayed there.

His friend Henri gathered up the folds of his toga as a footman opened the carriage door.

"Madame D'Arbalêt will not mind that you have brought me?"

"*Mon ami*, it is a *masked ball*. No one will know whether you were invited or not." Something tore as Henri pushed forward. "Name of God! How did the Romans conquer the world wearing garments like these?"

Claude eased himself through the opening in a rustle of straw and leaped lightly to the cobbled street. Clearly, their hostess believed in doing nothing by halves. Even the footmen were costumed in the gaudy orange and blue-striped doublets and pantaloons of the Vatican Swiss Guard. Henri followed his glance with raised eyebrow.

"Well, that is original. But I doubt they will be guarding the pope. If Madame has invited her usual *habitués*, the guest list is likely to be weighted in the opposite direction."

"Truly? I would not have believed you such a sinner." Claude smiled.

Henri shrugged and straightened his wreath of vine leaves. "Oh, these days we are all decadent. Fortunately, it is not necessary to name one's sins, only to drop a dark hint now and again. When you tell them that you have been in Brazil, *you* will be quite in fashion."

My friend, you have no idea. Claude remembered a courtesan called Corquisa, and the flicker of swords in the light of a bloody moon. His business tonight was with another, very different lady who called herself Manon.

"First they must find out who I am," he said lightly, drawing the straw fringes of his headdress over the brim of the hat to veil his face.

Henri shook his head. "Merely to see the mask will give them a thrill. Did you not tell me it was given you by some kind of native priest?"

"He was a *cacique* of the Truxa tribe whose life I saved when hunting wild pig in the *sertão*—the back country—of Bahia."

"You will be a great success, I assure you," replied Henri, leading the way up the curving drive.

The mansion was another relic of Napoleonic pretension. Light from crystal candelabra shifted through open doors and windows. At the entry, Henri presented his card of invitation.

"My friend is the Baron Claude Delorme."

"Monsieur Thibaudet, Monsieur le Baron, you are welcome. You will find refreshment in the blue salon."

And music, Claude found as they pushed through the crowd, was available everywhere, wafting in different keys and tempos from consorts of instruments tucked into the corners of the various rooms as the forests of the Amazon rang with the competing cries of myriad birds.

"Madame has bagged a fine collection of the famous and infamous," murmured Henri. "The fellow dressed as the Devil is a young poet called Paul Verlaine, whose book of Saturnian poems caused quite a stir last year. The gentlemen garbed as Sarastro from *The Magic Flute* calls himself Eliphas Lévi and is reputed to be a master of esoteric lore."

Claude nodded without paying much heed. He was here to find a woman, not a man, and some of the things he had seen in Brazil would make a poet's blood run cold.

They had scarcely entered before two young women costumed as nymphs seized upon Henri and carried him away. Claude continued on alone. In that collection of bright fabrics and glittering paste jewels, his painted leather and straw attracted curious looks. They spoke of a world where these fantasies were real. He told himself that the outfit was only a disguise, but he could feel his body swaying, his booted feet beginning to carry him with the feral tread he had seen when the cacique danced.

The music was loudest in the ballroom, where fantastic figures whirled, their images repeated endlessly in the mirrors that lined the walls. But Manon's slender shape was nowhere to be seen. He glimpsed instead his own reflection, and for a moment the blaze of the candelabras became firelight, the ballroom a clearing in the *sertão*. He saw the figure of the *cacique* weaving among the Beings of Light that the sacred drink had summoned, that fluttered about him like so many birds. Then the dark shape of a crow flapped past and they were only costumed dancers once more.

In the gaming room, a murmur of conversation rose above the click of dice and the soft slap of the cards. Beyond the curved backs of the baccarat players, he caught a flash of green. The line of a lifting arm struck instant recognition. That surprised him. He had thought the memory of Corquisa would insulate him from the physical response that at one time had made him Manon's slave.

Claude felt in his pocket for the hard edges of the box that held the emerald. For the past two years he had labored to lay the foundation of a new fortune in the Santo Pedro mine, all that remained of his family's fortune. Once he had planned to return to Manon with a new mistress, decked in emeralds, on his arm. But surely a better revenge would be to give her the jewel, so that every time she wore it—and she would be unable to resist—she would remember what she had lost.

Tonight she was garbed as a serpent in viridian satin that sheathed her supple figure from breast to hip and clung shockingly to thigh and calf before it trailed across the floor. She sat perched on the padded arm of a chair, clinging to a florid gentleman in the diamond-quilted doublet of Pierrot who was sweating beneath his mask.

A close-fitting cap formed the serpent's head. Her arrested pose as she saw him was very like that of a snake he had once surprised in the *sertão*.

Her lips tightened as he halted before her and bowed.

"Is that a costume of Brazil, monsieur? I had a friend who went out to that wild land—" One graceful hand played with a tendril of golden hair.

Was it possible that she did not recognize him? Claude's skin was still bronzed from work outdoors, and he no longer minced like the *boulevardier* who had been her lover.

"If you would honor me with your company, perhaps we might find that I know him. . . ." Gruffly, he offered his arm. She smiled and started to slide off of the chair, then made a little moue of frustration at the constriction of her gown.

"I am a hunter from Brazil, mademoiselle, accustomed to carrying off my prey," said Claude, in one swift movement gathering her into his arms. The florid gentleman dropped his cards and began to protest, but she only laughed.

"Is he your new beloved?" Claude asked in his own voice, and felt her stiffen in his arms. Until now, she had not been sure, but even without sight he would have known the supple form beneath the satin hide.

"He thinks so . . ." she replied, and then, "In the next room there are curtained alcoves. We can be private there."

As he settled Manon on the cushions, she tipped back her mask.

"Claude, is it really you?" she gestured nervously. "Put off that straw and let me see you!" With a curious reluctance, he set the headdress aside, realizing only now how the role, or perhaps the spirit of the *cacique*, had armored him. But Manon was still looking at him with more than professional appreciation. "Oh, you *have* changed!"

"You are the same," he responded, realizing even as he spoke that it was not true. Still slim, she was more finely drawn, her complexion almost translucent, the good bones pressing against the skin.

"While you have been dancing with the savages, I have been learning the ancient wisdom of our own land." She drew a handkerchief from her decolletage, coughed discreetly and thrust it back again. "Monsieur Pierrot—" she nodded scornfully in the direction of the gaming room, "has the privilege of paying my bills, but I have a teacher now who shows me marvelous things. Master Zabadon has the secret of youth eternal, Claude. With his aid, I will never be less than I am now. Come to my salon on Sunday evening, and you will see. . . ." She extended a slim hand and although he still desired her, it was all he could do not to recoil.

"I have brought you something from Brazil," he said abruptly. As she opened the box, the calculation in her eyes gave way to wonder. The emerald glowed in the candlelight, shaming the satin of her gown.

"Oh, Claude! Claude . . ." With trembling fingers she lifted the golden chain. Green fire swing hypnotically, then he fastened it around her neck so that the emerald pulsed upon her breast. "Oh, how beautiful. My dear," she said meltingly, "I have missed you so. . . ."

In another moment, she will be telling me that Monsieur Pierrot disgusts her, Claude thought. *She will say that she always believed in me, that she sent me away for my own good. She will not say that she wants me because I am once more wealthy, but that will be the truth behind her words. . . .*

He got to his feet. "Then you will not forget me. Mademoiselle, *adieu.*"

If he stayed, he would not be able to leave her, and then the whole cycle would resume. Snatching up the headdress, he made his way blindly toward the door. The roaring in his ears was so loud, he did not know if she had called his name.

಍ଓଣ୪ଌ

When Claude could think again, he found himself in the garden beside a fountain whose crystal drops reflected the light of colored lanterns. Before him stood an enormous crow. He blinked, focused, and the impression of enormity vanished as he realized he was looking at a gentleman in an evening cape whose edges had been dagged to suggest wings. A hood drawn up over his head joined a beaked mask.

"Monsieur le Baron, *bonsoir*." The stranger spread his wings in a bow. "I trust you have been refreshed by the cool night air."

"I am well, Monsieur le Corbeau," said Claude, amusement mastering his surprise. "My thanks for your concern."

"And Mademoiselle Manon, is she well also?"

Claude stiffened. "What do you know of her?"

"I know that you are correct to be concerned. The master she follows treads a dark path."

Claude's amusement abruptly disappeared. He knew better than to return to Manon's bed, but it would seem that he was still bound to her, if only by chivalry.

"What do you mean?"

"To learn more, you must explore paths that a man of your class does not often essay. But I see from your garments that you have already done so." Teeth flashed beneath the mask as the man smiled. His accent belonged to Brazil.

The leather poncho rustled as Claude rose. "What must I do?"

"There is a bookshop on the Rue de Clichy in Montmartre called the *Bibliothèque Lyons*. If you were to appear there at about four o'clock of the afternoon, you might find those who can advise you."

"Will you be there?"

"Oh, I may turn up anywhere. If you take this road, you will surely see me again." The crow cape swept up as the stranger laughed. A few steps made him one with the night, leaving Claude staring.

The noise from within had diminished, and the *cacique's* headdress held no more magic. It must be growing late. Time, he thought, to find Henri and go home.

Striding up the avenue on a fine autumn afternoon with the pearly dome of Sacré-Cœur rising like a cloud from the hill before him, Claude found it hard to believe in secret societies and evil magicians. He had put off last night's fears when he replaced the straw and leather of the *cacique's* garments with a new coat of fine grey wool. His old clothes had been hopelessly behind the fashion, and in any case, a new breadth in chest and shoulder made them unwearable. In the clear light, his memories of the night before seemed a fantasy. Magic belonged to Brazil. This was Paris, where the Age of Reason had been born.

If it had not been such a fine afternoon for walking, he might have turned back, but somewhat to his surprise he found the bookstore almost immediately. Bins filled with tattered volumes had been set out beneath a sign that showed an ancient god with a raven at his feet. Lettered in gold were the words "Bibliothèque Lyons", and below them, "J. Rondelle."

Claude paused just within the door, breathing in the powerful scent of old paper. Tiered shelves stretched to the ceiling, crammed with books thick and thin. Beyond the counter at the far end was a door, but he could see no one.

"May I assist you?"

The voice came from above him. Recovering, Claude looked up and saw a fair-haired young woman with a smudge of dust on her nose perched on a ladder, a book bound in blue leather in her hand. Additional volumes were stacked precariously on the upper rungs.

"I was expecting to meet someone here—" he covered his confusion with a bow.

Still on her perch, she inclined her upper body in a suggestion of a curtsey, a motion that suited her rounded figure well. "The bookstore belongs to my father. I believe he is drinking wine with the gentlemen you seek in the back room."

Claude watched appreciatively as she slid the blue book into a space on the shelf and reached for another volume, then he made his way past the counter. The door behind it opened to a cloud of tobacco smoke and a babble of speech that trailed off as he stepped inside.

"Excuse me, your daughter—"

"Ah, Célie. She must have liked your looks if she directed you in here without coming to ask . . ." replied a rotund gentleman with thick glasses whom Claude supposed must be Monsieur Rondelle.

Claude shrugged. "She was up a ladder at the time."

The others laughed. In one of them he recognized the nobly bearded Eliphas Lévi, looking rather less imposing in a black frock coat that had seen better days. Of the others, one wore the open collar and loosely-tied cravat of a denizen of Bohemia, and the second was a young man whose coat was even more fashionable than the one Claude wore.

And what, he wondered, did they see when they looked at him? The gentleman he had been? Or the man of action he had become?

"My apologies if I intrude," he said uncertainly. "I was invited by a—gentleman—whom I met last night at Madame D'Arbalêt's ball. He wore the costume of a crow . . ."

"Ah, Monsieur Marabô!" exclaimed the young man of fashion. "Did I miss him? I was hoping to see him there!"

"He did not give me his name," Claude said stiffly. "I am the Baron Delorme."

"You are welcome. My name is St. Cloud."

"Are you a Seeker?" asked Lévi. Claude met the older man's deep gaze, trying to understand the question.

"Only in the sense that I seek to do a little good in the world when I can." That would cover what he had done in Brazil for the courtesan Corquisa, what he hoped to do now for Manon.

"That is as good a path as any to the Way," said Monsieur Rondelle with a laugh.

"So why did Monsieur Marabô send you here?" St. Cloud asked.

"A . . . friend has become the student of someone called Master Zabadon. I am concerned about her safety."

The atmosphere in the room chilled.

"He leads a lodge known as the *Société du Lys Noir*," Lévi sighed. "I counsel you to remove her from their influence as soon as may be. The dreadful orgies so often attributed to those who study the secret doctrine are for the most part fantasies of the Christian bourgeosie, but there are some deluded souls who profane the Mysteries by seeking to make them real."

"We have no certain knowledge," added the Bohemian, an artist, to judge by the stains on his hands. "But it is said that Master Zabadon's followers do blood sacrifices there . . ."

"It is said . . . " Claude echoed, "but what do you *know*?"

"There are some things it is better not to know," muttered the artist darkly. "Baudelaire and his imitators sing of the flowers of evil, but they are *poseurs*, more concerned with the frisson created by the thought of evil than by the thing itself."

"By their fruits shall ye know them," murmured Lévi, stroking his beard. "There are some who would ban all study of the Mysteries, but the Wisdom of the Hidden Temple that has guarded the truth behind all true religion since the beginning is far older than this pursuit of evil for the sake of Power. Study of the occult lore should ennoble the spirit and purify the soul. We do not have to risk the contamination of direct contact. It is enough to observe what becomes of the disciples of Master Zabadon."

"Young Stuyvesant, who threw himself off of the Pont de l'Archevêché," said St. Cloud.

"And Dumaille, who bankrupted himself funding Zabadon's search for the Potion of Youth . . ." muttered Rondelle.

"But he is not dead!" objected the younger man.

"He might as well be—lives in a hovel and cringes when you call his name! To think that he was once a scholar." He shook his head with a sigh. "I can't count the books he bought from me. I wanted to buy up his library when his possessions were auctioned off, but all the books were gone."

"Gentlemen, you have said enough to alarm me," Claude interrupted them. "If my friend is truly involved with this scoundrel, how do I break his spell?"

"You must go to the lady and reason with her," said Rondelle. "If she still cares for you."

It is my emeralds she cares for now, came the bitter reflection. He should forget Manon, start anew with someone like the bookseller's daughter, Célie. But the old protective instinct would not be denied.

"And if that does not serve?" he said then.

"I will seek the counsel of the Ascended Ones," Lévi said slowly. "I have long believed that those who serve the Light have the obligation to oppose the forces of Darkness. Perhaps the time has come."

ఌርଥ୫୨ଓ

During the remainder of that week, Claude was on the watch for Monsieur Marabô, but although he often heard crows calling in the trees, he did not encounter that elusive gentleman. By Sunday evening, the crisp fall weather had become a cold rain. To Claude, his blood thinned by two years in Brazil, it seemed that winter had already arrived, chilling both body and soul.

As he walked he fingered the folded paper, covered with Hebrew letters and magical sigils of protection that Monsieur Lévi had inscribed for him. It reminded him of designs he had seen drawn in chalk at a crossroads with candles and offerings in Brazil. Had the one tradition inspired the other, or were both part of a greater mystery? In any case, to carry it could do no harm.

Just outside Manon's door, he noticed the feather of a crow on the cobbles and slipped that into his pocket as well.

Manon had redecorated her lodgings while he was away. The drawing room was now hung with a rather heavy flocked paper in dark red, the chairs and sofas covered with velvet in dark jewel tones. Manon herself wore black lace over maroon taffeta and a curious necklace of garnets that glowed like drops of blood against her white skin.

Claude paused in the doorway. A thin girl in brown was playing the piano. The other woman wore grey and lilac with a mourning brooch. The pale skins of the men suggested that they did not often see the sun. It was not difficult to identify Master Zabadon, a man of medium height with flowing, silver-shot hair, dressed in a white suit that would have been commonplace in Brazil but was startling in the gloom of a Parisian October evening. Claude would have known the man in any case, the faces of the others turned constantly toward him, like flowers to the sun.

Flowers of evil? he wondered. These people did not seem wicked so much as lost. Even Manon, who as he recalled retained her self-possession even in the throes of passion, covertly tracked Zabadon's movements even when she was speaking to someone else.

The servant announced him and Manon fluttered forward in a rustle of silks, but it was Zabadon whose gaze, open and luminous, held his. Eliphas Lévi had spoken with a venerable dignity, but this man exuded charisma. Claude felt his skin tighten. He had seen eyes like that in Brazil when men were possessed by Powers.

What are you? he asked silently, and found himself stroking the crow feather in his pocket as if it could reply.

"Good evening," said Master Zabadon. "You must be the Brazilian of whom all the world has been telling me. You have been blessed by a hotter sun than shines on Paris, but I see you are a gentleman." His laughter let Claude know that this was to be taken as a pleasantry.

"I left my pelts and feathers at home," Claude smiled politely.

"So I perceive," came the reply. "I have been hearing about the witch-doctor costume you wore to Madame D'Arbalêt's ball. I understand that it is unique—perhaps one day I might persuade you to show me. You understand, I have a professional interest in such things. These primitives sometimes retain surprising glimpses of the True Wisdom."

For a moment memory filled Claude's vision with bright fluttering images. Had he really seen the Beings of Light, or were these the memories of a brain disordered by the brew called *Jurema* that the *cacique* had given him?

"In their own setting, I found their intelligence no less than my own," Claude said blandly.

"Mademoiselle Manon has perhaps told you of our studies." Zabadon's dark eyes glowed. "A man of your experience could be quite valuable, and you might find that the Mysteries of the Old World as compelling than those of the New."

Claude had half expected this, and found it interesting that the magician had chosen to try flattery. What, he wondered, had Manon told him? Their eyes met, and for a moment Claude felt an odd sensation, like a pressure within his skull. Anger flared as he recognized the attempt to invade his mind, and the feeling eased.

"You must understand that after so long abroad, my affairs are in disarray. It will be some time before I am free to pursue other interests, but certainly, once I am free. . . ." He let the phrase trail off with a bland smile.

"Of course. But now I am sure you would wish to speak with our hostess, so I will detain you no more." With a royal wave, Master Zabadon turned to the thin gentleman with whom he had been conversing.

Manon came towards him, slipping her handkerchief back into the bosom of her gown.

"Now do you see why I call this man my teacher?" Her eyes glowed as they never had in the days when she swore that Claude was her dearest love. "Is he not wonderful?"

"He impressed me greatly," Claude replied with some truth. "But so do you. The dress becomes you, but I confess I had hoped to see you wear my emerald."

The color that rose in Manon's cheeks made him realize how pale she had been. "I would have done so, but Master Zabadon says that the green vibrations are bad for my health just now, and I must only wear red jewels." She took a small box from a mahogany table, and set it into his hand. "He says that you must take this. Soon I will be better," she smiled winningly, "and then you may give it back to me!"

Claude bit back the retort that there had been nothing wrong with green vibrations on the night of the masked ball. He had never heard of a courtesan refusing an expensive gift, especially Manon. She must be ill, or more bewitched than he had believed.

"Then I must trade my emeralds for rubies," he said, tucking the box into the pocket of his vest.

"Oh yes!" she replied with a brittle laugh, coughed into her handkerchief and laughed again. "Yes, indeed!"

ଓଔଷଓଈ

In the nights that followed, Claude slept badly, haunted by dreams in which Manon fled toward some faceless terror. In an attempt to dispel those visions, he returned to the bookstore and persuaded Célie to walk with him and once or twice to have dinner in a café. She seemed a vision of health and sanity in comparison to the guests at Manon's salon, but when the dream changed, it was Célie who was running down that dark tunnel, equally oblivious to her danger. He tried to warn her, but each night she seemed farther away.

On the fourth night, he was wakened by stealthy movements in his dressing room. For a few moments he lay very still, wondering why the thief had not tried the desk or collected the silver in the sitting room. Perhaps he was looking for the cuff-links and jeweled stick-pins that were part of a gentlemen's wardrobe. Or perhaps he had heard that the Baron Delorme had brought a fortune in emeralds back from Brazil.

Claude heard the squeak as his steamer trunk was opened, and then the rustle of straw. With that, he guessed who had sent the thief, and what he had been told to steal.

At the emerald mine, he had formed the habit of sleeping with a knife beneath his pillow. Now, without conscious thought, it was in his hand. Soft-footed on the carpet, he slipped across the room and eased open the door. The dressing room had one small window, through which a little moonlight showed him a dark figure. In the next moment, the thief leaped up to face him, the bag that held the cacique's costume swinging. Claude ducked as a blade flashed in the other's hand, then feinted with his own, the moves he had learned at the mine coming back to him.

Steel clashed and scraped as they closed, stumbling over the clothing swept from shelves. The thief's arm came around in a swirl of cloth, trying to catch Claude's blade, but the sharp edge sliced free. Claude strove to grapple with his opponent, but the thief was serpent quick and serpent strong. The knife flickered; Claude ducked and drove beneath it, but his opponent evaded wth a quick twist, crashing into the wardrobe.

Claude straightened, knife ready. The dark shape swayed, muttering in a thin high voice that made his skin crawl. He saw it grab the bag with the costume and felt his own arm move in slow motion as he tried to respond. The paralysis held him as the thief fled. The click of the front door released him, but by the time he reached it, the moonlight showed him only an empty road.

ಬಿಂದು

"We apologise for asking you to meet us here," said St. Cloud, indicating the wooden tables where laborers and tradesmen were drinking wine. Faded playbills were tacked to the walls. The establishment, clearly a place where the working class mingled with the *demi-monde*, was called *Le Corbeau*. Claude had found that amusing when he arrived. He was not amused now.

"The bookstore is watched, you see."

"Monsieur Lévi's lodgings have watchers as well," added the artist, whose name, Claude recalled, was Lebrun. "Corporeal and astral, though his wardings have turned back any attempts to do more, and he knows how to veil his movements so they did not see him come here." He turned to the older man. "I warned you not to fare out on the spirit road to spy on the *Lys Noir*. I told you how it would be."

Claude sighed. Strained muscles still reminded him of last night's encounter. He had not thought he wounded the intruder, but in the morning, the floor of his dressing room had been splattered with red. He thought the thief had been too small and agile to be Zabadon—some boy, perhaps, whom he had hired for the deed.

Lévi sighed. "It was my mistake. For so long I have opposed the forces of materialism and tyranny. I had forgotten that those who work evil in the world of the spirit can have great power."

Claude poured more wine from the carafe. It was a harsh country red, the color of Manon's garnets. A waiter passed, bearing a flask of absinthe to a gentleman in black who sat in one of the darker corners. The liqueur glowed emerald green . . . like Manon's eyes. . . .

"I have renewed the wardings on my own home," the occultist went on. "I can do the same for you—"

"Do not trouble yourself," Claude replied. "I saw no suspicious loiterers. And why should they bother? As I told you in my note, they already have what they wanted from me."

"But what do they want it *for*?" asked St.Cloud.

"Power . . ." Lévi said heavily. "It is always Power that the Enemy seeks, whether to rule men's bodies, or their minds, or their souls."

"Zabadon is like the man who will take whatever strange herb or liquor he can find, hoping for the inebriation that leades to inspiration," Lebrun said then. "I was that way myself, until I learned that the Doors of the Infinite may only be opened by patience and discipline."

Sometimes, thought Claude, *one has to kick them down.* His nerves twitched with an itch that only action would relieve. He tried to tell himself that the *cacique's* costume was no more than a souvenir of an interesting experience. Let it gather dust in some other man's closet. And yet—

"He might have a reason," he said unwillingly. "When I wore it at the ball, my perceptions . . . changed." And Manon had sensed a difference in him. He remembered once more the wiry energy of the person with whom he had grappled in the dark, and an unwelcome suspicion began to grow. If she had been the thief, then magic had surely been at work, to make her so strong.

"So we may perhaps have pagan spirits to deal with as well?" Lévi sighed.

"Perhaps," Claude agreed, "but the costume comes from a very different world, and I think it might take time to understand."

"Do you?"

"Not enough . . ." he said slowly. "But too much for my peace of mind."

"Do you still wish our help to save your friend?" the occultist asked then.

"I do not know whether she is endangered or she *is* the danger," Claude replied. "But I have been attacked, and so have you. I learned in Brazil that ignoring enemies will only encourage them."

"We have found out more about Zabadon's associates, but we do not yet know where they meet. Before we can act we must gather our forces, we need to learn—" began St. Cloud.

The door slammed open. Monsieur Rondelle stood in the entrance, cravat askew and a swelling bruise on his brow. As his wild gaze fixed on his friends, he staggered forward.

St. Cloud eased him into a chair and thrust a glass of wine into his hand.

"Célie!" Rondelle whispered when he could speak. "They took Célie!"

"Who? Speak, man!" The artist gripped his hand.

"Dourdonais, the young man that we saw with Zabadon, and two toughs. They knocked me down and took her away."

Claude gripped Lévi's arm, his chair nearly crashing into the corner table behind him.

"You talk so glibly of magic! What is all your learning good for if you cannot find Célie?"

"Do you think we are living in some fairy tale?" growled the old man. "High Magic requires preparation and ritual. That cannot be done in a day."

"I'm not sure we *have* a day!" exclaimed Lebrun.

"What will they do to my girl?" Rondelle covered his face with his hands.

"Why not ask your lady friend? It is her fault that this has happened!" Lebrun turned on Claude. "You know where *she* lives—"

"No need," came a lazy voice from behind them. "I can show you where the black lily grows."

The gentleman in the corner had come forward. He was, Claude saw now, dressed quite correctly in a black tailcoat and pantaloons that strapped beneath his boots, though the red and yellow striped waistcoat was perhaps a little gaudy for afternoon wear. It was only the dark cloak that had reminded him of wings.

While the others sat staring, Eliphas Lévi got to his feet and bowed. "Monsieur Marabô . . ."

If Claude's request for help had indeed led to Célie's abduction, they ought to blame Marabô himself, who had told Claude about the *Lys Noir*, but meeting that sardonic gaze, no one ventured to say so.

"Lead on, then," Claude stood. "I will follow you."

⊂⊃⊂⊃⊂⊃

In the end, all of them followed, in two carriages that deposited them in a decaying neighborhood near the Seine. Claude had his sword-stick, and the others had provided themselves with clubs, with the exception of Monsieur Lévi.

"I am no man of my hands," the occultist said solemnly. "There is no time to return to my temple and prepare for a battle on the spiritual plane in my accustomed way, but the time has come to test the disciplines by which I have lived for so many years. As above, so it shall be below, and without, as it is within. If you will deal with those threats that are visible, I will do what I may against the invisible world."

Night had fallen, and the street was deserted. The wind off the river felt dank and cold. But as their oddly assorted band marched toward the old warehouse, Claude found himself smiling, and only then realized that the life of a gentleman had become as constricting as the fine coat he wore. He laid it down outside and slipped the sheath from his swordstick. He had no doubt of his ability to handle the effete specimens he had seen in Manon's drawing room with fists alone, but the bravos Monsieur Rondelle had described sounded more formidable.

As they approached the doorway, Monsieur Marabô stepped aside. Claude recalled now that the man had promised only to show them the place, not to fight beside them, and wondered why he had expected more.

"Many thanks for your guidance," he said shortly. "I would ask only that you stay nearby so that someone may report our fate if we fail."

"But of course," came the reply. "If you will take advice, go quietly through the door."

"Pray they have not locked it," muttered the artist.

Marabô laughed softly and leaned forward. Claude heard something click as he touched the lock.

Inside, the sweet stink of incense lay heavy on the air. Lebrun crossed himself. Claude heard a whisper that must be Lévi, praying. Curtains of black velvet had been hung on frames to create a room within the warehouse. Moving softly forward, Claude separated the nearest and peered through.

The space was uncertainly lit by black candles, set in a pentagram drawn in chalk upon the floor. Was it their smoke that made it so hard to make out the figures that moved within? A sonorous, dissonant chanting rose and fell, grim with purpose, even though he could make out no words.

"They have raised a circle of power," said Lévi at his ear. "It is meant to keep out alien spirits, but it may keep them from seeing us as well." He pushed through the curtains, and the others followed him.

Black-robed figures were posted by the candles at the five points of the star. Two dressed in white stood before an altar on which Claude could just make out a pale female form. The barely seen barrier kept him from moving forward, as if he forced himself against a wind.

The chanting ceased.

"The planets are aligned, the spirits satisfied. It is the hour of destiny!" the resonant voice of Master Zabadon rang out. "Come, my sister, and take this sacrifice. Her blood shall be your blood, her youth your youth, her life yours!" There was a pause, and then a murmur Claude could not make out. "My beloved, believe, this is the only way. Look at me and know that I speak truly. I was born when the Sun King ruled France, but I will never die! Strike, and you will reign forever at my side!"

"On the table—that is Célie!" Rondelle's hand closed painfully on Claude's arm. At his cry, the nearest black-robe turned.

"In the name of the High God and all His holy angels, be opened!" cried Lévi, drawing a complex sigil in the air. The air before them cleared, and they burst through.

The artist, who was nearest, swung his club as the black-robe drew a dagger. As the others started toward them, Claude caught Rondelle's arm and dragged him forward Lévi, still intoning invocations, puffing behind.

The woman bound to the altar was indeed Célie. To one side stood Master Zabadon. Claude snarled as he realized that the magician was wearing the *cacique's* leather poncho over his robes. Facing him stood Manon, nearly as pale as her white gown. An evil triangular knife wavered in her hand.

"Get that blade away from her," he hissed to Rondelle. "I will deal with the man!"

Or try to, Claude thought as Zabadon turned to face him, raising the heavy ritual sword two-handed. *I wonder if he knows how to use that thing?* Against it the slender blade of Claude's sword-stick seemed a wand. Behind him came the grunt and scuffle of a fight. Someone cried out, but he dared not look to see who had fallen, for Zabadon was advancing with the lithe tread of a jaguar, his lips drawing back in a feral smile.

Claude feinted and lunged, disengaging as the heavy sword came round, and realized in consternation that the thing projected an aura of force that pushed his blade aside. He no longer feared his own weapon would be broken, but how could he strike when a single parry protected Zabadon's entire torso?

To draw the magician away from the altar was the only thing he could think to do.

The light dimmed as first one, then another candle was knocked over. Two of the black-robes were down. Lebrun and St. Cloud stood back to back, flailing at the other three. The *cacique's* poncho flapped as Zabadon swung, sending a ripple of light along the fringes. Had Zabadon learned to wake its magic?

The images painted on the leather seemed limned in lines of light as well. Zabadon's gaze shifted as sparks began to whirl around him, and the blow that would have taken off his opponent's arm went awry.

"You should not have stolen the poncho," Claude cried, remembering where he had seen those lights before. "Behold the *Encantados de Luz!* The Beings of Light have come!"

As Zabadon swung frantically at the little lights, Claude lunged once more. The slim steel slipped beneath the poncho to pierce the magician to the heart. The sparks spiraled around him like maddened butterflies as he crashed to the floor.

Claude whirled, and a stab to the calf brought one of the bravos down. Leaving Lebrun and St. Cloud to finish the other two, he sprinted toward the altar.

Rondelle sprawled across his daughter's body, blood pouring from his side. Manon tried to pull him away so she could reach the girl, but with his last strength the old man held fast. Claude grabbed the courtesan's arm and flung her to the floor, setting his heel on her knife as he used his own blade to sever Célie's bonds. Lebrun had finished off his opponent. He hurried towards them, saw what had happened and helped the weeping girl to sit, cradling her father in her arms.

Manon lay curled on the floor, coughing. As Claude bent over her, he realized with sick understanding that the blood staining her lips was her own. But even a wounded serpent could still strike. He knelt beside her, tossing her knife across the room before laying down his sword.

"Manon . . ." he said softly. "Is it the consumption? Why did you not tell me?"

She shook her head. Her skin was too white. He should have recognized that pallor before. "He promised me life! He gave me the power to take the magic garments. He said her blood would cure me. He promised me. . . ."

"Zabadon is dead," Claude said flatly.

"Then I will die," she whispered. "I have nothing now."

On the altar Rondelle lay still. Lebrun was holding Célie, murmuring softly, and she seemed to find comfort in his arms. It was just as well, Claude thought grimly. To Célie, he would always be the one who had brought her father to this doom.

Heart wrenched by guilt and pity, he looked down at Manon. "You have *me*," he said softly. "As long as you need me, I will take care of you."

Something dark moved on the other side of the room. Claude turned, fearing one of the black-robes had revived. Monsieur Marabô stood by Zabadon's body with the cacique's poncho in his hands. White teeth flashed in a swarthy face as he pulled it on.

"Don't touch—" Claude began, but the man was laughing. He stared. He had never noticed that the central image limned on the garment was a crow. Marabô was a younger version of the *cacique* who had given him the costume, with the look of a drummer in red and black whom he had last met at a crossroads in Brazil. Why had he not seen it before?

"This power doesn't belong here." The soft, accented voice was clear. "Best I keep it, don't you agree?"

"Was all this no more than a way to bring it here?" A jerk of Claude's head indicated Célie and Lebrun weeping over Rondelle, St. Cloud clutching a wounded arm, Eliphas Lévi gazing around him with tragic eyes, and the fainting woman who lay in his arms. "I would have given it to you, had you asked."

"You choose your roads," replied Marabo. "I only open the door."

The folds of the black cloak lifted like wings as he settled it around him. For a moment his grin gleamed above it. He turned. For a moment Claude glimpsed the great shape of the crow, then there was only the dark.

THE BIWA AND THE WATER KOTO

by Francesca Forrest

Francesca Forrest currently lives at the edge of a swamp in western Massachusetts, but at one time she lived in a thatched cottage in England, and at another, in Kyoto, the ancient capital of Japan. She has also studied classical Japanese literature and history. Her previous publications include an entry (the firefly bellflower) in *The Field Guide to Surreal Botany* (Two Cranes Press, 2008) and a short story ("The Oracle") in the YA issue of the online journal, *Coyote Wild*.

     About "The Biwa and the Water Koto" she writes, "Biwas have been played in Japan since classical times; in the famous story by Lafcadio Hearn, "Miminashi Hôichi (Earless Hôichi)," the biwa player sings the *Tale of the Heike* to the ghosts of the Heike warriors. Kappas, for their part, are well known in Japanese folklore, and water kotos, literally "water koto caves" (*suikinkutsu*) are also real, although none, to my knowledge, is actually big enough to walk into, and none has been proven to be the home of a kappa."

"I have a small problem," Tadahiro said, propping himself on his elbows. He leaned forward and slid the shoji door open to reveal a rainy night, a temple garden of shadows and silhouettes, shrubs deep in meditation. "Larger than small, actually. Quite large, in fact."

Yuko looked up at him. Had they been laughing only minutes before? Now his face was grave, his tone sober.

"What possible problem can burden someone as well-loved as you? Everyone, including the crown prince, wants you for a biwa instructor. All the ladies forget their husbands and their lovers when they hear you play. Unless some rival or slighted lady wishes you ill?" Yuko couldn't repress a twinge of jealousy at the thought of all those admirers. She sighed. Her pious intentions, a retreat at this temple, had been sincere, but it would clearly take more than copying out lines from the Flower Garland sutra to free her from earthly attachments.

"It's not the music that's the problem, but the instrument. When I first started helping the abbot tune up his playing, I borrowed one of the biwas from the imperial treasury for him to use—it seemed only proper, since he was an imperial prince before retiring from the world. Unfortunately, I borrowed it rather unofficially . . . and now the treasury wants it back. For some reason, the abbot says I'm mistaken about the biwa, and that it has belonged to the temple all along. Not only will he not return it," continued Tadahiro, frowning, "but he has banned me from the temple grounds. I shouldn't even be here now."

"Th-that doesn't make sense," said Yuko, stunned. "Why should he do such a thing?"

Tadahiro tilted his head. "I haven't the faintest idea."

"When must you return it?"

"Within the next few days."

"And if you fail?"

"Then I become a thief. A thief who's stolen from the imperial treasury," said Tadahiro, looking Yuko full in the face.

Yuko tried to speak, but words wouldn't come. She dropped her eyes. When she looked up, he was gazing out at the garden again.

"It's getting light. I must go," he said. Yuko pushed herself up abruptly, and the robe that had been covering both of them slid off her shoulders.

"My retreat lasts three more days," she said. "I'll look for it. I'll find it for you."

⊱❦⊰

Yuko's hand was as unsteady as a small child's as she attempted to copy more verses from the Flower Garland sutra later that day. Her thoughts returned to Tadahiro's words, and at noon, when she turned in her completed work, she decided to see what she could learn from the taciturn monk who had come to collect it.

"In the chapter I've just copied, it says, 'Unobstructed, the Buddha's concert of wonderful sounds pervades all lands of the ten directions.' The abbot plays a number of musical instruments, doesn't he? I've heard that he practices with the crown prince's biwa instructor. Are they likely to play together before I leave?"

From where she sat behind a screen, Yuko could not tell whether the monk's prolonged silence reflected anger, confusion, or some other emotion. At last, he spoke.

"The abbot has recently embarked on a program of soul-cleansing austerities. I do not believe he intends to give a performance any time soon."

"I see. Well, then. I suppose he must have returned the biwa the instructor lent him, from the imperial treasury. I had been hoping to hear it—it's said to have a lovely sound."

"The abbot has never used a borrowed instrument," the monk said sharply. "The temple has its own biwa, a treasure brought over from the land of Kara two centuries ago by our founder."

"Really? Then that must be a lovely instrument as well. Would there be any chance of my seeing it?"

There was another long pause from the other side of the screen. Then,

"I'm afraid not. That biwa has a destiny, and it goes where it needs to go. And right now, it has chosen to remove itself from worldly affairs."

"Certainly all things have their own destiny," Yuko murmured, happy to end the conversation.

It has chosen to remove itself. Could the instrument have been stolen, or worse yet, destroyed? The thought made Yuko sick. If the biwa was irrecoverable, then Tadahiro could not be saved. Perhaps it was hidden away. Maybe the abbot was engaging in austerities to atone for worldly desires, worldly desires that extended to claiming the imperial biwa for the temple.

Yuko would have to search all the temple buildings, which meant that she would need more freedom of movement than was generally afforded a lady of high degree. Fortunately, Yuko had long ago discovered the solution to that problem: one had simply to change one's degree. Any of her attendants would be more than willing to trade places with her for a day, but it was Ukon who had played this little game with her in the past and Ukon whom she trusted most. The following morning, it was Ukon who dressed in Yuko's elegant but cumbersome layers of robes and combed her hair into a black river down her back.

Yuko, for her part, tied her hair back and put on Ukon's plain robe and hakama skirts. Directing Ukon to say she was feeling unwell and not to go to prayers, Yuko slid open the doors of her quarters and stepped out onto the veranda.

Wonderful! The breeze, the sunlight! Why couldn't the doors to the veranda always be open, wide open?

One of the monks crossing the courtyard, seeing Yuko, bowed and started to approach. By walking purposefully away, Yuko avoided a conversation. She'd need to decline a bit more in degree, clearly, if she wanted to walk about unnoticed. She studied the garden. Over there, men were pruning the azaleas and the boxwood. Near the main hall, a man swept the stone path. Yuko sighed. All men. But here, coming through a side entrance, was a girl with a basket of flowers on her head.

Flowers for the altars, thought Yuko. *This girl will visit every building in the temple, and no one will give her a second glance.* Yuko hurried to intercept her.

"Excuse me! Hello! You! Please, come speak with me." What a botched salutation! But how do you call to someone you don't know, someone of no rank?

The girl hurried over. Indeed, the next moment she was standing right in front of Yuko, balancing her flowers with one hand and staring at Yuko full in the face, eyes wide. It was most disconcerting.

"Yes, my lady?"

"I have a favor to ask of you. I'd like you to let me take the flowers to the altars."

The girl made no reply, but her mouth drooped and her eyebrows drew together, creating wrinkles on her young brow.

"And, if you will allow me, I have a present for you," Yuko added, trying to keep her voice gentle and calm. She slipped off Ukon's thin silk overrobe and held it out.

"For you."

"R-really?" The girl set her flower basket down and ran her fingers over the silk.

"Yes. Take it."

The girl hesitated, then lifted the robe up and touched the silk to her cheek. She flashed a startling, bright smile.

"Thank you, my lady! You can take all the flowers, that's just fine!"

With a little effort, Yuko was also able to persuade the flower seller to lend Yuko her jacket and leggings, and in return, she helped the flower seller on with Ukon's hakama skirts. The two made the switch in a secluded spot behind a stone lantern and a giant boulder.

The flower seller spun around in her temporary finery, smiling, and smoothed her hands down over the robe and hakama. She gave another face-splitting smile, then bowed deeply to Yuko and made her way from the courtyard with eager, bouncing steps totally unlike those of any lady in waiting.

Alone and unobserved in the temple courtyard, Yuko eyed the basket of flowers. Could she balance it on her head the way the flower seller had? Probably not; better to carry it on her arm. Lifting it into what she hoped was the suitable position, she headed for the storehouse. What better place for a biwa to retire to than a storehouse?

Before a wash basin beside a small shrine to Miroku, the Buddha to Come, a strange noise caught Yuko's ear, a sound like someone plucking the strings of an instrument. Not a biwa; the notes were more like those of a koto. But no, that wasn't quite right either. The notes had a metallic air, reminiscent of a bell—a tiny bell, a distant bell.

Yuko took a step closer to the shrine, and the notes grew ever so slightly louder. A shiver traveled down her spine. Whose music was this? She peered at Miroku, his seated stone figure, his head tilted as if lost in thought. *His?*

More notes sounded, light as air, but liquid as water, and seemly born right out of the earth. The earth's music?

"You there—are you planning on delivering those flowers? Yesterday's are drooping; the altars could use some fresh ones."

Yuko turned her head, though her attention was still on the ethereal sounds, and her eyes met those of one of the novice monks. His eyes lingered on her face, not sun-darkened, like the flower seller's, but pale from a lifetime hidden in the inner rooms of her father's mansion. He grew pale and took a step back.

"You're not the flower seller," he whispered. "You're dressed like her, but you're *not* her."

Three notes, random and beautiful, hung in the air. Then another, then two more.

"Do you hear that?" whispered Yuko.

"You—you must be a fox spirit in human form!" The novice glanced over his shoulder, but the activity of the morning had given way to noonday stillness. No one was about. He wiped his hand across his head.

"Do you hear that?" repeated Yuko. "Where is that music coming from?"

"You mean the water koto?"

"Water koto?"

"Yes; look." With a trembling hand, the novice took the ladle from the wash basin in one hand and poured the water over his other hand. It fell onto the rocks in front of Miroku, and instantly there came a series of notes, echoing as if resonating in an underworld hall.

"It comes from down there," the novice said, keeping his eyes averted from Yuko's face. "There's a metal chamber down there, like a buried bell. It plays for days after any rainfall—water trickles down into a pool at the bottom of the bell, and make the notes we hear, just like a koto being plucked. Is—is that what drew you here? The music of the water koto?"

Another note reached Yuko's ear, different from the others. This one truly did sound plucked, and not like a koto, but like a biwa. Then came two more such notes, horribly flat and twanging miserably. And then more otherworldly notes from the water koto.

"Yes," murmured Yuko. "Yes, this is what drew me here." She reached for the ladle, placing her hand just below his on the handle, so their fingers were nearly touching. He looked up, and she held his eyes with her gaze.

"You said there's a chamber down there. Can you take me to it?"

The poor novice's mouth opened and closed like a carp's.

"If you don't want me to place a spell on you, you will take me there immediately," said Yuko, standing as straight and tall as she could and trying to look as much like a fox spirit as possible.

The novice hunched his shoulders and nodded. Silently he led Yuko out the side entrance of the temple and along a path that wandered down the side of a steep hill. Halfway down was a cleft in an outcropping of rock, tall enough to admit a man, but narrow. The novice turned to Yuko.

"I don't think even a fox spirit should go in there," he said.

"Fox spirits live for music like this," replied Yuko.

"There's something else besides music in there." The novice frowned. "Listen," he said in a rush, "the abbot always used to come here to meditate and to play the biwa. Then last month, he came back to the temple pale as a ghost, and without the biwa. He was ill for days, and he's never been back since."

Then that really was the imperial biwa I heard, thought Yuko. But why did the abbot leave it underground? The novice had a point: the water koto might play of its own accord, as drops of water trickled into the subterranean pool, but who was playing—or attempting to play—the biwa?

"Please don't go down there," begged the novice.

"My magic will protect me," said Yuko, with more confidence than she felt. Then, as an afterthought, "You needn't come along. You have other duties."

"Yes! Yes, I do—thank you!" He gave the most perfunctory of bows and hurried back the way they had come at twice the speed of their descent.

Yuko stepped into the cleft. Cool damp wafted up to greet her, and blackness. She glanced back at the brilliant sunlight. A real fox spirit would be able to carry the sun's rays along in a paper lantern, or would make its eyes glow so brightly that it didn't need one. Looking back, she spied an oil lamp set in readiness on a ledge in the wall. The abbot hadn't been here for a month. Would it still be filled?

It was, and equally fortuitous, the tools for lighting it lay right beside it. With a minimum of fumbling, Yuko lit it, and by its shy flame made her way in careful steps deeper underground.

The path curved around and down, and after about a hundred paces, Yuko noticed that the pinpoint of light from the lantern gleaming on walls not of rock but of bronze, smooth and high. She lifted the lantern up, and flashes of red and gold shone through an overlying lacework of green patina. The narrow path upon which she stood, slick with moisture, disappeared into a pool of water. Yuko took a step backward.

High overhead, at the apex of the bell, a patch of daylight was faintly visible, and in its light Yuko could see drops of water sparkling as they fell. When they struck the pool below, musical sounds filled the space. Unearthly.

Yuko held the lantern out over the water, moving her arm slowly in a wide arc. There! flickering in and out of view, a smooth rock protruding from the water, large and broad enough to sit on. The abbot must have come to that rock and in the darkness harmonized his music with that of the water koto.

Yuko caught her breath. Someone or something was sitting—well, lying really—on that rock now. She strained her eyes to make out who or what it was. Unmoving, it appeared to be a pile of discarded robes. Could the abbot have left in so much of a hurry that his robes stayed behind? And where was the biwa? Yuko leaned over the water with the lantern. This time, the flame flashed off the mother-of-pearl inlay on the front of the pregnant-bellied, long-necked form of the biwa, resting beside the robes.

Yuko drew back the lantern and its little sphere of light. The rock, the robes, and the biwa melted back into blackness.

How to reach the rock? Yuko held out the lantern again, but could spy no bridge, no stepping stones. Could she wade over? All right then, if there was no other way.

She stepped into the water. The shock of the cold made her fingers tingle, but the water reached no higher than her ankle. Another step. Now the water soaked through the flower seller's white leggings, but only to her knees.

Another step. Nearly there.

On the rock, the pile of robes stirred. Yuko stifled a scream. She tried to take a step backward. Something twined about her feet and held her fast. Panicked, she pulled back, but only succeeded in losing her balance.

The lantern hit the water and went out with a hiss. Yuko struggled to break free of the entanglement. Water pressed in around her chest. It lifted her hair out from where it had been hidden in the jacket and gave her garments the weight of lead. In a moment, if she couldn't get free, she would surely be pulled under. Horror drove Yuko to kick and twist more fiercely.

Her arm hit something hard and smooth—*the rock!* She tried to hold onto it, tried to pull herself up, but whatever had caught at her legs had a will, and its will was to have her submerged in the water. With a cry, Yuko made one last effort to gain purchase on the rock. This time, her hand hit the biwa.

At the ringing echo this produced, there came a splash. Suddenly, Yuko's legs were free. She pulled herself out of the water and huddled on the rock, shivering.

Beside her, something stirred. Yuko froze. She didn't want to go back into the pool again, but what was she trapped with here on the rock? The movement ceased, and she heard a faint groan. Whatever she was sharing the rock with, it seemed in worse shape than she was. She reached out, and her hand touched patterned brocade, then arms, chest, and—she drew her hand away, very wet. An open wound. Yuko pulled the robe over the wound and pressed the cloth to it. Hands tried feebly to push her away.

"Stop!" she said, "I'm trying to help you."

"Yuko?" Weak though the voice was, it was clearly Tadahiro's.

THE BIWA AND THE WATER KOTO

"Tadahiro! What's happened to you?"

Something broke the surface of the water. With a wet *slap, slap*, it climbed onto the rock and settled itself beside Yuko, exuding an aura of mud and fish.

"Wicked thief," said a gravelly voice. "He tried to take away the biwa. Now he'll be my dinner. The biwa stays. Must sing to the water music again. One day, some day, like before."

Perhaps an evening shower was passing through in the upper world, for suddenly a whole arpeggio of notes tinkled and echoed in the water koto. The creature imitated the sound, its voice rising in hoarse chirps. Then came an unhappy, discordant twang from the biwa, and a long exhalation of dank air.

"But it won't play, won't play for me, no. Not never," the creature said to itself.

"It's a kappa," murmured Tadahiro, barely audible.

A kappa. Yuko felt her heart drop right out of her. Kappas were malicious water spirits that dragged people into the water and sucked all life from them.

"Is that what's happened? Has he stolen the life out of you?" cried Yuko.

"Not all of it," he whispered. "Maybe half." But he sounded less than half alive.

"You can be next," offered the kappa.

"No, thank you! Didn't you want the biwa to sing to the water music?" asked Yuko, turning toward the gravelly voice.

"It doesn't sing anymore," said the kappa, with another deep sigh.

"I can make it sing," Yuko said. "And *he* can make it sing better. Better than the one who used to come here. He can make it sing . . . make it sing so the drops of the water koto will hang in the air to listen."

There was silence for a moment, into which came the notes of the water koto.

"Even better," said Yuko slowly, "he can teach *you* how to make the biwa sing. But not if you make him your dinner."

"Ehh, he's half gone already. Let him be my dinner, and you teach me to make the biwa sing."

"I can't teach you; only he can."

A wet, webbed hand wrapped itself round Yuko's right wrist, and a heavy weight settled itself on her pelvis. Unbalanced, she fell back and hit her head. Fireworks exploded before her eyes. Another webbed hand pinned her left shoulder to the rock. Weight pressed her stomach and chest as well, making it impossible to breath.

"So I fix him up, have you for dinner instead?" suggested the kappa. Unable to breathe, Yuko couldn't answer, could barely hear Tadahiro say, over the buzzing, roaring sound in her ears,

"If anything happens to her, I'll never teach you anything. I'll ask not only the biwa but also the water koto to never sing to you again."

Yuko felt her wrist and shoulder released, and the weight lifted from her hips and chest. She filled her grateful lungs with air. The buzzing in her ears faded, but it was several moments before her dizziness passed.

"But I'm *hungry*," grumbled the kappa.

"Where are you more hungry—in your stomach or in your heart?" asked Yuko, and as she did, more drops of water fell from above, and ethereal notes echoed in the bronze chamber. The kappa crooned back.

"The heart," it said, suddenly. "Yes, heart. All right. Move over. I'll fix him." The kappa pushed Yuko away from Tadahiro, and she heard it blowing steadily and unwaveringly. The noise stopped, and some minutes later, a rustling of cloth told her that Tadahiro was sitting up.

"What are you doing here?" Yuko whispered.

"When I left you, I thought I heard a biwa in the garden. The next day, I managed to slip in when the Minister of Ceremonies came to offer prayers. I asked one of the monks

THE BIWA AND THE WATER KOTO

where the abbot used to practice. He brought me to the entrance."

"Almost exactly the same as me, then," said Yuko.

"Teach me now!" demanded the kappa.

"The first step is learning how to hold it," said Tadahiro. "You can see in this darkness? Good. So watch where I rest the body of the biwa. Do you have the plectrum? The piece of ivory to strum it with? Ah, good." Tadahiro drew the plectrum across the biwa's strings once, then stopped to tune it. He strummed again, and the biwa sang out resonantly in the bronze chamber.

"Now you try."

"Can't. Won't sing for me."

"It will. It wants to sing for everyone. It will sing for the lady. Listen." Yuko felt the biwa, placed gently in her lap. Tadahiro's hand closed on hers, passing her the plectrum.

"Try 'The moon on the moors of Toya,'" he suggested. "You play that one well." Yuko played, and in the rests, the water koto answered her. When she finished, the kappa sighed. Yuko hesitated, then presented the biwa to him.

"Rest the body in your lap," she said. "The way I did."

The kappa strummed once. The sound was tentative, but musical.

"Ahh," said the kappa.

"It takes a while to learn to play like the lady does," said Tadahiro.

"Stay and teach me."

"We need two instruments," said Tadahiro. "One for me to use and one for you. I need to bring another."

"All right. Go fetch one."

"Unfortunately, I can't bring another one unless I take the one you've got now," said Tadahiro.

"No. This one is for me. The other man left it here. Mine now."

Yuko suddenly remembered the monk's words. "This biwa has a destiny. It has to go where it needs to go," she said.

"It needs to stay *here*," said the kappa.

"No, it's done what it needs to do—it brought you a teacher. But it needs to find someone else now. Its music is like the Buddha's voice—it reaches out to all the world, and where its sound reaches, sufferings cease. Let the instructor take it; he'll bring you back a rosewood instrument better suited for a beginner."

The kappa grumbled, but Yuko heard him thrust the biwa toward Tadahiro.

"You stay, though," the kappa said to her, and his hand clamped down on her ankle.

"No, she needs to come along with me," said Tadahiro firmly.

"No, no, no, no!" said the kappa, tightening his grip. "You won't come back. No lessons, no biwa, no dinner—no good!"

"I promise we'll come back," said Yuko. "And you won't miss us, because you'll be composing."

"Com . . . pose . . . ing?"

"You hear the music of the water koto all the time. Pick out the pattern of its notes and play them on the biwa until we return."

"Notes. . . ."

As the kappa repeated the word "notes," two more drops of water echoed like tiny bells or chimes in the chamber of the water koto. The kappa chirped an echo.

"Yes," said Yuko. "Bring together many notes."

"If you do, I can teach your song to other students," said Tadahiro. "The kappa's water koto composition, for the biwa."

"Hoho! Water koto composition, for the biwa!" exclaimed the kappa. "Yes!" He released Yuko's ankle. "Go, go! But come back."

In the darkness, Tadahiro's free hand found Yuko's and squeezed tightly. On unsteady feet, they waded into the pool and toward the path to the outer world on the other side, while behind them the kappa sang to the water koto.

TRIAL BY MOONLIGHT

by Robin Wayne Bailey

Robin Wayne Bailey is the Nebula Award-nominated author of numerous novels, including the *Dragonkin* series, the *Brothers of the Dragon* trilogy, and the *Frost* saga, among others. His science fiction stories were recently collected in *Turn Left to Tomorrow,* and his work has appeared in many anthologies and magazines. He lives in Kansas City, Missouri. Visit him at his website: http://www.robinwaynebailey.net

Readers of the first *Lace and Blade* had the delight of meeting Lady Elena and the highwayman Ramon Estrada, each harboring their own secrets. In this poignant and action-filled sequel, Robin draws us even deeper into the mystery of their entwined lives.

The Lady Elena Sanchez y Vega sat upon a white horse atop a high hill in the three-quarter moonlight and watched the coach that rolled smoothly along the southern road from Santiago de Compostela and Vilagarcia toward Pontevedra. A pair of lanterns dangled from the front of the coach, shedding amber light on the black, lacquered woodwork and on the hard-packed road. The team of four perfectly matched black horses trotted at an easy pace, while the driver gazed watchfully ahead and from side to side.

A moment later, a second coach appeared on the same road, its lanterns swinging back and forth in the darkness as its horses clopped along. The glow of the lanterns glinted on the side of the coach and hinted at a shape that might have been a crest. A pair of riders followed close behind.

Elena frowned as she studied the strange caravan. *Who would brave the forested roads of Galicia so late at night?* she wondered. From her high vantage, she could hear the creak of the wheels and the fall of the horses' hooves. A shade rustled in the window of the second coach, and a feminine face peered briefly out. The lamplight illuminated sharp, dark eyes that seemed, impossibly, to stare directly at Elena.

A low growl in the trees drew Elena's attention away from the coaches and reminded her of her true business. She sniffed the air. Cursing herself, she touched the clasp of her cloak, but before the garment could fall away, her horse whinnied and reared.

At the same time, a black shape sprang at her, knocked her from her saddle. She hit the ground with bone-jarring force.

Yet, even as she fell, her hand went to the waistband of her trousers, and she curled her fingers around the butt of a pistol. Dazed, she took quick aim. The shape sprang at her again, red eyes burning with hunger and anger, jaws slavering. It reached for her with claws as long as her forearms.

Elena fired.

The bright flash of her pistol lit up the hillside, and a cloud of gunpowder swirled against the moon. Twisting in mid-leap, the shape gave a howl of pain and crashed into the thick boll of a tree. Then, shaking a great, hairy snout, it rose on powerful legs and turned toward Elena again.

Elena flung her empty weapon aside as she stood up. "You're the last, Pedro!"

Clenching one fist, she ripped open the neck of her silk blouse. The moonlight warmed her face and throat, the soft cleavage of her breasts. Her heart raced with a wild rhythm. "When I kill you, the lineage of Cortez will come to an end!"

Elena threw back her head and howled, a savage sound that echoed from the top of the hill and through the trees. Fire ignited in her belly, burned her from the inside out. Her pale skin ripped open, toughened, and sprouted thick fur. Her bones reformed, grew larger, and her muscles throbbed with arcane power. She transformed, and the change brought both agony and joy, pain and pleasure. All her animal senses came alive.

In the Spanish night, the two werewolves charged at each other. Claws flashed amid snarls and howls. Blood sprayed the leaves and grass. One tried to break away; the other jumped on its back, sank teeth deep into shoulders and neck. They tumbled down the hillside, earth and stones cascading around them, until a thicket ended their fall.

Then, one hand stretched toward the sky. Moonlight kissed the claws. A pair of howls, a slashing stroke—

Blood fountained in the darkness.

With a cry of triumph, Elena rose from the bushes. Her hunched shape slowly straightened, and the red glow faded from her eyes. Her wounds, which were many, knitted, closed and healed. She looked down at the human body of Pedro, the last lieutenant of the sorcerer, Cortez, and prayed that a legacy of evil was done.

☙❧

Ramon Estrada rode quietly along the old coast road north of Pontevedra. A gentle breeze whispered in the night and stirred the folds of his pale silk cloak and the loose sleeves of his open shirt. Beyond the edge of the cliffs, the ocean surf boomed. The scent of salt tinged the air.

Tugging on the reins of his white mount, he paused and studied the sky. He knew the myriad stars by name, the many constellations and asterisms.

"There is Arcturus," he murmured to himself as if greeting an old friend. "And there, Spica." But it was the waxing moon rising over the pinnacle of a distant wooded hill that drew his attention.

He thought of Elena as he stared into its enigmatic glow, wondered where she was, what she was doing, why she sometimes slipped from their bed in the dark of night. He loved her as he had never loved anyone. He could admit it to himself, if not to her. Yet, they each kept secrets, and those secrets were keeping them apart.

A bright shooting star rushed across the firmament. Ramon Estrada watched it from the corner of his eye and noted the fine trail of smoke that lingered across the heavens. The faintest smile turned up the corners of his lips as the vapor slowly dissipated.

Then, through the boom and crash of the distant surf, another sound touched his ears—the creaking of coach wheels and the clip-clop of horses' hooves. Vehicles on the road so late at night were not common, but Ramon Estrada took his opportunities when they appeared. Reaching into the waistband of his trousers, he extracted a mask of glimmering silk, placed it over his eyes, and tied it securely. Next, he loosened his sword in its scabbard and checked his pistol.

Ramon Estrada guided his horse to the center of the road and waited. The wind rustled his thin cloak, and the moon shimmered on the fabric. In the darkness, he looked exactly like what the locals of Galicia believed him to be—a ghost.

The coach rounded a curve where the road came nearest to the edge of the cliffs. Pools of yellowish light from swinging lanterns cast a weird glow, and from the center of that radiance, four powerful Friesians emerged, as if through an otherworldly doorway. Behind them came a coach, ornate in its polished lacquer and woodwork.

Beneath his mask, Ramon Estrada raised one eyebrow and silently congratulated the coach's owner. The supernatural appearance of the strange contrivance surpassed his own.

Still a distance up the road, the coach stopped. The horses snorted as the driver rose cautiously to his feet, whip in hand, and stared at Ramon Estrada. For a long moment, all was quiet as driver and highwayman studied each other. Then, the driver made warding gestures with his free hand.

"*Fantasma!*" he called. "Begone! We have no business with spirits this night!"

Ramon Estrada answered in low tones, knowing his voice would carry even over the surf and the wind. "But I have business with you, *Señor*," he said. "From sunset to sunrise, I own the roads, and all who would pass must pay the highwayman's fee."

The driver hesitated. A leather shade eased up over one of the coach's windows. A woman's veiled face peered briefly out. Ramon Estrada could not hear her words, but the driver immediately drew a pistol from his waistband, aimed it, and fired. The flash lit up the road. The horses whinnied and pranced, and the coach lurched.

Still blocking the road, Ramon Estrada sat calmly in his saddle. When the gunsmoke cleared, the driver stared, as if unable to believe his eyes.

"I didn't miss!" he shouted. "I never miss!"

The pale highwayman responded with a sardonic chuckle. "*Lo siento, amigo.* Now I must double your fee."

The veiled face withdrew into the coach and the shade descended. The driver growled and slowly put his pistol down, his movements deceptively slow and cautious. Without warning, he flung himself down on his seat, snapped the reins, and cracked his whip over the horses' backs. Hooves tore at the earth, and the beasts leaped forward. The coach charged straight for Ramon Estrada, the driver's clear purpose clear to run him down.

Unperturbed, Ramon Estrada drew his own pistol and carefully aimed. The coach came on, closer and closer. A loud explosion—a flash!

The driver screamed as the whip went flying from his hand. His body jerked back against the coach, then tumbled sideways. For a moment, it looked as if he would fall into the road, but he caught the low rail on the side of the seat and voiced a second long cry of pain.

Ramon nudged his mount with his knees, and the steed danced lightly out of the coach's path. The conveyance raced by in a mad rush as the frightened and wounded driver scrambled to retrieve the dropped reins.

The highwayman knew exactly where he had placed his shot. The driver would not be using that whip, nor his pistol, nor anything else, with his right hand for some time. With half a grin, he tucked his own pistol back into his waistband, turned his steed, and prepared to give chase. But then, he jerked hard on the bridle. His horse reared in protest and stamped the ground as its rider twisted in the saddle to look over his shoulder.

A second coach came around the bend in the roadside. It looked even more ornate, more polished than the first. The lanterns on its rails burned with a deeper, sputtering light, and it moved with a strange silence on well-oiled wheels with black-clad riders, one on either side, like guardsmen.

Two fine coaches and two riders on the road to Pontevedra at midnight. It was more than unusual. It spoke of some purpose, and Ramon Estrada didn't think it could be good. He hadn't noticed it at first, but there was something ominous in these coaches with their black lacquer and black horses.

Galicia was a land of mystery and strangeness. The locals called it haunted, and not without reason. He was not the only one who prowled its hills and cliffs; his recent experiences with the sorcerer, Cortez, provided ample proof of that. Now, as he observed this unlikely caravan, his skin crawled.

It was warning enough for Ramon Estrada. He spurred his horse directly across the second coach's path, startling its team and its driver. He kept on going, riding into the darkness and into the concealment of a copse of trees.

The leaves, silvered by moonlight, shivered in the breeze. On the road, the coach stopped momentarily. Swords drawn, pistols in hand, the riders searched the edges of the road, circled the coach, but they ventured no further. Finally, the driver called them back, and they continued on after the first coach.

The highwayman rode out of the trees into the middle of the road to watch the last fading glow of the lanterns. He was not a man given to premonitions, but he knew trouble when he saw it.

Somewhere far away, a wolf howled. Ramon Estrada chewed his lip, removed his mask, and steered his horse for home.

ಆಲ್ಬಡ್ಬ

With hours to go before dawn, Elena rode quietly into the barn and unsaddled her horse. She had no real hope that Ramon was still asleep; he was as much a creature of the night as she. But if she could wash away the blood before he saw her, it might go a long way toward avoiding an argument. They were having too many arguments lately.

As she set the saddle down, a long shadow crept across the floor of the barn. With the moon at his back, Ramon stood in the doorway. She gave a small gasp and straightened. Then, she frowned. It wasn't easy to sneak up on someone with her wolfen senses, yet Ramon always managed it.

His dark eyes sparkled with disapproval. "How am I supposed to keep you in clothes?" he asked as he touched her arm.

Her blouse hung upon her in shreds. Her trousers were little better. She regarded him for a long moment, then put her finger through a rent in his shirt.

"I could ask the same of you, Ramon," she said with a hint of sarcasm. "This looks very much like a bullet hole."

Ramon Estrada grabbed her in both hands with a grip so tight he hurt her shoulders. His gaze burned into her, and despite herself, Elena knew a moment of shock and fear. Her heart quickened. Then her own gaze narrowed, and she knocked Ramon's hands away. She pushed him back and clenched her fists.

"I don't like to be manhandled, Ramon Estrada!" she hissed. "I don't care how angry you are with me!"

Ramon squeezed his eyes shut and slowly shook his head. "I'm not angry with you, Elena," he answered in a quiet voice. "I don't approve of your nightly hunts, but I understand . . ."

"Don't patronize me!" she shouted, interrupting him. She shook a fist under his nose, then recoiled as she noted the blood that covered her skin—not her own, but that of the creature she had just killed. Even in the dark barn, she could see the rich red blood, feel the stickiness of it between her fingers, smell its maddening odor.

Elena glared at Ramon. Suddenly, his heartbeat was loud in her ears. She could hear the blood rushing in his veins, feel the heat of it. He smelled rich, sweet. For an instant, he was not the man she loved at all. He was just—food.

Her skin began to tingle and burn, sensations that marked the beginning of her transformation. And she wanted it! She wanted it!

Horrified by her own thoughts, Elena dropped to her knees. She stared at her bloody hands, and began to tear the ribbons of cloth, stained with Pedro's blood, from her arms.

"My God!" she muttered. "What's happening to me, Ramon? What have I become?"

It was a momentary lapse. She got quickly to her feet before Ramon could answer. Elena Sanchez y Vega was not a woman to cower. She was in control of herself again.

Nevertheless, she stepped away from Ramon, no longer trusting herself to be near him, and away from the moonlight that spilled through the barn door.

"I'm leaving, Ramon," she announced in an icy voice. "I can't stay with you anymore."

"Shut up, Elena," Ramon shot back.

Her mind churned. She was a monster, a killer. No matter how she tried to control her transformations, sooner or later, they would control her. Her thoughts flashed to her little brother, who was asleep in the main house. She didn't dare to keep him near her, either.

"I'll make arrangements to send Alejandro to Barcelona. To a school, perhaps."

Ramon grabbed her again and shook her. "Shut up!" he ordered. "Stop it!"

His eyes bore into her with passion and anger. This time, when she tried to knock his hands away, he held on, flung his arms around her and drew her tight against him. Unexpectedly, his mouth came down upon hers.

She tried to protest. "Ramon! Listen!"

But he didn't. Ramon swept her up in his arms, carried to her a stack of fresh hay and knelt down gently with her. His movements were tender, but determined. As he kissed her face and throat and breasts, he tore away the shreds of her garments.

Elena stopped fighting. Her skin burned again, but with a welcome and exciting heat. Finally, with a deep sigh, she pulled Ramon down on top of her and began tearing at his clothing. Turnabout was fair play, after all, and she savored the feel of his naked, muscled flesh.

Dawn found them still in the haystack, slumbering in each other's arms. When a warm shaft of light speared down through the upper loft door and touched Elena's face, she snuggled closer into Ramon's arm. The songs of barn swallows disturbed her only slightly. Still, she clung to delicious sleep.

But when a deeper shadow fell across her eyes, she rubbed her nose, untangled herself from Ramon, and sat up. Then she shrieked. Her twelve-year old brother stood over them, his face pale, his mouth wide-open.

"Alejandro!"

Ramon Estrada shot awake and grabbed for his sword. Then, recognizing the unexpected invader, he reached, instead, for his cloak. With awkward haste, he spread the silken garment over Elena's body and his own. In her embarrassment, however, Elena ripped it from his hands and wrapped herself, leaving Ramon scrambling with a handful of strategically placed straw.

"Thank you for sharing!" he grumbled as he covered himself in the scratchy stuff.

"I could say the same to you!" Elena shot back. She looked to her brother. "Alejandro! Go back in the house this instant!"

The blond-haired boy stood as if paralyzed, his eyes still wide, jaw still agape.

"*Go!*" Elena ordered.

Alejandro licked his lips, then spun and ran out of the barn.

Elena sighed. "I think it's time for you to have a talk with him."

Ramon gave her a quizzical look and seemed about to protest. Instead, he pushed her back and snatched away the cloak.

"Later," he whispered. "I'm hungry again, and you look like breakfast." He rolled on top of her.

"Funny you should say that," she answered as he nibbled her throat. "For a moment last night, you looked like dinner."

They made speedy love, then sprang up and brushed away the pieces of hay that covered them both. Ramon grinned as he slipped into his trousers and boots. Elena wrapped herself once again in her lover's cloak. Together, they exited the barn, hurried across the lawn like youngsters sneaking home in the morning, and entered the ranch house through a side door to Ramon's bedroom.

"I must bathe," Elena said as she plucked another piece of hay from her hair. "Ramon, can you see to Alejandro and get his breakfast, please?"

Ramon pursed his lips tightly and nodded as he unwrapped her again. "We're a family now, Elena," he said, suddenly serious. "Don't forget that."

She kissed him, then tossed him a shirt from the closet. He slipped it over his head and adjusted the laces at his neck, played with the buttons on his sleeves and left the shirttails untucked. All the while, he watched her. Finally, mindful of the boy, he turned to leave.

She stopped him, calling his name in a low voice. "It's over now, Ramon," she said. "Pedro was the last. I don't have to hunt anymore, and they will never come after us."

Ramon answered with a grim nod. Pontevedra's citizens would not unlock their doors at night, nor unshutter their windows. Not for a long time. There had been too many killings, too many rumors of werewolves and ghosts, too many men like the sorcerer, Cortez. The tales and legends of haunted Galicia were no longer just tales to the townspeople, whose lives had been marked with terror, and he shared some blame for that.

He remembered his encounter with the pair of coaches. He'd not yet told Elena about them. Right now, however, it was time to think of Alejandro. In a very short time, the boy had become like a son to him. Alejandro and Elena mattered to him in a way that nobody had mattered in a very long time.

"I'll make breakfast for all of us," he said, "but hurry."

Alejandro was not in his room, nor anywhere to be seen. Ramon thought little of that. They lived on a ranch, after all. The boy had chores and performed them without complaint. He kept his own secrets, too, and secret places, like all boys. Alejandro would come when breakfast was ready, consume everything put before him, and then vanish again to ride his pony or swim in the nearby lake.

Ramon prepared a simple breakfast of toast and apricot jam, cheese, coffee and milk, and as he set them on the dining room table, he smiled at the sound of approaching footsteps. But it was not Alejandro.

Looking fresh in clean trousers and a white blouse with her wet hair tied back, Elena swept through the doorway. She wore a ruby pendant around her throat now, and the jewel glimmered in the light. The stone was special—it allowed her complete control over her transformations, even during the full moon. She wore it now like a promise to him.

"You're going to make some lucky woman a wonderful husband," she said as she noted the table.

Ramon held her chair for her. "What is the size of your dowry?" he teased. "I cannot be had cheaply." He cast a glance around as Elena reached for her coffee. "Now where is that boy? Alejandro!"

Alejandro didn't answer. Ramon frowned, and Elena set her coffee aside, untasted. It wasn't like the boy to avoid breakfast. Had the encounter in the barn upset him so much?

Elena pushed back her chair and rose. "I didn't propose," she said, continuing the banter, but there was a note of worry in her voice. "Let's look for him together."

They moved through the ranch house and out into the yard. "I'll check the barn," Ramon said. "Perhaps he's gone riding."

He walked briskly away and checked the stalls. Alejandro's pony was still there. The hayloft was empty.

Elena came into the barn, her manner agitated. "He's nowhere in the house. I looked in every room."

"We'll find him," Ramon answered. He knew the reason for Elena's worry. "Cortez is dead, Elena. He can't harm the boy, or anyone."

Elena bit her lip, and her body stiffened. "There were two coaches on the road last night," she said. Then a new look came over her face, and she touched his chest. "The bullet hole."

She was an observant woman. "I encountered them," he answered. "The driver took a shot at me. He'll never use that hand again."

"There was something . . . strange about them. I sensed it at the time, but Pedro attacked me and I had my hands full. What are these people doing here, Ramon? Who are they?"

Alejandro came suddenly through the door and glared at them as he put his hands on his hips. "Are you two in here again? What does a man have to do to get fed?"

Elena clapped a hand to her breast and sighed with relief. "Oh, so you're a man now?" She started toward her brother. "I'll feed you! Get inside, and I'll beat you with a loaf of bread!"

Ramon sighed also as he watched them cross the yard. It gladdened his heart that the boy was all right, and he chided himself for dark thoughts. The morning had started well. Very well, indeed. Yet, one small incident had changed everything, leaving him with an inexplicable sense of foreboding.

ଔଓଃଃ

All day long, Elena kept watch. Inside the house, she stayed near the windows. When she was outside, she scanned the horizons. She tried to conceal her edginess with light-hearted banter and easy laughter, by making special lunches and favorite dinners. But when Alejandro asked to ride his pony, she said no.

When the sun went down, they gathered in the parlor. She huddled with Alejandro over a game of chess and quietly discussed opening moves and strategies while she watched out the window. Ramon took a well-worn Bible from a shelf and curled up in a large chair by a lantern. Elena watched as he turned the pages.

He seemed to be studying the same passages over and over. "What are you reading?" she asked between chess moves.

"Genesis," he answered. He looked up and stared past her through the window with a strange, faraway look in his eyes.

"Again?" She couldn't hide a small frown. He often sat reading those same pages without ever explaining why. When she asked, he would say nothing. She found his silence irritating. After awhile, she let Alejandro win and suggested bed for all of them.

Even in Ramon's arms, she found little rest. When she slept at all, she dreamed of hunting. Mostly, she tossed and turned and tried not to wake her lover. Sometimes, she reached toward the bedside table and felt for her ruby pendant. She didn't need the talisman—the moon was not yet full. Still, it reassured her.

A soft knock sounded at the bedroom door. Elena and Ramon sat up at the same time as Alejandro stepped over the threshold with a finger to his lips.

"There are people outside," he whispered. "Strangers."

Elena sniffed. "Go back to your room, Alejandro, and wait." Ramon was on his feet, reaching for his clothes and the sword he always kept close, but she was not so eager for her little brother to see her naked again. When Alejandro departed, she sprang up.

"At least six," she told her lover as she snatched up garments of her own. "I can hear their horses. Two in the barn, and the others around the house."

"Leave them to me," he said darkly.

She reached for her boots. "Why should you have all the fun?" But before she had the first boot on, she glanced toward the night table.

Her ruby began to glow, to burn with a red heat that seared a mark into the polished antique wood. Elena grabbed for it, but the heat stung her fingers, and she snatched her hand away. The talisman was her most precious possession!

Alejandro ran back into the room. He'd dressed himself and carried the slingshot Ramon had made for him. "They set fire to the barn!"

Elena sniffed the air with her sharpened senses. *"Díos!* Not just the barn! The house is on fire! Ramon, get my brother out!"

Sword in hand, Ramon grabbed Alejandro's arm and steered the boy from the bedroom. Elena leaped to the window, tore away the curtain, and stared outward.

Red flames licked the walls of the barn, danced over its roof. Her horse, Ramon's, and Alejandro's pony raced out through the gaping doors, followed by a pair of sorrel mares. The panicked animals fled into the night.

An angry curse escaped her lips. New flames flickered on the other side of the glass. Ignoring the increasing heat and the danger, she lingered at the window. A line of riders galloped toward a hill in the distance. A black coach waited at the summit. Even in the night, she could see it.

Elena knew enough. Rolling across the bed, she snatched her ruby pendant. She would not leave it behind, though it burned her hand. A drawer in the night table contained her pistol. She took that, too, and raced from the room.

Smoke snaked through the hallway. Flames licked under the door to Alejandro's room. The parlor was already an inferno.

For the first time, Elena's animal senses played against her. She felt a rising panic, an instinctual fear of fire. She fought it, though, and dashed into the kitchen. Fire burned outside that window, too, and the glass shattered from the heat before she could react. Still, there was a door. Elena jerked it open and dived through a veil of flame.

She hit the ground rolling. "Ramon!" she called, as she scrambled up. "Alejandro!"

Ramon and her brother were nowhere to be seen, but a pair of riders charged from around a corner of the burning house straight for her. Elena brought her pistol up, too late. The weapon discharged, but the shot went wide as her assailants caught her arms, snatched her into the air, and carried her toward the coach on the hillside.

※ ※ ※

Ramon and Alejandro dashed around the side of the house, just in time to see Elena borne away. Ramon aimed his pistol and fired, but if the bullet found its mark, neither rider reacted. The boy would have given chase, but Ramon stopped him. They could never hope to catch the riders on foot.

Something red glimmered on the ground in the light of the flames. Ramon Estrada bent and snatched up Elena's ruby talisman. Curling his fingers tightly around the arcane jewel, he stared in the direction the riders had gone.

"Go to the lake, Alejandro," he told the boy through clenched teeth, "to the place where we fish. Wait for me there until I come for you."

Tears shone on the boy's cheeks as he looked up at Ramon, but he hesitated only long enough to pick up a stone for his slingshot before he sped away.

For a long moment, Ramon stared at the inferno that his house had become. He had lived here for a long time, but only recently had it become a home.

He gazed toward the distant hilltop and sensed, as much as saw, the movement of the coach as it rolled away. Whoever they were, they had come specifically for Elena. They would regret that.

He considered the talisman he held. The ruby had felt warm at first, but was beginning to cool. He slipped it into his pocket and went in search of his horse. Along the way, he would find a hollow tree, as well, a hiding spot where he kept another set of clothes.

He glanced toward the moon as it climbed toward zenith. Before it got much higher, the Highwayman would ride again.

೫ಌ෫ಌ

Even in the night, the tracks of the heavy coach were easy to follow. Ramon Estrada rode across the hills, down into a valley where a narrow path led to the Pontevedra road. By the time he reached it, he suspected where the tracks would lead.

The streets of the town were deserted. Here and there, the light of a lantern glimmered through window shutters, indicating that someone remained awake. Even the *tavernas* were closed and locked tight. The hoofbeats of his horse seemed to echo among the buildings. A dog growled from an alleyway. A cat dashed across his path. Otherwise, all was quiet. A hush hung over the town like a pall.

Still, he remained alert, his masked gaze sweeping from side to side. Down every street he rode, down every alley, past the commercial liveries and stables, wherever a coach might be hidden. When he reached the far side of town, he stopped, turned his horse in a slow circle, and studied the moonlit road. He spied fresh tracks again in the soft dust.

A cold anger filled the highwayman as he steered his mount in the direction of those tracks. Elena's captors were a bold lot. They had ridden right through the middle of town. He wondered—not for the first time—why he was not following a trail of blood.

Why had Elena not transformed and freed herself?

Ramon Estrada rode southward, contemplating the answers with a grim expression. When the tracks abruptly disappeared, he dismounted. At first, he thought it some trick of the moonlight, but the marks of the heavy wheels and its mounted escort simply ended as if the caravan had vanished.

It only confirmed the suspicion he had resisted—sorcery!

Ramon Estrada took the ruby pendant from his pocket as he stood up. The coach and riders might have continued southward. They might have turned off the road and gone east or west. He hated sorcerers, but he was not so easily put off a trail, nor was he without resources. Bending down again, he pinched a few grains of dust and sprinkled them over the ruby. Then, he held the talisman by its chain and let it spin. The moonlight struck it, and it sparkled with red fire.

He thought of Elena, to whom the jewel was bound. The ruby was part of her, and she part of it.

"Which way?" he asked.

The talisman continued to spin and sparkle, but it also began to swing on its chain, back and forth at first, and then in a widening circle, and then back and forth once more. Finally, it stopped swinging altogether. Defying gravity, it strained ever so slightly in a westward direction.

Ramon Estrada rose to his feet. A cold chill brushed over him. To the west, where the cliffs loomed above the sea, stood a structure that he knew too well, an abandoned Spanish fort that only one man had dared to claim.

Joaquin Cortez!

Thrusting the ruby back into his pocket, he leaped upon his horse and took off on an overland course. He needed no tracks to find the way to that cursed place. He and Elena had fought Cortez there, defeated him with his own magic, and rescued Alejandro.

This night, Ramon Estrada would fight another battle there for the woman he loved.

ଔଔଈଓଈ

Elena regained consciousness slowly. Her head throbbed from the blow to her skull, but the grogginess shrouding her senses suggested something more at work. Drugs, perhaps—or sorcery. She fought to open her eyes. What she saw caused her to gasp.

Joaquin Cortez stared down at her.

He was exactly as she had left him, on his knees, rigid, his face contorted with horror as his own magic was turned against him. He still wore the leather collar he had meant for her—the very same collar Ramon had slapped around his neck. She was back in Cortez's fort.

Yet, it was not Cortez who regarded her, only his corpse. His flesh was rotted and hung in strips on his bones. His eyes were gone, as were his fingers. The birds and the insects and the weather had taken their toll.

Elena felt a stirring of guilt. She had not killed Cortez, only left him paralyzed, to die from time, thirst, starvation and exposure.

A woman's voice spoke from behind her. "He was your lover once."

"He was a monster," Elena answered, her throat raspy. She tried to sit up, but found herself bound by heavy ropes. "He meant that collar for me, and worse for my little brother."

"He was my son."

Elena squeezed her eyes shut. Then, with an effort, she rolled over and looked at the old woman who spoke.

The woman's dress was finely made, a shimmering black with a high neck of white lace. Large hoop earrings of gold dangled from her earlobes, and a ruby not unlike Elena's own gem glittered on her bosom.

Elena remembered her first sight of the coaches on the road, the veiled face that seemed to look across the distance straight at her. Elena barked a short laugh. "He must have been a great disappointment to you."

"Indeed, he was," the old woman answered with a shrug. "Still, he was my son. But more importantly, he was the thirteenth member of a powerful *hungaro* coven." Her dark eyes burned as she loomed over Elena. "How is it that he should fall at the hands of a mere strumpet?"

"Strumpet?" Elena laughed again as she struggled against the weight of her bonds and managed to sit up. With barely concealed surprise, she noted the ring of men and women who stood around her in the torchlight, twelve in all.

Cortez would have been the thirteenth.

"Strumpet?" Elena repeated, inclining her head in open mockery. "You're one to talk, Inez Maria Cortez y Velasquez. Yes, I know you. You've slept with half the heads of state in Europe, or with their sons. Or their daughters."

Inez Maria Cortez y Velasquez pointed a bony finger. "Your life is on the line, girl," she said in an icy voice. She swept her hand around the room, indicating the others. "They are your jury and your judges, not I!"

"Old whore! You lie as easily as your son!" Elena had little chance for justice in such a court, nor did she look for it. She shook her head, tried to clear away the fog that muffled her senses.

Cortez's mother seemed to read her thoughts. "Don't try to change. We have the power to prevent it. You won't escape that way."

"We? It takes all of you, doesn't it?"

One of the other coven members spoke. "Enough! Take your revenge, Inez. Waste no more of our time."

"Dissension in the ranks?" Elena twisted around to get a glimpse of the speaker and noted the bandage on his hand. The driver Ramon had shot! She looked back at Inez. "You're not as powerful as you think, old woman."

Inez Maria Cortez y Velasquez grabbed a handful of Elena's hair and jerked her head backward. In her other hand, she held a knife. "I have enough power to cut that collar from around Joaquin's neck and lock it around yours!"

Elena tried to hide her fear. What could she do against so many? "Cut me loose, you cowardly sow, and I'll lock my hands around your neck!"

A scraping sound ratcheted suddenly through the chamber. Inez Maria Cortez y Velasquez froze. Elena shot a look around, unable to determine where the sound came from. It came again. The coven members grew uneasy. The women drew knives like Inez's. The men pulled pistols from their waistbands.

Like a ghost, Ramon Estrada emerged from the darkest corner. The wan torchlight shimmered on his cloak and mask, his white garments, and it glittered on the blade in his hand. He drew the point of that blade across the stone floor to make the grating sound a third time.

"The way you talk, Elena," he scolded. "Don't you ever try to make friends?"

"I've made you, Highwayman," she answered. "More than once. Do you like me in bondage?"

The coven member with the bandaged hand raised his pistol and fired. The flash lit up the chamber, filling the air with acrid smoke. A second pistol fired, then two at once.

For a moment, the room was silent as Ramon fixed Inez with his gaze. Another pistol fired. One of the women threw her knife. Ramon caught it effortlessly and dropped it on the floor. The bandaged driver rushed at Ramon, raising his empty pistol like a club. The steel point of Ramon's sword came swiftly up to pierce the driver's good hand. The pistol clattered, and the man screamed.

Inez Maria Cortez y Velasquez spun about to face Ramon. Her skirts swirled about her, and her shadow danced over the floor like that of an immense bat. She pointed her knife at Ramon and began to chant, raising her other hand as she muttered.

For an instant, the torches seemed to grow brighter, and the room wavered in the strange glow as if the air were liquefying. The rest of the coven joined in.

Elena felt as if her head was being squeezed in a vice. She struggled in her bonds, suddenly afraid not just of the coven or Inez, but also of Ramon!

Ramon reached out, caught Inez's wrists. The knife fell from her grip as he drew her close. His eyes bored into hers, and she tried to shrink back.

"Save your spells," he warned. "You will gain nothing but death if you persist."

"What are you?" Inez shrieked, asking Elena's question.

Ramon drew the old woman closer still. "I will not play games, nor risk more murder tonight. Look at me! If you have power, then open your mind and see me truly—if you dare. Then remember me. Remember my story!"

Inez's breath came in ragged gasps. Her eyes widened, and her jaw gaped as she dared to meet the iron hard gaze of the man who held her. Time seemed to stand still. Then, her old lips quivered.

"No!" she rasped. "Oh, no! It cannot be! I—I do see you! I know—*the mark!*"

She writhed and tried to pull away, but Ramon held her in an unyielding grip.

"Who am I, old woman?" he demanded, his voice the barest whisper. His words were for Inez alone. "Say my name."

Elena strained to hear.

"Son . . . !" Inez's voice was little more than a harsh, despairing croak. "Son of Adam!" She collapsed to her knees, her mind seeming to crumble. "Cain! You are *Cain!*"

Ramon let Inez go. The old woman sprawled at his feet, shaking and sobbing, but the highwayman was not done with her. Bending low, he whispered into her ear.

"My curse is upon you," he said with chilling calm. "Never come to Pontevedra again. Never threaten my family."

Inez's knife lay at his feet. Ramon picked it up. "Now, let's unwrap this pretty package." He cut Elena's ropes, and Elena tried not to shrink from his touch.

ఴ⌘ఴ

"I heard, Ramon," Elena said nervously after a deep silence. The fort was long behind them before she spoke. Pontevedra, too, lay behind them. She didn't know where they were going, but she clung to Ramon, riding behind him bareback on his horse through the darkening hills, more afraid than she wanted to admit. "I don't understand."

"Forget what you heard," he answered in a tight voice. "It's better for both of us if you forget."

She leaned her head upon his shoulder and shivered. "What is the Mark of Cain?"

She felt him tense. After a long moment, he answered. "Immortality."

Elena digested that. "Your soul." She shivered again. "If you can't die, you are denied the promise of heaven?"

It seemed too horrible to contemplate, yet she couldn't turn her mind from it. She swept the countryside with her gaze, taking in the stark nighttime beauty of the Galician landscape. "You had Eden," she whispered.

Ramon stopped the horse and looked around with her. "Sometimes," he said, "when things are right between us, I think I've found Eden once again."

She still couldn't grasp what he was telling her, but she understood enough. Ramon or Cain—he was a man with a heartbeat that she could feel, with warmth and breath. He trembled as if he, too, were afraid, and she knew suddenly that whatever he was, whoever he was, he needed her.

After all, what promise of heaven did she, a monster, truly have?

She glanced upward and touched the ruby talisman at her throat. The moon hung over the top of a low hill, igniting the distant trees with pale fire. It would be full in a few more nights.

"I love you." She sat up straighter, and when he didn't respond she gave him a teasing shake. "Tell me your name, *Señor*."

He started the horse forward again and steered toward a silvery lake.

"I am Ramon Estrada," he answered, but he spoke the words without conviction.

THE PILLOW BOY OF GENERAL SHU

by Daniel Fox

Daniel Fox is a British writer who first went to Taiwan at the millennium and became obsessed, to the point of learning Mandarin and writing about the country in three different genres. The first novel, *Dragon in Chains*, is now out from Del Rey. Before this, he published a couple of dozen books and many hundreds of short stories, under a clutch of other names. He has also written award-winning poetry and plays.

Here, he offers a multi-layered story about the price of obsession, but also about the other side of that dark human experience: compassion and, ultimately, redemption.

Any man, every man can find himself pinned by a moment, heart-stolen, abruptly turned around.

The same is no doubt true of women also, but General Shu was not much concerned with women.

Nor, to be honest, had he been too much concerned with men before this, except as units in a calculation. Shu was no master commander, he had no gifts at warfare or leadership; his talents lay in provision, in negotiation, in anticipation of need. The army was such a size, the river was this broad: it could be crossed in two days, with this many boats brought from here and here. Shu knew. How and where the boats were likely to be

THE PILLOW BOY OF GENERAL SHU

hidden, that too. And he wouldn't forget provender for the men during this delay, nor for the horses; neither would he forget to propitiate the river-gods, to ensure an easy crossing.

A spy captured, a ransom to be paid? Ask Shu, how much is reasonable. A city taken, a levy to be raised from its no doubt grateful citizens? Ask Shu, how much they can afford. A city not taken, its walls manned and its gates barricaded? Ask Shu whom to bribe and what to offer. This was his genius, and why he had to be a general. He would never win a battle, but he could make any battle winnable, if a well-fed and rested soldiery was enough to win it. If not, he was still the man to buy a victory, if someone on the other side was only prepared to sell.

He followed the army, rather than leading it. Necessarily, he followed close. This day, heavily astride an indignant horse not accustomed to the work, he huffed into the public courtyard of the provincial governor's great house. The dignified comforts of his carriage were stuck in highly undignified mud a mile behind, and a succession of urgent messengers had only demonstrated how essential it was for him actually to be here. The governor was a fool, and twice a fool to be so swiftly overtaken by his follies; the more military generals, they were all fools too, by dint of long practice. If they were allowed their head—the governor's head, in this instance, along with those of all his household—then the army's forward march would be delayed by a month or more, while it lingered to pacify a restless and unreliable province.

Shu's mount might be unexpected—he kept a saddle-horse for show, largely, the occasional brief parade—but his face and figure were not. A soldier ran to seize the horse's bridle and haul it to a welcome halt; another brought a blessed mounting-stool, to save him the indignity of an ungainly slither to ground.

Fat men should not ride horses. That had been his overriding thought all this way, all the sway and jar of it, every bruised and aching measure of his flesh. Probably, fat men should not be soldiers at all. His bones were padded most unsoldierly, and he knew that he was mocked.

He patted vaguely at his distempered horse's neck, because he was a decent man and truly bore no grudges. Then he had sweat-froth on his fingers, and had to wipe it on his skirts. Horses make poor plotters; their revenges are immediate, though some are lasting. He was sore now, and he would be more sore tomorrow.

No matter. A horse was a passing sorrow. What happened here would be enduring, whichever way it went.

As briskly as he could manage, Shu bustled through to the inner courtyard, where the generals would be sitting now in judgment.

In some respects at least, he was too late. There was a bamboo framework rigged up beyond the gateway, with a man hung from it. What was left of a man. Nothing clung to him except his blood, no vestige of an earthly rank, but still he was no doubt, no doubt at all, late governor of this province.

Well. Shu had not really expected to save him. If a man will stand, will declare his public allegiance to an emperor in fast retreat and close the gates of his cities against the horde that pursues, he cannot expect kind treatment from that horde when his own gates are broken, as broken they will be. What can withstand a horde?

One dead man was not a catastrophe, except perhaps to himself. His whole house was another matter. Trying to stride, Shu scuttled past that foul and dripping scaffold, to where the lords of men—his fellow generals, he reminded himself, and none of them blessed with the seal and authority of the generalissimo, as he was himself—sat in conclave in the shade of a pavilion.

Uninvited, unexpected—they had no doubt been counting on the mud to keep him out of their councils, out of their hair—he sat himself among them, sweaty and disordered and utterly disagreeable. Whatever they wanted to decree, he was determined to disagree with it; and his voice carried more weight than all of theirs combined, for which they would never forgive him.

Not a man to haver or dissemble—not when so simple an act as sitting chafed his thighs, and it was their fault entirely for being so precipitate, for causing him to hurry—he said, "So: you have killed the governor, then. How many more?"

"None yet, but of course his family—"

"Of course his family must be let live," Shu grunted, in a mockery of agreement. "If you slay his family, who had no hand in his folly, then you must slay all his councillors who were as guilty as he; and by the time you have slain their families too, and reached perhaps a little further towards the officers who carried out the governor's orders, then the whole province will be in terror of you, for who among them can be innocent where their masters are so guilty?"

"So they should be in terror," said General Ho. "A rebel province deserves to cower before the blade. Yes, and feel its bite."

Actually, of course, these men here were the rebels, but Shu forbore to say so. Instead, "Will you leave half your force behind, to impose this terror?"

"No, of course not. We pursue the emperor . . ."

". . . With these people at your back, all churned about with hate and horror."

"We do not fear peasants!"

"No? Perhaps you should. It's these peasants who will feed you on the march and through the winter. Or not. Their mattocks have more power than your swords, in the end."

A shrug from General Ho. "We have heard all this from you before, Shu."

"You have. And I was right before, and I am right now, and you know it. You knew it before I came, or you would not have waited for me," blithely ignoring the fact that they had not. "Half the late governor's family would already be dangling from that scaffold in their blood, while you distributed his women among the soldiery, while you kept his daughters for yourselves."

Which was to say, *You are all my lap-dogs truly*, and they knew that too, and resented it with a smoky fury that would bring grief soon enough to someone, but not to him.

A boy came with a tray, and squatted in the corner to prepare tea. Good. Tea was soothing for turbulent minds. He himself was hot and thirsty after the discomforts of his hurry. He would be glad of tea, and the chance it offered to speak of other matters. The army's swift advance, the boy-emperor's desperate retreat, the generalissimo's sure success: all of these were proper subjects to be raised and praised over the perfumed pleasures of the tea-cup.

And meantime here was distraction for the eye too, no need to dwell further on the grisly horror in the courtyard. He could watch instead the boy's slender grace over kettle and charcoal-pot in the wreathing steam and the shadows. Watch as his sleeve fell back as he reached for the tea-bowl, see how a glimpse of line and movement could define the perfection of a wrist. . . .

The boy came forward on his knees to serve Ho and then the others, one by one. Now, watching, Shu was no longer distracted. He was snared, rather. In the grim light from the courtyard, the boy had a still-ethereal beauty, as though death and horror could not mark or mar him. There was no tremble or hesitancy in his fingers, no fear in his eyes, only the shy deference that was proper. His thick black hair was as tame as oil and fingers could achieve, not quite a porcelain smoothness; that privilege was owned by his skin, which was immaculate. Nothing about him was as coarse as his clothes. He was like polished jade, Shu thought, that could never be debased by the sacking it was wrapped in.

Shu shifted his stool a little at the table, to see the boy better when he retreated to his corner, to the kettle and the brew-

THE PILLOW BOY OF GENERAL SHU

things. Let the other generals argue between themselves; they could make all his own points for him anyway, and believe them better from their own lips than from his. Let them imagine he was listening, governing in silence. What he wanted was in his sight, more and far more than he had come for, more and far more than he had ever hoped to find here.

In truth, he had expected to find the generals dividing up the house and its treasures between themselves. Having forestalled that, prevented it, now he wanted one of its treasures for himself. A son of the house might have been difficult to claim, but a serving-boy? He could surely manage that, without giving Ho distemper . . .

He was, perhaps, more obvious than he thought, less subtle than he liked. General Ho was saying unusually little, being altogether too complaisant. Waiting, perhaps, for an opportunity to spring. Well, Shu would not give it him. If Shu knew one thing, he knew how to wait. He could ride away from here on that appalling horse, and send later for the boy. . . .

The boy was coming forward with fresh tea: a forward boy. He was kneeling at Shu's side, his bare wrist brushing Shu's: a careless boy, except that the gesture had been entirely careful. As was the catch of their eyes together, the boy's dark and luminous, enticing, pleading. An importunate boy. And an alert one, seeing Shu's interest and responding to it, seeing something for himself therein. In all of this, a desirable boy; and more, seen closer, still a beautiful boy.

Shu said—no. Shu tried to speak and had no voice, and had to pause and clear his throat before he could say, a little thickly, "Boy. Who rules this house, with your master dead?"

"His sons are gone, lord," fled, the boy must mean, which might perhaps be another reason why the governor hung alone on his scaffold there, "so my mistress, I suppose. If you do not?"

A grunt, and, "Perhaps I do. Smart boy. Where may I find your mistress?"

The boy told him but wouldn't show him, wouldn't follow into the women's quarters. A whole boy, then, and keen to stay that way. Shu sent him instead to wait in the outer courtyard, with the abominable horse; and let the weight of his own authority carry him crushingly over all tradition, into another man's harem.

A dead man's, and Shu made a kinder invasion than it would have faced without him. Which perhaps they knew, these frightened women and their eunuch servants; word travels swiftly, incomprehensibly, through a house that stands under pain of destruction. They welcomed him as best they could, better than he should have expected. No shrieking, no cowering, only silent and rapid conduct to the new widow in her grief.

She was genuinely grieving, he saw, though perhaps not for her husband. She had closed the shutters, against any view of his dangling body; that was just as well, though nothing could have shut out his screaming. He must, Shu thought, have screamed. Perhaps a lot, perhaps for a long time.

". . . A kitchen boy?" she repeated, bewildered.

"His name is Shen." A cautious boy, a deep boy.

"Is it?" She waved a hand vaguely. "Of course, take what you want . . ." meaning, *You will anyway; you have already taken my husband, my life.* And then she said what she really meant, what she really mourned, "My sons . . . ?"

"They are gone," he said, "which was wisdom, and may have saved their lives. They will not be pursued, and perhaps they have not gone far. They may send a message," if they were not too wise to be so careless. "If you have the chance to reply," if they hadn't ridden far and far, beyond all telling, "tell them to lie low until the last of the army has moved on. Whomever we leave here as governor, he will have instructions; they should be safe to return, if my word has any weight behind it."

And he patted his great comfortable pillow of a stomach, to show her that it did.

THE PILLOW BOY OF GENERAL SHU

There would be no second journey on the atrocious horse; Shu waited until his carriage came eventually to collect him. His brother generals were gone by then, long gone in pursuit of the endlessly-running emperor. Shu might have waited indoors, in comfort, with his boy, but the house was too much troubled already. The last thing its mistress needed was a late-lingering and most unwelcome guest.

Instead, he put the boy to the horse's bridle and led them both out onto the road. Here there were no comfortable benches or blossom-trees to give a perfumed shade, no fish rising in drowsy pools, no gods in niches, watching: only the road, endless and empty. But there was at least a wall at their backs, to screen them from the house and vice versa; there was a post to hitch the horse to, freeing the boy to attend to his new master.

Who was stranded suddenly, his mouth opening and closing like a stranded fish, as he approached and backed away from saying various variously stupid things.

He was master here, he told himself sternly, and he could simply look if he wanted to, if he chose. He did want, but he chose not. He chose to gloss his looking with speech, as if he could draw the lad into an easy, natural conversation, as if a general and a kitchen-boy could ever match mind to mind in comfort. By the side of a weary road, say, after a bad morning, while they waited with a thread-thin patience for a carriage that was tediously slow in coming.

As if he had ever had the skills of common discourse, as if charm and subtlety and insight came to hand, to mind as readily as tonnage and mileage and usage, as if words were numbers and could all be made to march in line. . . .

"Can you read, boy?" It was how he was accustomed to deal with the world, by means of questions, answers, facts.

"No, lord."

"Ah." He had, to be frank, small use for a kitchen boy. He had no kitchen, nor any immediate prospect of a house to put it in. He might have found legitimate employment for a secretary. Clutching at straws, "You can be taught, perhaps, if you are quick to learn. Are you—?"

A smile, small and quiet, enough to break the heart. "I am told so, lord."

"Good. That's good."

Even so, he could never be quick enough. The sharpest mind needed years to learn its characters; Shu would not have years to justify his boy. Not months, even. He would have no time at all. As soon as the news was out, as soon as the boy was seen in his shadow. . . .

Well. His brother generals had their personal servants, their body-slaves and favourites. He was entitled too. They would laugh only because they always laughed, as people always had. There was no harm in that.

At last, young eyes conjured what they waited for. "Is that your carriage, lord?"

"Is it?" He saw, perhaps, something breast the rise; yes, certainly, a shape coming down, lit by occasional sparks within its own shadow. "I expect so. I hope so. What can you see?"

"It is, it's a carriage. It looks mighty large, lord: wheels higher than my head. And drawn by, drawn by . . ." He hesitated, shaded his eyes with his hand, looked again, looked around for startled confirmation. "Drawn by *fire-horses*?"

Shu chuckled. "Not quite," though the boy earned credit for the attempt, and for his courage too. Likely this was his first brush with the spirit world outside of gutter-magic, a fire-spell or a murky potion. Nine boys out of ten would have been running by now.

This boy stood and stared, and now it did feel entirely natural and easy for Shu to let his big blunt hand with its missing finger rest on that slender neck, to feel bones and tendons and the surge and suck of young blood beneath soft and supple skin.

To grip tight enough for reassurance, to shake him gently as a sign of adult authority in this new world, to let him know where he belonged now, here at Shu's side; to murmur, "Don't be afraid, Shen. That is your home now," *this is your home now, beneath my hand,* "and no matter if demon-cattle draw it forward day by day. Only the view changes. You'll learn."

"Yes, lord."

"You should perhaps begin by learning to call me master," as he was not a soldier and couldn't be a scribe, could only be, what, a house-boy in this curious snail-shell house. . . .

"Yes, lord," he said complacently, twisting in Shu's grip to press a daring cheek against his arm. Unless it was the defiance that was daring, and the cheek that was complacent. Shu couldn't tell; he had no experience, nothing to draw on. This world was abruptly just as new to him, implicit with things stranger and far stranger than a carriage drawn by unearthly creatures.

It reached them at last, a vast square block of a wagon hauled by six great black beasts with fire in their bones and smoke beneath their hide. Sometimes he thought they were only fire and smoke, and their physical shape was pure illusion. But it was an illusion that held good, mile by mile and month by month; that was solid wrought iron that muzzled and yoked them and linked them to the traces, and those were very real hollows that their hooves left, bitten deep into the road.

Shu had paid his price to have them, and still thought them a bargain. He'd bargained with a demon for a herd to draw the wagon-train, to keep up with the army in its chase; that deal had been made with prisoners' blood. But then he'd needed six more for himself, not to be left behind, and the cost of those of course had come to him.

There were those who thought he'd lost his finger in the war, on his climb to rank. He'd never seen any reason to disabuse them, but actually he'd spent it on the war, which was a very different thing.

☙❦❧

Shu had designed this carriage himself, though he had never needed to be so coarse as to say so.

Screens folded out from the walls, to divide the interior into separate small rooms: a reception chamber, a place of work, a bedroom.

No kitchen.

With the screens folded back and his things packed away for travel, it seemed bleak enough, a poor space to offer to a boy even for his own use, let alone as an expression of his master. Shen seemed delighted even so, finding his way swiftly from the clever hinges in the walls to the challenge of the chests, how some of them opened out to make furniture while they still contained Shu's papers and scrolls, his brushes and inks, his clothes and cushions and bedding.

"This one? What does this do," poking and prodding with delicate ineffectual fingers, "how does this unfold. . . ?"

"That one," laughingly, reaching to pull him to his feet where he came lightly, easy to the touch, "that one is just a chest. . . ."

☙❦❧

No kitchen, but it didn't seem to matter. When the light failed, when the carriage stopped, Shen made tea over a charcoal fire outside. Shu drank it at his desk, reading the reports that were already coming back to him from the vanguard. He made calculations, made notes, wrote instructions in swift clear characters on thin strips of paper. By the time those had been rolled and slipped into bamboo tubes, sealed and sent away with runners, there was food: jewelled rice with egg, hot and spicy and delightful, neatly and delightfully served.

THE PILLOW BOY OF GENERAL SHU 135

At length—when the bowl was empty, essentially—he remembered to ask, "Have you eaten too?"

"Oh yes, lord. With the men." And, in response to a blankish frown, "I made congee for the guards. After so much work, digging this out of the mud, they needed something hot."

Of course they did. Another day, any other day, Shu would have known it, would have seen to it himself. Today—well, today he nodded, but said, "In the future, feed them, certainly, but take your own meals with me." And, when the boy seemed likely to protest, "It is an order."

"Yes, lord."

And then the boy was clearing away the empty dishes, and Shu need only sit back and watch him move in the lamplight; and he thought this might almost be all he wanted, just to see beauty in action, in private, and know it to be his own.

But there was more, inevitably, more to come: a time when the bed had been laid out and all the lamps dimmed bar one, and in that depth of shadow he could watch as Shen slipped the coarse tunic off his shoulders and let it fall, revealing himself to be entirely the boy, entirely the body beautiful.

And then that same implausible boy—unlooked-for ever, unexpected utterly, irresistible now—stepped forward and put his slim fingers and his urgent attention to undressing Shu. It was a more complicated procedure, with buttons and sashes and lacings to be addressed, but there seemed to be an astonishingly short time—and that to Shu, who was the acknowledged expert in the study of time and work—between those firm, determined hands easing off his slippers and those same hands unknotting his breech-cloth and setting it aside.

And then returning to his body, impertinent, imperious; and if Shu were aware of the contrast at all—the great sagging ageing bulk that was himself, against the lithe slender subtle ivories of youth—it could have been only for a minute, before any notion of himself as a separate creature, a mockable man, was stripped away entirely in the hot damp bewildering wonder that the boy made of his bed.

⊰❦⊱

Messengers came, continued to come all night, as ever, and were for once delayed till morning.

At some time in the night, the wagon-train that followed the army caught up and overtook. This was commonplace, Shu's own order. He liked to bring the demon-cattle through on night-roads where he could, not to alarm the peasantry. The men could rest just as easily by day, and the cattle saw perfectly well in the dark.

What was unusual was his being in his bed but yet awake to hear the creaking of ropes and axles, the hot breath and stamping of the beasts, the low calls of the men who worked them.

In bed and awake and not solitary, that was unheard-of. He would have resented sleep this night, that might snatch away a moment's understanding of slender bones and solid flesh, skin pressed stickily against his skin, a weight sprawled uncomfortably across his legs and a head nestled into his shoulder.

A head that stirred, that lifted, although he would have sworn he had not uttered a sound or twitched a muscle; a body that shifted itself as though reading his discomforts, settling more snugly against his side; a voice that murmured, "Lord?"

"Did the wagon-train wake you? It's nothing, it'll pass by and be gone," as this night would, and all the world be new in the morning.

"My lord was awake," Shen said, as though he had read it in his sleep and so roused as a good boy ought.

"It doesn't matter." Indeed it had been a quiet joy, a treasure to be held against uncertainty, the possibility of loss.

"No, lord," a kiss to his chest, an interlinking chain of kisses, "but now we are both awake," a hint of teeth at his breast, at his nipple, "and it would seem a shame to waste that happy chance. . . ."

Time was a wagon-train, a series of moments, passing by and gone.

☙❧

In the morning there was tea again, and congee for all in the open air around the conjured fire, even for Shu—"Eat, lord," laughingly, "eat with us this morning, and this evening I will eat with you"—and so on, the everlasting haul along roads that unreeled like silk from a bobbin but never so smoothly.

Shu sat on his well-padded rump in his well-padded chair, jolted and bumped none the less. He read and scribbled charcoal notes and struggled to think clearly, and every hour called a halt so that he could write his orders properly and send them off via his tail of messengers, and the only unusual thing in that was the struggle, and the only unusual thing in his carriage was the boy, who was the cause of it all.

By day's end they had overtaken the wagon-train again in a familiar game of leapfrog—Shu being happy enough to startle peasants with his own turnout, if it saved him the inconveniences of travelling at night—and all but caught up with the rear echelons of the army, stalled now at the same river that had delayed the emperor. Stalled, but not for so long; the emperor had no General Shu to organise boats fetched down from a lake on wagons that would themselves float like boats to carry troops across beside the bridge that other troops were mending with timbers cut from the woods that fringed that same lake and carried on those same wagons. . . .

All day he had been arranging this and all that it implied. All day he had been talking softly to his illiterate boy, explaining every message received and every message sent, every consequence. It helped, he found, to keep things clear in his own head. Shen was a perfect audience, interested in everything, asking occasional pertinent questions, rolling and sealing Shu's papers as he wrote them. If fingers occasionally brushed skin, if eyes more often brushed eyes, that was more than a perquisite, that was an incentive.

After two days, it was no longer a surprise to find someone else at his elbow, in his eyeline, in his bed.

In less than a week, it was already a habit to look around for him, those times, those few times that Shen wasn't immediately there: as though something were wrong in the world, a little out of kilter, that needed a boy's light body to rebalance it. He had never strayed far. He might be walking with the guards at the rear of the wagon, chewing ox-hide and listening to their tales of the war; he might be riding up front with the wagoners, learning to crack a firewhip and drive a team of hell-cattle. Boy-like, he wanted to be everywhere, but he always came back to Shu.

By the end of that first week, Shu still didn't have a rank, a position to put to the boy or what he did, that curious mixture of the most intimate services and the most practical. "He is my servant," he would grunt, knowing how inadequate that was, so general it seemed both meaningless and untrue, both at once. And a betrayal, that too.

☙❦❧

The first time he heard someone else's appraisal, it was one guard speaking to another: "Where's he off to, then?"

"Who—oh, the general's pillow-boy?"

"Who else?"

"Looking for a duck, he said. For the big man's supper. Promised me the wings if I can find him fresh mushrooms for tomorrow. Not sure I trust him, but . . ."

But Shu knew for certain sure what he could expect for supper, tonight and tomorrow. And he understood a little more about his boy's systems of supply and barter, and was impressed by how swiftly those systems had been set in place, knowing as he did a little about the subject. And he knew a lot more about how his boy was seen and spoken of.

He wanted to be angry, but that was difficult. Shen was more, so much more than a bed-warmer—but even to Shu, what counted for more? What did he treasure more than the nights, the long slow sleepless nights? The rest of it anyone could achieve, anyone trained to cook and run errands and care for a man's small comforts on the road. The nights, though—well, no one else could suffice for that, because no one ever had.

Even so, Shu resented the phrase and would not countenance it. The first time one of his brother generals used it to his face, he was angry almost to the point of indiscretion. Only a lifetime's training held his temper, schooled his face to its common neutrality, let the moment pass.

Shen himself cared not a whit what they called him. "Body-servant," he said, rubbing oil lingeringly over that great edifice that was Shu's body, "pillow-boy," adjusting the pillow beneath Shu's head, "catamite," dipping his head just briefly to kiss Shu's straining cock, "what difference? They are not here, they don't know what I am to you, or you to me. They can call me what they like."

"And me?" Shu managed, struggling a little for the air. "How should I call you, then?"

A bright smile, and, "You should call me Shen. And you should call me when you want me. I am here."

It was inevitable, of course, that all the army knew he kept a boy. It was inevitable too—because he did not like it—that all the army would come to call Shen his pillow boy. He learned to live with it, as he learned to live with the boy: day by day, moment by raw new moment. When Shen's physical presence was no longer startling to him, when indeed he took it almost—*almost!*—for granted, he could still be startled by something inside himself, an abstract of Shen, how the boy lay curled within his thoughts and deeper yet, in heart and head together.

Day by day, the boy made his life so much easier. So many little things he no longer had to think about or order: his clothes were washed and mended; whenever he was hungry, there was food; a hundred errands a week, he only had to ask and Shen would run them. A hundred more, he didn't have to ask. The boy anticipated with all the discreet grace of a spirit servitor, sworn and bound.

In all the stories Shu had ever heard, true or otherwise, there was a price to be paid for such service. He had paid his own price for his demon hauliers; sometimes in the darkest reaches of the night, he would dread the day this new price fell due. And reach a heavy arm across the boy in hopes of protecting him, at least, when that day came. Hell is inexorable and debts are not forgiven, but it should not be the innocent who pay.

Here was a message for General Ho, where he should billet tonight, where his supply-wagons would be looking for him.

Here was a message for Captain Hao Cho, here one for Captain Lin, one for the quartermaster on the wagon-train.

There could be a dozen such at every stop, and the boy was illiterate. But he only needed telling once, which paper was to go to whom. He would roll them into their bamboo sleeves and seal them and hand them out to the waiting messengers with never a mistake. Shu didn't trouble to check him any more. Perfect trust: it was a rare and a wonderful gift.

And, he was sure, must be paid for.

Sometimes he roused in the darkness and found himself alone, which was unexpected now, new now, terrifying, wrong.

There would be lamplight, though, beyond the bedroom screens. He would call softly, and Shen would come at once, with apologies. He had been sleepless, bitten by the night mare or roused by the wagons passing. Better to find something to do when he was wakeful, he would say, than to lie restless in the bed and risk waking his master. He had been grinding inkstone for the morning, perhaps; he was sorry if the noise of it had woken his lord, but he knew a way to make him sleep again. . . .

Perfect trust.

ଊଊଊଊ

General Ho broke the seal, unrolled the paper, read it and grunted discontentedly. He hated to lose even a day in this endless chase. Shu was right, though, Shu was always right: he was short on supplies, and the men would benefit from a rest. And be hotter on the trail thereafter, knowing that the emperor had gained a little, not enough. . . .

He gave his orders, then, or Shu's orders, rather:

"There is a dry river-bed ahead. We will drop down into that, and make our way along it to a certain point, described on this map here," an enclosure in the bamboo. "Camp there, where the wagon-train will look to find us in the morning."

And meantime the troops could sleep late, comfortable on soft dry silt; and if the emperor's rear guard had left any spies behind, the chasing army would seem to have vanished from view. They would have no idea where the rebels were, or in what numbers, or where they might reappear. . . .

ଊଊଊଊ

Captain Hao Cho, Captain Lin: their orders had them marching their squads through the night, to meet up before dawn at a lakeside rendezvous.

This lake was artificial, made by the damming of a river long ago. It supplied the headwaters for a canal now, long and straight, navigable for a hundred miles, more.

The emperor had loaded all his supplies onto barges, Shu's message said; these convenient waters were saving him days, saving his army the work of carrying and hauling.

Only break the dam, the orders said, and the lake will drain itself dry. The canal will have no water, and all the emperor's goods will be stranded in a muddy bottom, all but inaccessible, irrecoverable. Men might work for days to break it, but each captain had a magician in his train. Those two together, working with the men, they should suffice. . . .

⊰❀⊱

The quartermaster's orders also had him hurrying all night. Nothing unusual in that, except that the hurry was more pronounced. A hundred of his demon-cattle were needed urgently, as draft animals to clear a calamitous rockfall where the emperor's retreating army had sabotaged the road.

His quickest way to deliver them would be to feed them into a certain dry riverbed here—the point marked on the map enclosed—and have men drive them hard with firewhips, stampede them up. The banks were too steep to climb; the animals would have nowhere to go but exactly where they were needed, faster than they could possibly be herded. . . .

⊰❀⊱

It was in the morning, then, when General Ho was looking out for his supplies, that instead he heard first the confused cries of his men and then a dull and rising roar.

THE PILLOW BOY OF GENERAL SHU

When he saw it, dark and thunderous, it was hard to understand: a wall that moved so fast, that engulfed so much, whatever it met it seized.

Men tried to scramble up the banks, and fell back as the soft soil crumbled beneath their weight, and were swept up in the flood of filthy brutal water. Nothing could stem it, nothing avoid it.

A few, a hopeful few leapt onto horses and tried to outrace it. The general was among them, for certainly he should survive this, he who had survived wars and revolutions, a dynasty and its fall.

They might, perhaps, have been lucky, but they met another wall coming the other way: a wall of smoke and fire and hoof and hide, strange flesh, a black stampede.

And hauled their horses cruelly to a halt, and turned to face the flood; and saw hopelessness and death, and turned again. And tried to charge the bank, tried to mount it by sheer force of will and spurs and fury, terror too.

And failed, and fell back, and were consumed.

ଔଔଔଔ

Shu heard the news perhaps even sooner than the generalissimo himself. People needed to be told what to do, and they were accustomed to have Shu tell them.

Also, therefore, he heard the reasons for the catastrophe and deduced the causes, more or less.

And closed his carriage door, and sat down with the boy Shen face to face, with a blade between them as the price that must be paid; and said, "It will come back to me, you know. Of course it will." In all its ugliness and confusion, with a slow and brutal death to follow.

"No, lord. The writing of the orders is . . . conspicuously not yours."

"To you, then. It will come back to you," in much the same tone of voice, all doom.

Shen was almost smiling as he shook his head. "You had a fall in the carriage here, my poor fat lord, and hurt your hand," and the bewitching boy's fingers took Shu's hand and laid it out flat and open on the low table, parallel to that lethal knife; and he set his own hand on Shu's forearm so that they sat slender wrist to fat wrist, pulse to pulse, "and all the world knows I am illiterate, no use to you at all in your work. It was a scribe wrote those orders for you, and not at all what you told him to write; he was a wicked man, suborned by a captain with a grudge. They should both have died for it, by now. Orders have been sent. Conspicuously your own orders, justice in due measure."

Shu shivered a little at the meticulous care of his planning, but it could still not be careful enough. "The generalissimo will have his magicians test this, they will ask questions in hell—"

"And will learn nothing to the contrary. I have a promise. And have paid for it."

There was a bandage, a clotted wound on his arm. Shu said, "You told me your knife slipped, slicing bitter melons."

"Yes, lord. Forgive me, I lied to you."

Now, at last, he might allow himself the callous rush of relief, that it must be someone else and not himself—or Shen!—on the cruel scaffold. And then, overwhelmed, appalled, "What are you, boy?" Ghost, devil, what. . . ?

"I was," Shen said, still careful, measuring his words, "I *was* my father's youngest son."

And suddenly—after all these days, all these long miles of looking at him—Shu could see the widow's lineaments picked out in his face, and knew then who his father was and how thorough this deception, how entire this revenge.

And there was a pot of tea on the table, which the boy had freshly made; and Shu gazed at it and said, "Do I need to be careful what I drink, from your hands?"

THE PILLOW BOY OF GENERAL SHU 145

"No, lord. Never."

He believed him, immediately and completely. But one thought leads to another, one new image to one that came before. Shu said, "You had us all in the one place, around one table, on that day. You served us all. You could have killed us all."

"Yes, lord, but I had no poison for the tea. And you were there," added gallantly, and perhaps a fraction late.

"Gods," with a shudder. And then, again, "What *are* you?"

And here after all was the price to be paid, and not after all Shu who had to pay it. The boy lifted those glorious eyes and looked at him, while his slim hand stayed clamped lightly around Shu's arm; and he said, "I am Shen, the pillow boy of my lord the general Shu. That is all I am, and all I will ever be."

MISS AUSTEN'S CASTLE TOUR

by *Sherwood Smith*

Sherwood Smith's literary accomplishments span the galaxy of imagination from Young Adult fantasy (her *Wren* and *Crown Duel* series) to adult fantasy (most recently, her *Inda* series from DAW) to space opera (the *Exordium* series with Dave Trowbridge), science fiction (collaborations with the late Andre Norton) and media tie-in novels. Sherwood's latest short story was "Court Ship," published in *Firebirds Rising* from Penguin, and her most recent books are *Treason's Shore* (DAW), *A Stranger to Command* (Norilana), and *Trouble with Kings* (Samhain).

In between writing and teaching, Sherwood participates in the SFWA Musketeers, enjoys watching The Three Stooges, and reads the letters of Jane Austen.

The generally accepted definition for 'genius' is *an extraordinary intellectual power especially as manifested in creative endeavor*. A simpler definition might be, *one who recreates*. In its turn, 'recreation' has its own polysemy. The irony is ingenious, I find.

Much has been written about the mysterious gap in Jane Austen's letters between 26-7 May, 1801, and 14 September 1804. Evidence indicates she had suffered a disappointment in love, but to protect Jane's privacy after the latter's death, her sister Cassandra burned all Jane's letters during that period.

The determined scholar glimpses her through mention in family letters beginning that autumn, and thenceforward until she reappears again in 1804. What happened during those four months? Jane's movements are detailed in a travel diary, which Cassandra never saw.

Here is the opening:

As you can see, I obtained this little travel book, with the intention of writing you an extended letter. I dare not claim the vaunted pinnacle of Volumes of Travel Reminiscence. My purpose is humble. Where would I post my letters? We are not so grand as to expect a convenient diplomatic pouch, or even some lieutenant carrying dispatches, as Charles had so confidently predicted. Naval lieutenants are not to be met with everywhere—especially as we plan to travel farther in from the sea.

What has happened, you ask? Permit me to retrace.

In the two days after I last wrote, the Endymion *arrived at Portsmouth, and Charles having got leave, posted to us at once. I can say 'at once' because it so occurred: it seems that the vessel carried passengers from Calais, among whom were a clergyman and his sister, Dr. and Miss Crawfurd. They offered a place in their Carriage to Charles, posting all the way to Bath, which demonstrates their good nature.*

At first Jane did not write what happened to spark that friendship, because she felt ambivalent about the cause.

The Channel crossing was made difficult by stormy, contrary winds, which confined the passengers to the officers' cramped wardroom. Charles Austen, one of Jane's many brothers, happened to be off-duty. He chuckled as he read from a packet of papers; on being encouraged by one of his fellow officers to read aloud to the company, he obliged. The text was *Lady Susan*, and when his audience lauded the story as not only funny but quite unlike anything they had ever heard, Charles admitted with scarcely concealed pride that it had been written by his sister. The packet, containing close-written sheets of *Lady Susan, First Impressions,* and *Elinor and Marianne*, was passed among the sea-faring Austen brothers to enjoy during their off-duty moments.

After the passengers had all disembarked and the officers were granted leave, Charles encountered the Crawfurds just as he was about to purchase a mail coach ticket. When it was discovered that they all had the same destination, the Crawfurds insisted he accompany them. No sooner had they rolled out of the inn yard than Miss Crawfurd begged Charles to while away the tedium of travel by reading more of his sister's tales, and so he took out Jane's most recent effort, *Elinor and Marianne*.

Amid much laughter over the Dashwood family, the blue gazes of brother and sister met in triumph. Charles kept reading.

※ ※ ※

L ast night, Charles brought his Benefactors to meet us. The Crawfurds began with "genius" and "extraordinary"—all the loud compliments I hate most, because, whether it's true or not, there is nothing one can gracefully say before strangers. But once they saw my discomfiture was real, and no fine lady bridling, they left off the Subject. That enabled me to enjoy the "We laughed out loud all the way" and "There was never a coach ride so short."

The delicacy the brother and sister displayed thus had more appeal than the exaggerations about Genius. He is a gentleman-like man of stylish appearance, and his sister young and while you know I would as soon fling my pen out the window than say "as beautiful as an angel," in this case it is very nearly true.

Jane Austen's code for "handsome and attractive" was "gentleman-like." She had never been effusive. Her earliest writings made fun of gushing language. Since Tom Lefroy had so recently gone back to Ireland, leaving her waiting for the proposal that both families expected, she had become more than ordinarily cautious.

*When the Evelyns called—bringing Mr. Thomas Evelyn, who shares with his Uncle the all-consuming Love of Horses—glad was the outcry at their unexpected Encounter with the Crawfurds, which three or four years of perfect indifference had delayed from the last. Once the usual nothings were said, the Crawfurds were so witty and full of engaging conversation, we were all soon talking and laughing, even Mr. Evelyn, who on rare occasion can be transformed from a Yahoo about Horses. We discovered similar Tastes in books—*Evelina *delightful—*Arthur Fitz-Albini *dreadful—Madame de Genlis fashionable—Smollett at his best when satirizing the Great but in execrable taste—so comfortable when everyone is in agreement without expectation.*

We went from Hesperus *to the continent. Miss Crawfurd, as both visitor and the prettiest woman in the room, was acknowledged the principal talker. She expressed a Desire to travel upon the Continent, to visit castles and places of antiquity. As soon as she uttered the words, the gentlemen all caught her idea.*

We were assured that everywhere there is peace, and everyone smiles: the Treaty of Luneville during winter appears to have given the Prussians Cause to put away their swords, and the negotiations beginning in London intimate that the French will trouble us no more. Charles insists that after their naval defeat at the Nile and their recent losses in Egypt, their adventures have ended.

Then Dr. Crawfurd declared that he had that morning received a letter via Diplomatic Pouch, inviting him to visit the Home of a Patron, and he is to bring any party he cares to invite.

Miss Evelyn exclaimed at once. You know her wish for Distinction through her drawings. Once she had spoken, I felt I could add my voice to the general outcry, without it seeming to be particularly aimed at Dr. Crawfurd, who even Cousin Eliza acknowledged as the most interesting man in the room.

I confess to you, who well knows my tastes, that a tour through crumbling castles with old moats would draw my eye and fire my imagination even if we are not to meet with a pack of ghosts, or a young lady dressed in white and bearing a single flickering candle as she runs weeping through the graveyard. I condition only for the moat not being filled with horrid creatures—or horrid smells.

Dr. Eldon Crawfurd's courtship of the reticent Jane was delicate, conducted not through compliments—he understood quickly that those resulted in silence—but through conversation. Those who listened to the tales of his travels gained the impression of a clergyman in the agreeable situation of having no present living, but as the inheritor of a sufficient fortune, in no immediate need of one. He once or twice alluded to his intellectual patron, a well-traveled and educated prince in the Austrian Empire, which added greatly to his impression of erudition.

Miss Crawfurd made her life with her brother, but she assured them in a witty aside that she did not have to depend upon him for her *menus plaisirs*. Miss Evelyn whispered to Jane during the bustle of getting the tea things ready, that she had once met them in London, where Miss Crawfurd presided over entertainments in her brother's house in Wimpole Street. Miss Evelyn added meaningfully that the Crawfurds numbered among their acquaintance people of rank and wit.

Jane commented to Cassandra that everyone likes to be known to have visited people of "rank and wit," even if one can make no claim to those distinctions themselves.

At first, the idea of the castle tour faltered with the Austen parents. But Dr. Crawfurd exchanged his seat next to Dr. Austen, and he explained in the smoothest, most sympathetic manner his conviction that a clergyman who travels and sees much of the human condition can bring more wisdom to a parish than one who has learned only through the threadbare sayings obtainable in published sermons. Dr. Austen was much struck by this observation.

Then Henry Austen, who had irritated the family by marrying their widowed cousin Eliza de Feuillide despite everyone's wishes, commented, "Of course you will not wish to go, Mother. You may find a comfortable home with Frank, or Edward, while we are gone."

Mrs. Austen promptly claimed her share in the prospective treat, adding plaintively, "I do not know why everyone would assume I would not be a good traveler. I am equal to anything that Father is, and why should anyone presume that I should not wish to go?

That settled the question. They would go. They had only to establish the means. When Charles reported that the *Endymion* would be ferrying to the continent a party of relations belonging to the first lieutenant and the captain, and that he would send off a request by post to gain permission from his captain for passage, the conversation turned to the important topic of what to take—Mrs. Austen stating that the first thought must be given to sheets, as she had heard that foreigners had no notion of proper washing.

&c;&c;&c;&c;&c;

*T**he journey to Portsmouth was agreeable. We talked and laughed the entire way, which shortened the distance by at least an hundred miles.*

Besides the Crawfurds, the party included the Austen parents, Jane, Charles, Henry, and Eliza—who had no interest in returning to the continent, where so many she knew had been beheaded ten years before, but the way Henry's roving eye had landed on the fair Miss Crawfurd, she decided the time had come to call on her extended relations. Mr. Evelyn could not be gotten to leave his phaeton and four, but Miss Evelyn had declared (with a cant of the head in the direction of the handsome Dr. Eldon Crawfurd) that an artistic Grand Tour would be something worth doing, and her cousin Mr. Thomas Evelyn (*his* gaze stayed on Miss Maria Crawfurd) offered to go as her escort.

The Crawfurds had to exert their considerable charms once the party was on board the *Endymion*. Mrs. Austen took an immediate dislike to the motion of the ship upon the water, and to the evil smells below the decks, despite the neatness of the arrangements. In spite of her list of alarming symptoms (punctuating a stream of messages to the captain to steady the boat, messages which Charles wisely offered to carry, so that the captain never saw them), they arrived without mishap on the continent. Here a magnificent array of hired *voitures* awaited them, ordered by Dr. Crawfurd.

Jane Austen was so pleased with new sights, sounds, everywhere people in curious dress speaking other tongues, and she found their new acquaintances so agreeable, she accepted the Crawfurds' generosity toward their entire party as part of their enormous charm. She had no apprehension of any purpose beyond the subtle social minuet of courtship.

Rotterdam pleased the entire party. Mrs. Austen's spirits rose at the sight of flower-boxes everywhere, and streets so swept and scoured that she declared she might walk abroad in her slippers and return without carrying one spot of dirt.

They set out for Cologne. The pleasantly undulating countryside was tidy, from the rows of the farms to the canals full of boats, but they had to stop frequently for Mrs. Austen.

They began their tour of antiquities at the Cathedral in Cologne, where they viewed the Golden Sarcophagus containing the Bones of the Magi. By the time they had heard the details of the martyrdom of Saint Ursula and the 11,000 virgins, Mrs. Austen was speaking of palpitations and nervous disorders again.

At this point the party split up. Mrs Austen insisted upon a stay in Holland, which she might enjoy at leisure while awaiting the others. Jane and Charles were surprised when their father also decided to remain behind, saying something unintelligible about being old—one is decided in one's tastes—clergymen today—it's the fashion to be familiar with Fordyce, but where Donne and the great Milton are forgotten, the old must make way for the new.

The Austens were a fond family. Jane was troubled on her father's behalf, but felt it was not her place to inquire into his reasons. Surely her father could not have found fault with Dr. Crawfurd, so witty, elegant, and fascinating! She decided her father sought an excuse to stay by Mrs. Austen. Charles would have pursued this matter, but Maria Crawfurd laughingly linked her arm within his as she claimed his protection on a walk about the town, and when they returned, in the bustle of parting he forgot to ask.

The next day, it was a smaller party that set out. The Crawfurds contrived to have Charles and Jane in their *voiture*; in the second carriage, Eliza was pleased to keep Henry beside her, with no more distracting company than Miss Evelyn (who hid her disappointment of Dr. Crawfurd in talking determinedly of antiquities, the proper use of the pencil in the making of shadows), and her disappointed cousin (who felt that Charles Austen had unfairly stolen a march by his walk about town with Miss Crawfurd).

As the carriage rolled alongside the river, Eldon Crawfurd offered to read poetry to the company. He read aloud well, pleasing Jane with his expressive interpretations of Cowper, and for a while they conversed on the spark of poetic genius. Was it inherited? Shakespeare's progeny was not famed. Was it taught? Socrates to Plato to Aristotle to Alexander the Great were the most obvious examples.

"But beyond that, I can't name many," Charles said.

"One might have to define greatness," Jane murmured.

Maria looked amused. "Do you claim that Alexander of Macedonia was not great, then, Miss Austen?"

Jane had not thought she was heard. She blushed. "I make no claims to scholarship."

But Eldon said, "We're not in school now. We are a private and informal company, with little to do besides conversation. I believe I speak for us all when I say, we may safely put forward opinions without the demand of academic proficiency."

Jane said, "Well, despite all we're told, what did Alexander accomplish, besides conquering a lot of people who probably would as lief been left alone, had they been asked? It is true he built the library at Alexandria, but anyone may build a library without being thought wise."

Eldon laughed. "You are not the first to make that claim against the Macedonian, and I find I must concur, unless one is given to admiring battles. We had a debate on this very subject when I was at school in Germany. One of my poetical friends made a case exactly like yours."

"Madame de Staël said much the same," Maria put in. "Though I believe some of her discourse was aimed at the First Consul."

"Madame de Staël," Charles repeated, sending an uneasy glance his sister's way.

Maria touched his wrist. "Oh, surely you are not going to exhibit tiresome country-town attitudes. Who is here to be impressed? We are quite alone, you a world traveler as is myself and my brother, and your sister the author of *Lady Susan*."

Jane reddened, and Maria mistook her blush of shame for bridling at a compliment. She privately thought Jane Austen affected, but went on in soothing tones, "Some say that to geniuses must be applied a different rule; Madam de Staël's recent publication on literature is very widely regarded, you know."

Eldon smiled. "Widely regarded from Scotland to America, where Thomas Jefferson has written in its praise. So much good will transcending national boundaries can only be considered a fine thing, after so many years of war."

Jane found herself in an uncomfortable dilemma. This was not the first time Maria Crawfurd had scorned country-town attitudes, which in Jane's view might better be characterized as scrupulous.

Maria took her silence for capitulation. "The Count whom we are to visit—he is actually a prince, you must understand, but we English translated his title as Count. He remarked about Madame de Staël that faces age, but wit never does."

Eldon laughed. "My sister would have both if she could."

A warning glance flashed between brother and sister.

Charles was frowning in thought. "You have mentioned the Count before," he said. "What can you tell us about him?"

Eldon replied, "He collects books representing all branches of knowledge, from many countries. He says it would require several lifetimes to read them all. Something, perhaps, all artists wish they could have." He turned to Jane. "Would not you, Miss Austen?"

"Everyone would like to possess youthful beauty and wit for ever," Jane said to him, glad to have bypassed the uncomfortable subject of Madame de Staël, and her irregular life. "Some never have either, which they regard as tragic. Some only think they do—"

"—which we regard as comic, when they are exposed," Charles said. "How I love Jane's pompous windbags! Anyone would take Mr. Collins for my old headmaster."

Miss Crawfurd pressed Jane's hand. "That is part of your great gift, Miss Austen, to expose falsity in all guises."

Eldon offered to read from Pope, and Jane's uneasiness subsided. She realized that, by degrees, she had relinquished the idea of marriage to Dr. Crawfurd, handsome as he was.

Friendship was altogether more comfortable; she was content that he might become a brother if Charles and Maria wed.

∽∞∽

Saturday, June 29, 1801. Hotel König von Ungarn, Vienna.
  At Ratisbon we were able to join up with the Danube as this river, unlike the Rhine, is polite enough to flow in the proper direction.

  I found it impossible to write aboard the boat, so you are spared my description of the wild forests and ruins and monasteries perched on cliffs, enough for a thousand Otrantos. You may apply to me for details, as I see my future self hovering beside your chair, helping your reading along with such questions as "What page are you on? Have you reached the boat yet?"

  Charles was distraught when Miss Crawfurd went walking with Mr. Thomas Evelyn. He paced about in a manner to satisfy any Young Werther. At least he did not rant verses of Klopstock at us, hindered as he is by not speaking German. Dr. Crawfurd once again brought forward the subjects of artistic creation, and of genius, until I began to suspect that some cause lay behind it. I can only suppose that either he or his sister think to commence author. I am minded to say that people who talk forever of writing without ever squaring to their page probably will never do it from some cause or other. But I might be mistaken.

  It is Sunday afternoon. We had to apply at the Embassy to discover a Protestant Church, with the result we attended Divine Service with a great many Diplomats. This will, I feel sure, constitute my own brush with Greatness, so I record it for your benefit, Cassandra, as well as mine.

  Speaking of which, we have paraded along the Prater with the grand and the chimney-sweeps alike, and we have obtained diplomatic passes to be conducted on the morrow *through Schönbrunn, which Miss Crawfurd assures us looks like a Cleaner Versailles.*

Miss Evelyn has bought new crayons for just this purpose. If someone hints at faults in her drawings—which are as flat as ever—she punishes them with medieval masonry and baroque styles until they agree with her sense of her own Genius, or run out of the room.

After hearing music wherever we go, I am almost sorry to depart on Tuesday for Buda-Pesht.

☙❧

With some deft handling on the part of the Crawfurds, the party that left Vienna was reduced yet again.

Charles would go at any cost, and the Crawfurds were determined that Jane would go with her brother.

Maria flattered and smiled Mr. Thomas Evelyn into bringing himself to the point, then turned him down. Having no interest in old castles or book-collecting counts who claimed to speak at least twenty languages, he remained in Vienna to seek the source of the horses he had seen exhibiting their skills at the Spanish Riding School.

Eldon did his best to disengage Miss Evelyn from the group, but she was as oblivious to hints as she was to criticism. She had determined that the fabulous castle of Count Dracula would aid her in achieving fame when she returned to England with her book of sketches, and she disclaimed any hardship.

Henry and Eliza did not have to be disengaged. She felt that Henry had had enough of Maria's bewitching conversation, and swept him off to a castle nearby, to which her own relations had fled after the French Revolution.

So it was just one carriage that left Vienna, and rolled into the vast woods to begin the long journey eastward.

And now, the Crawfurds began to approach their purpose.

"You will discover," Maria said one morning as the carriage rolled across a bridge, "that the Count is fascinated with the latest theories of scientific discovery. If you have any interest, you will find the latest publications at the castle, far as it is from any modern city."

She smiled on Charles, who smiled back, hopelessly besotted. To be so beautiful, and so well-informed about the world!

"Just last year I attended a lecture on electricity by a fellow who spoke before the Royal Society," Charles exclaimed, not including the fact that a fellow lieutenant had all but dragged him and his fellow officers in order to fill chairs for his father, a learned man but no public speaker.

"I attended a similar lecture in Paris," Eldon said. "You have probably observed how scientists will travel between nations, or at the very least correspond with one another, quite ignoring the struggles of governments. The most exciting discovery of late has been the principle of the galvanic spark."

Charles had been bored into lockjaw by his friend's father, but now was glad he'd been forced to listen. With a glance toward Maria, he said with tolerable ease, "Galvani's theory of animal magnetism is quite exploded. Alessandro Volta proved that there was a magnetic spark not in the dissected musculature, but in the metals used to mount them."

Miss Crawfurd said, smiling, "The Count sent a message to my brother while we were in Paris, requesting him to procure the newest publications on that very subject. Did you read the latest theory, putting forward the notion the spark of life can be imbued in living organisms?"

Charles shook his head, having to give up his pretense of scientific expertise. "My duties have kept me out at sea."

Maria patted his hand. "Of course. While you sailors labor so admirably to protect our borders against invaders, ideas cross quite freely. They are there to be met with when you gain liberty."

They stopped at an ancient inn that night, and had the drawing room to themselves. They agreed to eat in company, without the ladies separating off. Maria had a capital idea—they would read *Lady Susan*, the men taking turns with the male characters' letters, and Maria and Jane the women's, as Miss Evelyn said she preferred to listen as she worked on the Ostrogothic ruin she had taken in swift sketches that morning.

The laughter this time was pointed, the Crawfurds enjoying how Lady Susan had succeeded in fooling the fools, Charles laughing because Maria laughed, and Jane swinging between pride and pain. When she retired, she wondered if all authors found their opinions mistaken for those of their creations. Perhaps this explained why so many books were published in anonymity.

✥

Bistritz—uncertain date.

It is very odd, Cassandra. I pride myself on being a rational creature. But as we traveled east, the land around us not only got wilder, it seemed somehow older, the darkness darker, the light more fitful, and night full of noises that make one sit closer to the fire. I told myself that particular area had long been controlled by the Turks, until scarcely a century ago, so the marks of our Civilization would seem the rarer, and signs of Eastern Civilization strange.

That does not reason away the constant howling of wolves.

But it is not our surroundings that disturb my thoughts so much as my company.

I see you looking satirical, and in truth, so should I, if I were sitting in my room at the Paragon, with the noise of Bath outside the window. Perhaps I ought to review Elinor & Marianne, *not just to correct the manifold errors I detected in my reading, but to remind myself of what my heroines learnt about the conflict between Reason and Passion.*

Miss Evelyn only speaks to insist we stop for a short time at every castle or ruin so that she may sketch it. The rest of us use the opportunity to walk about, and breathe air that is not enclos'd in a Carriage.

Charles pines if Miss Crawfurd is not by. She is as bewitching as ever when she is among us, always ready with a fund of easy conversation and wit. She speaks constantly of the power of Youth and Beauty, as if there is nothing of importance in life but these. Am I rational to own to these Misgivings? Cassandra, I hardly know what I write; the candle is already guttering (I was in a reverie between every sentence) and the wolves howling abominably.

The Crawfurds promise that they have saved the best for last—that we shall love Castle Dracula, and that its Count is so honored to receive us as guests, that he will meet us to conduct us the rest of the way.

Wolves—there goes the candle, I can scarcely see to write.

If I hear chains, or a shriek, I believe I will change my name to Clorinda.

ଓଃଠଃ

Jane had just written the above when the maid, a thin young girl, brought hot water. Jane thanked her in French as she handed her a vail.

The girl's mob cap trembled with her nervous effort, but she darted forward and thrust into Jane's hand—a rosary! Then she darted out again, the remains of the water in her pitcher sloshing.

Jane did not know whether to regard this scene as comical or pitiful. Hearing a commotion in the shared parlor, she went out, and found the Crawfurds and Charles.

When she opened her hand to disclose the rosary—and a homely, rough thing it was, the beads carved from wood by no delicate hand, the crucifix also made of wood—Miss Crawfurd drew her skirts aside and made a noise of disgust. "Fling it out of the window!" she exclaimed.

Dr. Crawfurd protested with a laugh. "My dear sister, it is merely a peasant icon, and a rough one at that."

Miss Crawfurd turned away in disgust. "I have a distaste for peasant superstitions." She added with meaning, "And you know the Count has a worse."

The clergyman said, "Miss Austen, surely you do not intend to collect idolatrous objects. You know what the church leaders have to say upon the subject of false pieties."

Jane realized it was the first time he had made reference to Church teachings in all their travels, clergyman though he was. Everything else—literature, science, history and famous people, especially people of genius—had been canvassed, but nothing about religious principle.

Here was part of the reason she could not consider him seriously as a mate. There was no time to consider this further, as a commotion in the outer room heralded an arrival.

I promised to lay everything out as exactly as I can describe. I had thought on meeting him that Dr. Crawfurd the handsomest man of my acquaintance, but he was nothing compared to Count Dracula.

He is tall, very fair. Light-colored eyes. I leave the excess to my fellow Authors, but when one is in his presence, one notices nothing else. In consequence, I scarcely questioned traveling at night. Nor did any of the others.

We were bundled into very fine carriages, all warmed with bricks, and so we raced into the night, pursued by the cries of unseen Wolves.

I do not remember the details of the journey. It might have taken all night; I just know that we arrived, weary and half-asleep, in a court lit by torchlight. In that uneven illumination, I gained the impression of great archways, perhaps in series. We drew up, the horses steaming, before a great door of ancient hard wood, studded all over with iron nails. This door was set in stone, conveying the impression of withstanding enormous force—whether of weather or other threats I could not say.

"Come within," the Count said.

The door opened with a screech of metal joinings, and a great many servants in livery appeared, conducting us into light and warmth. My senses were alert now, aware of iron wheel chandeliers overhead, and behind the rattle of chains and the grating of bolts securing that massive door.

The tired, bewildered guests were overwhelmed by the magnificence of the castle. The light within was quite bright, though not the familiar hue of beeswax candles, or oil lamps, much less the faint, noisome glow of tallow. From the chandeliers hung silver lanterns, each containing a flame of sorts, burning from a source mysterious to the Austens. (Miss Evelyn paid the lights no heed; her attention was all for the carved gargoyles over the archways, which she could already hear herself explaining to a rapt audience were surely Byzantine in origin.) The air smelled of old stone.

"Welcome to my house," said Count Dracula. "My people will make you comfortable. Your journey has been long. I am aware how far from the civilized world my land lies. We will all meet again after you have had your rest, and then I will conduct you over the castle, that you may explore, and sketch, to your heart's content." He gave Miss Evelyn a slight bow.

Jane was led away by a girl not much older than the one who had given her the rosary, which lay in her pocket still, as she'd had no time to pack it before the sudden and surprising departure.

Jane closed her hand around the comforting wood as she observed the lowered eyes and meek manner of the servants. Unlike the people they'd seen in villages and on the road, these servants did not wear religious emblems at all.

On impulse she drew from her pocket the rosary. When the servant saw it, she stood still as stone, gazing with such desperation that Jane extended her hand. The girl reached tentatively, and then clutched the gift, her eyes closed, tears leaking from them. "Thank you, thank you. Now I may be free," the girl whispered in broken French. And she flitted out before Jane could speak.

❧☙❧☙❧

I sit in this room with a single light, the bitter smell of iron-gall ink heavy in my nostrils; I will shortly get to why. I said I must lay it all out rationally, though what I am about to retail will make you think I am dreaming.

Not that things seemed ill at first. I slept deeply on our arrival. Already my mind was turned about, as what seemed night was actually day, though we could not know it, as the shutters in our windows were nailed tight. We all slumbered the same number of hours, or perhaps we were wakened by some agency I did not detect, but we appeared in a refectory at about the same time, everyone looking weary still, except for Miss Crawfurd, who entered with a light, dancing step, smiling at us in triumph. It was she, and not the Count, who commanded the silent servants to bring the breakfast, which was well cooked and plentiful.

The Count made his appearance when they had finished, and said that he would conduct them over his castle himself.

Miss Evelyn had her sketchbook and crayons ready to hand, but the Count offered her arm to Jane.

They traveled through several well-proportioned rooms, handsomely fitted up. The Count related the history of the castle, using the royal 'we' and speaking in the immediate, giving so vivid a description of attacks and battles engaged in by his Norse forefathers, whom he named the Szekelys, he conveyed an unpleasant sense of having witnessed these spectacles.

Charles only half heard. He walked along on Maria's arm, gazing at her in blissful admiration. Miss Evelyn paid scant attention: she was too busy storing up details of ancient artifacts, and trying to decide where to begin sketching first. Visions of a royal exhibition had begun to take shape in her mind.

The Count gazed down into Jane's observant eyes and talked about the purity of his northern racial blood, breeding leaders since before the time of the Romans. He looked for evidence of awe, but instead heard in her breathing and saw in the tilt of her button chin that she did not appreciate the details of impalements and beheadings any more than she was impressed by the necessity to cleanse the countryside of lesser races, which were identified by their swarthiness of skin and grossness of feature.

By the time they had walked the length of three great rooms, the Count had shifted his discourse to the number of Royal Houses with connections to his, giving an account of royal gifts in evidence, from an ancient hunting tapestry to a pair of dueling sabers affixed to a wall above a carved and gilt escritoire.

Miss Evelyn stayed behind to sketch that last while the others mounted the stone steps spiraling up a tower to reach the upper level. Jane, looking everywhere, noticed that the sound in a tower was odd: a whisper far below sounded like a rustle next to one's ear. But then one stepped around a corner and the rushing of the wind outside snatched away all sound but its keening.

Dr. Crawfurd's voice speaking her name caught at her attention. ". . . with Jane? He promised that any poets or writers I brought would be mine."

Miss Crawfurd's distinctive laugh echoed up. "*Tais-toi, cher* Eldon! Remember what you did to Johann Hölderin! To beguile the best blood is not enough to earn its mastery. . . ."

Then they were around the turn.

The Count looked down at his prize genius. "Do you have a question, Miss Austen?" He smiled.

Jane had learned to observe smiles. This one was complacent, the smile of expectation.

"Thank you, no," she said. She was small and round-cheeked, and the Austen manners were always good, for she had been raised by enlightened and rational people. Self-control was of paramount importance to the Austens. To people for whom it was not of paramount importance, the Austens could be misunderstood.

At the tour's end, most of the company dispersed to rest again. Jane returned to her bed chamber, but she found it so cold and uncongenial, with its nailed shutters warding the light, she left it again.

Remembering the many conversations about the Count and his library, she sought that room in hopes of finding something to read in order to distract herself from inchoate worries.

The library was a long gallery of a chamber, with bookshelves extending up the walls so high that the mouldering volumes at the top were in reach only of a ladder. A fire roared in a fireplace wide and deep enough to hold entire trunks of trees. The tables were enormous, probably hewn from the trees too large to put into the fireplace.

Miss Evelyn sat at a corner of one table, within the warmth and light from the fire, finishing her gargoyles. The room was otherwise empty, so Jane perused the lettering on the spines of the shelved books. Many were in Latin, or in unfamiliar alphabets, so she turned over some of the titles lying on the table. These were recent, some works from the Encyclopedists, and several medical texts, most of them in Latin. Topmost was William Harvey's work on the circulation of blood.

Next to it lay a pamphlet upon the same subject, printed in French, with a great many underlinings, and notes in Greek and Latin. Jane remembered the odd words about blood she had overheard in the tower, and turned over the pages. The theory stated that blood injected into someone else's veins would carry to the receiver the qualities of the donor. Therefore, the blood of a king would convey the royal heritage, and likewise, the blood of a genius would, upon circulating through the recipient, carry the qualities of genius. The question only remained, how much blood must pass into the recipient until the effect would become noticeable?

There was a note below, in a strong handwriting: *You must take it all to gain the effect entire.*

Jane stared down at those words, remembering all the conversations about genius, blood, electricity and galvanic sparks. Her sense of formless worry had sharpened into a distinct apprehension of threat when the Count spoke from the other side of the library. "Do you understand now, Miss Austen?"

Jane looked up. "Understand what, pray?"

"Come, come. You are perceptive and intelligent. My acolytes claim genius on your part, a claim I am prepared to accept. Maria is as discriminating as she is ambitious."

'*Maria?*' Jane wondered if Miss Crawfurd and the Count had come to an understanding, of which her poor brother was unaware. She glanced at Miss Evelyn, but she had fallen into reverie, her gaze turned toward the fire, and her hand dropped loose upon her sketch.

Jane turned back to the Count. "I perceive in this text a theory about blood circulation. I know from family experience that medical practice dictates the letting of blood, that impurities may be driven out. I have not learned of better blood being successfully put *into* a person's veins."

Laughter met her words. Jane whirled around, considerably startled. It was not the affected titter of girls new to company, or the quiet laughter of well-bred people, but a tinkling sound, like the play of silver hammers on glass. She found so inhuman a sound issuing from human mouths to be unsettling.

Miss Crawfurd stood just inside the doorway, smiling in triumph, her blue eyes so wide they reflected the burning lights overhead. Jane looked past her to several young women. These advanced with graceful, drifting steps to stand beside the Count. Jane gazed at their parted red lips that revealed prominent white teeth, with lengthened canines of a type never filed by dentist's hand. She would never call those teeth *natural*, yet they appeared to be Nature's make.

"Blood can be taken, Miss Austen," Miss Crawfurd said. Her teeth were normal, but her smile was avid, her voice low and breathless. "It can be taken by those who have the will and the power to reign, ever young."

"Even so old a race as mine can learn modern ways," the Count said, laying one hand on the pamphlet, the other hand indicating his companions.

Jane's gaze lifted to his face. Her pupils contracted when she noticed for the first time his strong white teeth, the canines wolf-long. "No more the indiscriminate feeding. We begin a new experiment, not just with the better blood of people of good family, such as your purblind friend here."

His hand indicated Miss Evelyn with negligent dismissal—and she did not move, did not seem to hear.

"What I desired my young friends to bring me is the blood of genius and innovation. You, Miss Austen, are possessed of creative genius. But never think that we take without trade, for we respect genius. You may become one of us, which will furnish you with many lifetimes of these other fools, the longer to exhibit your talents."

"Lifetimes?" Jane repeated, her heartbeat quite wild.

To the Count and his companions, her fear was evident, but also the longing which the idea of *lifetimes* for writing engendered.

"Your culture's assumption that humans are just below angels is a comforting but erroneous assumption. The Vampire is above human in all ways: strength, vitality, and intelligence. There is only one circumstance which we do not share with the thoughtless animal breeding of the generality of humanity: we are not born as vampires, we are made."

"Vampires?" Jane had never before spoken the word. She had read enough tales to understand what was meant. It would be easy to dismiss the evidence of her eyes as the fervid imaginings of authors penning horror tales, but she knew that the stuff of novels derives out of the truth of experience.

The Count made a gesture that took in his castle. "The superstitious fools regard the transference as magic, but we are the possessors of galvanic impulses ill-understood by you with short and blinkered lives. My lanterns, burning without apparent source, are the easiest understood manifestations." He indicated the steady illumination of those iron wheel chandeliers overhead.

Jane folded her hands tightly against her. Even in the face of the irrational, she would remain rational, and polite. "May I put to you a question?"

"Please." He smiled with those terrible white teeth. "I have been reading from your work while you were slumbering. The creator of *Lady Susan*, which is so witty an exegesis upon the groundless moralities and pieties of your culture, will surely come to a swift comprehension of my offer."

Jane did not explain that *Lady Susan* was a cautionary tale, and unsuccessful at that: all its *soi-disant* wit and cleverness came to nothing when Henry went ahead and married his cousin

Eliza de Feuillide. The failure of her message was as great a reproach as the Crawfurds and the Count's conviction that its sardonic ironies represented her own views.

She had already made her decision about the eventual publication of *Lady Susan*—which would not happen.

If she survived this *rencontre*.

She asked politely, "It is on the blood of humans that you feed, is it not?"

"Entirely." Miss Crawfurd laughed gently as she came forward. "I have begun my transformation; you can see yourself the effect." She raised her arms and twirled around. "Do you think I was born to this beauty? I assure you, I was not. And you will be the same."

"Do people consent to surrender their blood?"

"If they are wise."

"Are those who refuse harmed?"

Maria gave her elaborately careless shrug. "Why worry about peasants or fools? There are enough of them in the world."

The Count said, "The effect is the same whether we take it or it is let by sword or other means as practiced by humanity upon itself every day: if enough is lost, the donor dies."

Miss Crawfurd tossed back her golden curls. "What are a few peasants more or less? They breed like rats. I greatly favor this experiment with better blood."

The Count's pale eyes flashed wide. Jane knew she was fully awake, and yet between one heartbeat and the next he was next to her. "You must make your choice, Miss Austen. Become one of us, or your corpse will be buried, unmourned, outside the castle grounds, and your writings forgotten. Because I assure you, if we permit this fool to live—" he indicated Miss Evelyn, "—and we probably will, as the English are notoriously inquisitive when too many of them vanish, she will never remember her visit here."

Miss Evelyn neither stirred nor spoke.

"My brother?" Jane asked.

"He will be our first consort," Miss Crawfurd said, smiling as she indicated the Count's young ladies. "He is entertaining enough for a little while. Who knows? In a few years, he might even become interesting, and make vampire consorts of his own."

The Count's long teeth were more terrible a threat than mere words. "Or, if you consent to join us, you may write a letter home, informing your family that you have found love here, and chose to remain behind. Your brother will be released to carry your missive home, with Miss Evelyn. You and my young friends, the Crawfurds, will join my children of the night, and live for ever."

"Taking the lives of others is evil," Jane said. "A breaking of one of the Ten Commandments."

"Broken every day, not only by your criminals, but your own governments."

"That may be true, but that does not make it right."

"Right! In my castle, *my* commandments are the only law we obey. Conduct her to her chamber, that she might reflect," the Count said to the vampires. "And make certain that she has pen and paper for her letter."

Jane's last glimpse of Miss Evelyn was of her vacant gaze, her profile outlined against the fire.

And so, my sister, here I am, writing to you as a way of setting out my thoughts. Now, what I have surmised is this: there is no use in refusing to believe the evidence of eyes and ears. There is indeed a terrible power in these Creatures.

But at the same time, that Power appears to have its limitations, though I was not told of those. Sunlight, I suspect, is one. There has to be a reason the Count only travels about at night, and keeps the shutters nailed. The most important question is this. Is there a second limitation on the vampires, one that goes beyond morality to the Supernatural? I refer to the rosary, specifically the Crucifix. Outside of the castle, even the most humble wore them, and moved about freely. The meek servants here do not have them, making me wonder if the these servants are forced to serve a vile purpose when they do not serve in other ways. In short, they are prisoners, which would explain the reaction of the serving girl to whom I gave my Crucifix. What power has this symbol?

My understanding of Holy Communion is that it is not the thing, but the essence of the thing which celebrates our faith, which furnishes the sacred connection to Providence. If that is true, then there is power not in the Crucifix itself, but in the faith behind it? Miss Crawfurd's response to the Crucifix in my hand just before the Count came convinces me that I am in the way of it.

Though my faith in Divine Providence is strong, I do not know that my dangling a Crucifix before these vampires will avert them. I was not raised to express my faith through this symbol. We speak less of miracles—though it seems here I am surrounded by anti-miracles—than of grace.

But if it is true there are Galvanic Sparks that can be Harnessed, and that faith (faith in evil as well as faith in good) provides the motivator for either the propagation or the limitation of Evil Powers, then Providence already gave me my own Power: my imagination.

And so I end this account, which either will be found when I am gone, or—if I succeed—you and I might read it together, and then burn it, because I will never tell the world of this experience. Only you will understand what was in my heart, or know of the power I once gripped in my hand. The power of force is evil. The power of imagination, I believe, can be used for good.

To that I will dedicate my life, however long I am given.

෴෴෴

Screams echoed through the castle, high shrill screams that shivered on the air like the rubbing of fingers round the rim of crystal glasses.

Jane was still writing when the door to her chamber was struck open by an angry hand, and Maria Crawfurd stood on the threshold, her eyes quite wild. "What have you done?" she demanded.

"I employed my genius," Jane replied, but her accuser was too incensed to suspect irony. So she explained, "I used my imagination to summon the galvanic powers gathered here, and described the opening of all locks, the unfastening of shutters, that we might gain the benefit of light and air." She pointed her quill at the window, from which slants of golden afternoon light patterned on the stone floor.

"The Count—what have you done to the Count? His face—he's transformed into a vile Semitic peasant!"

"I described him with the countenance he despises most," Jane said. "I hope his new face will teach him compassion, if not wisdom."

"You *stupid* fool!" Maria advanced on Jane. "He's *gone!* The vampires are all gone down to the crypt and locked themselves within!"

Actually, that was not quite true. One remained, watching.

"My brother is trying to rouse them now—it might be months—it might be *years* before they dare emerge!"

Jane had packed her belongings. "I trust they will have cause to reflect. After all, if one is to claim to be a superior being, should not one's actions reflect a superior standard of civilization?"

Maria's face twisted with hatred. "And so, with your hypocritical countrified convictions you condemn us all to a short existence and ugly old age. Jane Austen and her duplicity! I am *glad* you will never amount to anything."

"I hope I am no hypocrite. But that is a battle we must fight every day, to choose what is right even when we are surrounded by foolishness and venality. Or evil." Jane indicated the rest of the castle with her quill, trying to hide how frightened she was.

"Fight for what?" Maria retorted. "The only battle worth fighting is against age, and ugliness. There is nothing I will not do to remain young and beautiful. Nothing."

Jane did not point out that the hatred distorting Maria's features did not make her beautiful now. Instead, she put pen to paper, and looked at up Maria Crawfurd with intent. "I think I will—"

Maria turned and fled.

"—put you in a book."

03෬෯෨

The servants stripped the castle of its treasures as they fled. The Crawfurds departed in the only coach, leaving the Austens and Miss Evelyn behind, but some of the servants—perhaps aware of who their benefactress had been—aided them in leaving.

In the chaos of departure, Jane Austen's papers vanished, but she was too hurried to search for them. By the time they reached civilization again, Charles Austen had recovered from Maria Crawfurd's spell, and Miss Evelyn had never noticed anything amiss. She had been too bespelled by her visions of fame to notice anything around her not made of stone.

Those visions had to remain just that. The world was not agog at her drawings, and as she had not thought to sketch any of her companions, even a later mention of having traveled with Jane Austen did not raise much interest, as she had no proof to offer but a cross-hatched series of ruins and gargoyles much like anyone else's.

As for Jane Austen, she had only sixteen more years to live—an eyeblink in the existence of a vampire—so she could not know that the Count and some of his companions would eventually dare the world again, nearly a century later. And because they had not learned either the compassion or the principles that Jane had tried to teach them, they were defeated, this time more permanently.

That left the castle to me—the one who had taken Jane Austen's papers, and who eventually obtained her other writings, as well as the subsequent imaginings of the men and women Jane Austen influenced, minds both wise and foolish, visionary and telluric.

It has been well over a century since the Count, driven by passion and greed, emerged to attempt the recovery of his powers, and two centuries since his first defeat via the pen in the small hands of a plain little woman. Though he desired the regenerative influence of genius, he did not understand its power.

I will not make the same mistake.

RENT GIRL

by Traci N. Castleberry

Traci N. Castleberry says she first met Orossy (that's or-OH-see) when he appeared in her novel in a tavern wearing a dress and she had to figure out a reasonable explanation as to why. "Rent Girl" takes place after the events in that novel.

When not writing, Traci spends her time fielding phone calls at a hotel, selling butterfly wing necklaces at a bayside tourist shop, turning online test scores into scientific papers for a psychologist, and taking lots of pictures at the San Diego Zoo. She shares her apartment with two cats, four saxophones, and a stuffed gecko named Guido. Three of her Clarion stories, *Hart and Soul, Stolen Moments,* and *Venom's Bond*, have metamorphosed into e-books that are available under her pen name, Nica Berry. Visit Traci and her alter ego online at www.orossy.com

In this tale of inner strength and the healing power of love, Traci asks some hard questions: How do we accept love when we believe ourselves to be unlovable? How do we reconcile and nourish the masculine and feminine aspects of ourselves, especially when the prevailing expectations force us to be only one or the other?

Orossy shivered in the cold, gray morning. Feisal's warm body curled beside him in the same bed they'd shared for the past month, in the same comfortably cluttered room. Yet Orossy felt far away, stifled, choked—

"'Rossy? What's wrong?"

He couldn't talk, trapped in a nightmare. Men surrounded him, held him fast. He couldn't breathe, couldn't get away . . .

"'Rossy? Another dream?" Feisal's voice brought him back. After a moment: "Another memory?"

With a nod, Orossy pressed his back against Feisal's broad chest and felt strong arms wrap around him. He still wasn't used to being able to trust anyone as deeply as he trusted Feisal. It scared him as much as the dream had.

"Want to tell me about it?"

He didn't. Not really. Nor did he need to; Feisal knew almost as much of Orossy's past as Orossy himself. "The tavern," he said. It didn't matter which day.

"Ah," was all Feisal said. It was all he needed to say. With his Healer's mind, he loosed threads of soothing dennar into Orossy's body. The panic ebbed, but the fear remained. "I'll make you some tea."

"I don't like tea." Orossy got up to follow Feisal anyway. Feisal tossed him a robe, and Orossy wrapped himself in the blue silk. "I'm sorry."

"Don't." Feisal looked at him with exasperation tempered by love. "I won't be able to sleep if you can't."

A light already burned in the kitchen. Jussi, the Lord Governor's steward, crouched beside the stove, dressed in working clothes, a gray jacket and pants. The kitchen, as always, offered comfort. Wooden panels covered the floor. Near the stove stood an oven and a short wooden table with a pair of three-legged stools. Shelves lined the walls, housing pots and dishes from all over the continent. A kettle of water boiled on the stove, and a plate of rice cakes sat ready. Orossy took one and nibbled on it. Jussi always knew what they needed.

Feisal raised an eyebrow. "Up a bit early, aren't you?"

The steward set out three stoneware cups, leaf-shaped in honor of the arrival of spring, and poured out hot tea. "Everything must be in order for your father's return."

The rice cake turned tasteless in Orossy's mouth. Lady's grace, what would the most powerful man in the territory think of his son's new lover? Feisal should have someone his equal, not a half-breed tavern brat.

"'Rossy?"

Feisal rubbed Orossy's arm. Orossy flinched. "Everything will be fine. He already knows about you."

Feisal handed him the cup. It smelled faintly of orange. Orossy wrapped his hands around it and shifted his gaze to Jussi. Whatever the steward knew, the Lord Governor surely knew.

Until Feisal's warm hand covered his, Orossy hadn't realized he was shaking badly enough to spill a few drops of tea. "It will be fine," Feisal repeated. "I promise."

"It will be different." Lady have mercy. As if it weren't bad enough to be the object of whispers and stares whenever he went out of the house or worked in the Infirmary. Now he'd be watched, measured, found wanting, inside the house, too.

Feisal ran a hand through Orossy's long hair, curling a lock around his fingers. "Don't worry. He'll like you as you are." He yawned. "Maybe I can sleep little more after all. Coming?"

"I should study." Forcing a smile, Orossy kissed Feisal on the cheek. Inside, he felt like screaming. *As you are*, Feisal had said. Did he have any idea how hard that was to figure out?

☙❧

Orossy dressed quietly in the dim light. Feisal was already asleep, twitching in his dreams. The Healer might not have Infirmary duty until mid-morning, but classes started early for Orossy. He rubbed his temples, already feeling a headache from the stress of lessons. His lack of education was another reason he felt inadequate. He had more dennar than Feisal, being able to read minds and emotions as well as heal, but he'd never learned how to use it properly. Lady's grace, he'd never even been able to write his own name until Jussi showed him last month.

He adjusted his uniform, a long-sleeved blue tunic, belt, and a matching pair of pants worn by both male and female students. The leather boots he would pick up on his way out; no one wore shoes inside the house. He cinched the belt and caught a shadowed glimpse of himself in the mirror, struck again by the image that could be either male or female.

Feisal loved men. Always had, which made Orossy worry. Surely it was only a matter of time before Feisal asked him to put away the feminine accoutrements and be as the gods had formed him. A man. And, more than likely, the Lord Governor would have his own ideas about an appropriate pairing for his son. Lord Maddren certainly wouldn't approve of an uneducated tavern brat who couldn't decide which sex he was.

Out of habit, he started to braid his hair in the feminine style. Catching himself, he pulled loose two braids, leaving one on either side of his face. The masculine style. It looked foreign. He could get used to it, couldn't he? For Feisal's sake? After all, Feisal had done so much already, teaching him that love was something more than the physical. Orossy owed him something in return.

He crept to the cabinet and eased the bottom drawer open. There lay the dresses he loved, along with the cincher and other accessories to enhance his femininity. For one last moment, Orossy ran his hands through the fine fabrics before he took everything out of the drawer and wrapped it into a bundle. As of today, there would be no more Rossa. She was dead.

Orossy bent over to give Feisal a kiss on the forehead. His lover's dreams were pleasant; a light touch of dennar ensured they stayed that way.

Leaving Feisal to sleep, he slung the leather satchel with his books over his shoulder. Jussi was still in the kitchen. Orossy thrust the bundle of clothes at the curious steward. "Get rid of these. Please." Not able to bear seeing what Jussi did with them, Orossy pulled his boots on and hurried out into the damp gray morning.

Two days. He had two days to turn himself into someone presentable and respectable, a man worthy of the Lord Governor's son.

☙❧

An education certainly seemed like a good way to become a worthy man, but every class only served to remind Orossy of how much he lagged behind the others. This particular class, the history and ethics of the city, had a mix of students, most of whom had some form of dennar. Orossy was one of two studying to be a Healer; far fewer people had the dennar for healing than for mind-reading and empathy, and those few were badly needed. Five or six students were the children of affluent council members. Others hoped to be apprenticed in various trades, but it was obvious that none came from a background like Orossy's. They talked and joked easily with each other. None of them had trouble with the subject material, having been born and raised within the city. As long as the teacher, Healer Deverrin, explained things aloud, Orossy could understand and remember. He'd always had a good memory. It was when they were expected to work out of their books that Orossy ran into trouble.

Like now, when he sat at a desk in the first row of an Infirmary classroom. Birdsong outside an open window distracted him as much as the muted thoughts of his peers. He'd first wondered if Deverrin picked on him because Deverrin was a Healer himself, but Orossy had since realized that the Healer took every chance he could to humiliate someone he thought undeserving of admittance into their elite order. Deverrin had only asked him one question all morning and Orossy had answered poorly, opening himself up for another round of degradation.

"No, Orossy, that's not correct. Didn't you look over your text?" Deverrin said with thinly veiled disdain. "Try again. Tomorrow I expect a *written* explanation of when dennar should and should not be used by a Healer, and you will read it to your classmates." He addressed the rest of the class, all of them fourteen or fifteen years old to Orossy's nineteen. Several of them were slouched, bored, in their chairs. "See that the rest of you study well enough so as not to follow . . . *his* example. Dismissed."

Orossy felt the usual heat flood his face. Everyone, it seemed, had noticed his change in hairstyle. As if it weren't hard enough dealing with differences in age and learning, he had to endure the constant stares and unshielded thoughts.

It's a gutter brat. How'd it ever sneak in here?

It's from Tavern Street. What made it ever think that it could be a Healer? I wouldn't ask it for help even if I were dying.

Orossy gritted his teeth and pretended not to be aware. Healers were supposed to be compassionate and open-minded, a creed Deverrin espoused while not practicing it himself. Deverrin collected a few papers and walked out of the room, trailed by a student asking questions. Orossy picked up his books to leave.

"What's the matter? Need some help with your homework?" a boy taunted from behind him. "Need someone to read to you?" A foot curled around Orossy's ankle and jerked, knocking him off-balance.

The books clattered to the floor. Fuming, Orossy bent over to pick them up. He hadn't told Feisal how bad things were; he didn't want his lover to think he couldn't take care of himself. For all his experience in dealing with adults, dealing with young men was completely different. He looked at them, the burly Hannik and the rat-like Johnen, wary.

"We can help, can't we?" Hannik said, jabbing his friend in the ribs.

"But not for free." Johnen leered. "We know how to get old Deverrin off your back, but it will cost you."

Oh, Lady. Orossy had a sick feeling in the pit of his stomach. "I'm not interested." A group of students blocked the door, curious to see how the conflict progressed.

"We want to see if all those rumors are true. Were you really a rent girl?" Hannik asked.

Orossy put the books in his satchel. "Yes."

The boys looked at each other and laughed. "Prove it."

Closing his eyes, Orossy counted to ten before he responded. "Not today."

"He won't do it for free. I told you," Johnen said.

"I won't do it at all." Orossy clamped his jaws shut, determined not to say anything else. He walked to the door, but the crowd didn't move.

Hannik jabbed him in the arm. "Because you're Feisal's catamite. Is that it?"

Until now, Orossy had ignored all of the jibes and remarks, because they were directed solely at him. But now they brought in Feisal . . .

A man defended his lover's honor. That much Orossy knew. He swiveled. "What did you say?"

Hannik glared at him, seemingly surprised that he'd actually gotten a reaction. "You heard me. Think you're better than the rest of us 'cause you're fucking the Lord Governor's son. You didn't earn your place here."

"Privileged little bastard." Orossy grabbed Hannik's collar. "You have no right to talk about earning your place. No right at all."

A few wide-eyed youths gathered behind their friend. Hannik spoke for them all. "We know you came from Tavern Street. How many did you sleep with to get in here? Did you service that old harridan Rewenna too?"

Rewenna was Feisal's mentor and the director of the Infirmary.

"Bastard." Orossy drove the boy backwards through the crowd and shoved him against the stone wall. Several other apprentices shouted at Hannik to fight back. Orossy spoke over them. "Apologize."

"For what? You don't belong here. Rent boy. Or should I say rent *girl?*" He snickered. "Even Deverrin isn't sure. What do you really have under that uniform of yours?" He made a grabbing motion toward Orossy's groin.

Orossy ignored the whistles and catcalls coming from the others. "Tell me something," Orossy said in his best rent girl voice. Rossa's voice. It frightened him how quickly she came back. "Have *you* ever been to Tavern Street?"

A glint of fear showed in the boy's eyes. "No."

"Then you have no idea what a rent girl's life is like. Let me give you a taste." He clenched Hannik's chin, turning the boy's face slowly from side to side as if he were examining a stock animal to buy.

Hannik tried to pry Orossy's fingers apart. "Let me go. You can't do this. It's against the rules."

Orossy cracked his palm against Hannik's cheek. The boy yelped. "Can't do what? Give you lessons? Isn't that what this place is for?" Orossy ground Hannik's head against the rough stone wall, savoring the boy's unease. "*Never* talk back to me. Keep your mouth shut or I'll do it for you."

Hannik trembled. The rest of the students went suddenly quiet.

"Do you know what you do when you go downstairs for the night?" Orossy continued to use Rossa's voice. "You wander through the crowd, looking for a potential customer, while the crowd looks at you. Some of them feel you up, to see if you might be to their taste." He demonstrated, caressing Hannik's cheek. The boy jerked his head away, but Orossy had already moved on. He pawed at Hannik's arms and chest, grabbing him bruisingly hard when he tried to get away.

"They call out, 'Come here, girl,'" he said, mimicking the rough voices of his customers. A little dennar, and Hannik felt the lewd and base emotions Orossy had sensed every night at the tavern. "'Think you're a tease, do you? I've got a few things in mind once we get upstairs.' And you choose one." Orossy kissed him on the lips, the barest hint of what the men would do later. "Even if he's the worst one there, you have to choose him, which is no choice at all, really. It's all about the money. No one cares about *you*. No one sees you as anything but a body to be used."

Truly frightened now, Hannik tried to shove Orossy away. Orossy caught the boy's wrists and pinned them against the wall. "Do you know what happens if you disobey your tavernkeeper, or if one of your customers complains?"

Hannik's brown eyes widened in terror. "Don't. Please, don't. I'm sor—"

Orossy kneed him square in the crotch. Hannik's high-pitched wail echoed in the room. Satisfied, Orossy let his victim go. The boy sank to the stone floor, agony etched in his face. From the corner of his eye, Orossy saw Johnen race out of the room. The other students tripped over desks and chairs as they backed away in mute horror.

"That's not all." With his booted foot, Orossy gave Hannik two swift, savage kicks to the ribs. When the boy moved his arms to protect his chest, Orossy knocked the wind out of him with a kick to the stomach. "Then, if he's not *too* mad, he'll leave you to see yourself out. If he's still angry, he might take you to bed to teach you a lesson, and that, I assure you, is not a pleasant experience."

Hannik continued to struggle for air, curled up and rocking back and forth in agony with his hands cupped around the tender, abused area.

Orossy forced Hannik onto his back and straddled him at the waist. He leaned over, propping himself up with his arms so he could look Hannik directly in the eye. "Let me ask you something else. Have you ever been hungry for a day, for a week? A month?" Hannik gave a tiny shake of his head. "Have you ever had to find food for yourself? Digging through icy water until your hands were numb and bleeding in the hopes that you'd find enough shellfish to make a decent meal?" Again came a shake of the head. "I was. I did, more times than I could count. I didn't have a well-built home, like you do. No food, no warm clothes, not even ugly uniforms like these!"

Fabric ripped as Orossy grabbed the laces on the front and yanked them apart. Hannik's bare chest showed lived red and black splotches. "I never knew my mother. My father drank the money I earned from begging. When I got too old, he sold me to a stranger who told me he'd find me honest work. Instead, he took me to a tavern. The tavernkeeper thought me pretty enough to be a girl, so a girl I became. One man after another took me to his bed. Some were gentle enough. Some . . ." He choked, remembering. "You wanted to know what it's like. I'll *show* you!"

Hannik screamed as Orossy used dennar to feed the boy exactly what he remembered: his first night at the tavern when Niklis had shown him exactly what he expected from a rent girl, the terror and pain and humiliation that created the hard, cold shell of Rossa, the slow numbing of all of his feelings so he could use her to survive.

Orossy broke the mental contact. Hannik's mouth hung open. "I had no hope of living past twenty, let alone an education or honest work. So don't you dare presume *anything* about me! I've lived through more in my nineteen years than you will in a lifetime, privileged little brat that you are. Don't you ever—" Orossy pulled Hannik up by the remains of his shirt and then slammed him down hard, "*ever* say I don't belong here, or that I didn't earn my place!" Another smack to the floor, and Hannik lay dazed and unmoving. Blood trickled from his nose.

Without pity, Orossy rose and headed towards the gaping onlookers. This time, they stayed out of his way. One or two mumbled an apology.

Rage-blind, Orossy didn't see Healer Deverrin until they collided. The Healer's voice was sharp. "Orossy!"

The use of his name broke through Rossa's hardness. Orossy stopped, disoriented. Fear and pain choked the room. He saw Hannik, *really* saw him, battered, bloody, and limp on the ground. He sensed the broken ribs, the concussion, the gathering bruises. Sickness filled Orossy's mouth. He must have looked like that after one of Niklis's beatings, and now . . .

Now he was no better than the tavernkeeper.

Deverrin grabbed his upper arm and shook him fiercely. "What in the Lady's name have you done?"

The rough contact rekindled Orossy's rage. He couldn't stand being grabbed and yanked around. He yearned to give his teacher the same treatment as Hannik until some small part of his mind checked him. This was no helpless, naïve boy but a man, a Healer with status and power.

Hannik's moans saved Orossy from any further rashness. In disgust, Deverrin let Orossy go and crouched down beside his student. Deverrin's eyes filled with fury as he used dennar to gauge his Hannik's injuries. He glared at Orossy. "Filthy gutter brat. The Healer's council will hear about this. So will the Lord Governor. If I ever see you anywhere near this building again—"

Orossy drew himself up to meet Deverrin's angry gaze. The Healer looked away first. Orossy gathered his shredded dignity and walked out of the Infirmary.

The Infirmary, located in one of the busiest districts of the populous city, was a fair distance away from the Lord Governor's home. By the time Orossy plowed his way through crowds, rickshaws, and narrow, winding streets to reach the quieter Noble's district, he was shaking badly. Guilt and shame replaced the surge of anger.

Lady have mercy, what had he been thinking? Not only had he attacked a classmate, but he'd also defied his teacher, a senior Healer. And on the eve of the Lord Governor's arrival! He'd ruined everything, all because he'd let his temper get the better of him.

He paused at the long, cobbled driveway that led to the Lord Governor's house. The building stood in the distance, with sloped, tiled roofs, well-kept gardens, and paneled doors that slid to enlarge various spaces or to let in more light. It was one of the oldest and largest houses in the city, and the finest. Orossy couldn't fathom what made him think he deserved to live in a place like this. Maybe he shouldn't bother going home at all.

Except then he'd never see Feisal again, and he couldn't bear that. The only way he would leave was if Feisal told him to. Resolutely, he headed up the path, steeling himself to meet whatever fate lay in store. Jussi met him at the door and, without saying a word, took Orossy's books and led him into the kitchen where he deposited Orossy onto a short, three-legged stool. The steward draped a wet cloth over the back of Orossy's neck. Orossy opened his mouth to explain, but Jussi gestured for him to stay silent. "Save your explanations for those who need them. I, for one, need your help with dinner."

He put a bowl of almonds and walnuts in front of Orossy along with a small paring knife. Grateful for the work, Orossy didn't notice how late it had gotten until he sensed Feisal come home. The Healer's fury hit him like the slap of a hand, filling him with a sudden, bright heat. Orossy took a few deep breaths to mentally center himself. It didn't work.

"He's not angry at you," Jussi told him. He poured two cups of tea and left just as Feisal walked in.

"Want to tell me what happened?" Still in his dark blue uniform, Feisal seated himself at the table across from Orossy and picked up a cup.

"What did they tell you?" Orossy asked, cautious. He slid the knife and nuts to the side.

"Lots of different things. I want to hear your version."

Orossy watched steam from his cup twist into the air. "It's my fault. I lost my temper. I shouldn't have kicked him."

"I hear that wasn't all you did," Feisal said with a chuckle.

"It's not funny!" Orossy's fist pounded the table hard enough that his cup of tea lost a few droplets over the side. "They wanted me to—" He broke off, too ashamed to say more. A whorl in the wood caught his attention.

Feisal waited a few moments before prompting, "To what?"

Heat flooded Orossy's face when he managed to speak. "To service them."

"Ah." Feisal took a long sip, his face thoughtful. "I assume you told them no?"

"Of course I did! I'm not . . ." He mentally swore at himself for stumbling again. "I'm not a rent girl anymore. No one owns me, and I'm not your cat—cat—" This time, he couldn't say it.

Mercifully, Feisal didn't prod him any further. "Good. That makes two things you're not."

He wondered how Feisal could take this all so calmly. "I'm not a student anymore, either. There are plenty of things I'm not. I don't know what I *am*." Grudgingly, he picked up his cup of tea, now cool enough to drink without wincing.

Feisal cocked his head and stared at Orossy. "Is this because my father is coming home tomorrow?"

Orossy mumbled his answer into the tea. "No."

"Are you sure?"

He wasn't sure, but he didn't want to talk about it anymore. "What are they going to do to me?"

The Healer swirled tea around in his cup. "I don't know. Rewenna is on your side, and there were plenty of witnesses that saw you provoked, but it's going to take a while to sort out. Beating is one thing, forcing dennar is another, and it's more serious. Instead of worrying about it, I'll tell you what," Feisal said with a mischievous grin. "Rewenna suggested rather strongly that I should take the day off tomorrow. I'll take you to the market district. You can pick out new clothes for tomorrow night."

"I'm sorry," Orossy said, suddenly guilty that Feisal had been forced to forego his duties.

"For what? That my colleague instills the same ill manners in his students that he possesses? Don't be an ass."

"Then I'd like to go." They'd hardly spent any time together, with Feisal busy at the Infirmary and Orossy struggling to catch up in class.

"Good," Feisal said, and kissed him on the cheek. "One last day to enjoy ourselves before Father gets home."

ଓଷ୍ଠଃ

Orossy had already known hundreds of ways to please a lover, but using dennar to do it was something new. Feisal had taught him, with infinite patience, how to use dennar to tease and cajole a body, how to bring a partner near climax and then to back off. Often, their sessions had lasted the entire night, leaving them bleary-eyed in the morning, but they were always gentle with each other, mindful that a Healer's dennar could hurt as well as heal if they got too reckless.

No so tonight. In the dim light of their room, Orossy clawed at Feisal's skin, desperate for the contact. His dennar traveled through Feisal's body, touching every part of him, memorizing him. Knowing that Rossa was still so close terrified him, intensifying the fear that he wasn't good enough for Feisal.

Feisal's loose hair, well past his shoulders, slipped through Orossy's fingers like silk. His skin was already warm and damp. Orossy sent his dennar to the pleasure points within Feisal's body, coaxing them from inside while his hands and mouth sought them on the outside. He focused all his attention, all his effort on it, wanting only to please Feisal, to give him something he'd remember.

"'Rossy."

Orossy heard his name, but he kept going. This had to be perfect.

"'Rossy. Don't. This isn't the tavern. You don't have to think like that any more."

Orossy opened his eyes to look down at his lover. Guilt stabbed through him. Feisal's dennar for mind-reading was weak, but when they were intimate he could pick up thoughts and feelings. "I'm sorry. I wanted—"

Two fingers pressed Orossy's lips together. "I know. Let me." The Healer brought Orossy's face towards him for a kiss. Feisal's hands were like magic; every touch tingled with dennar, warm and exciting. It was a trick Orossy hadn't learned yet, and Feisal enjoyed taunting him with it. Dennar-laced fingers tickled his face and neck, to his chest, belly, and lower, until Orossy thought he might die from need.

Feisal wouldn't let him, of course. Here, he was safe. It was such a blessed relief to be in accord with someone, to trust. Not like the tavern, where Rossa had become more than his name.

Feisal had seen behind that façade to the real Orossy. Making love hadn't always been this easy or wonderful; it had taken time, and Feisal had been careful and understanding. The Healer loved him, he knew, but tonight Orossy had a desperate need for proof.

His lover knew it, although the ease and sincerity with which Feisal made love to him hurt. *I don't deserve this,* Orossy thought, but kept it sheltered from Feisal's dennar. The Healer was so kind and gentle and earnest that Orossy couldn't believe that he'd been lucky enough to find him. It wouldn't last. Nothing this good ever could.

"Yes, it can," Feisal murmured in his ear. With the exquisite control he'd learned over the years, Feisal wrung every bit of stress and tension from Orossy's body, leaving Orossy unable to think of anything besides what Feisal was doing to him. The Healer took his time, ensuring that Orossy was completely aroused before bringing him to a full, delicious climax.

Afterwards, when they were both sated and spent, Feisal held him close. Even so, Orossy felt cold, as if a frigid wind blew against his bare skin. If he closed his eyes, he could still remember the boy he'd been, starved for love as well as food. "I'm not like that anymore. I'm not naïve. I'm not hungry."

"You're not alone, either," Feisal said with a squeeze. "I'm here, 'Rossy. I'll always be here for you. My father coming home won't change anything."

Even with Feisal's reassurance, the cold didn't leave him.

⊰⊱⊰⊱

The next morning, Orossy fiddled with the silk jacket and pants, wondering why he found it suddenly difficult to secure the fastenings of a men's jacket on himself when he'd had no trouble doing it on someone else.

Feisal lounged on his bed, watching, and trying not to laugh. He was already dressed, his mauve shirt hanging rakishly open. "Are you sure that's what you want to wear?"

Orossy felt the heat rush to his cheeks. "I'm sure."

"You look miserable."

Done, finally, Orossy shook out the sleeves. "Your clothes are too big on me. That's all."

"It's not all, but . . ." Feisal came up behind him to adjust the shirt, running his hands over Orossy's shoulders and arms. "If it's what you want, then it's fine with me."

But what do you *want to see?* Orossy wanted desperately to ask, but held his tongue. He agreed with Feisal that he looked odd. Feisal's clothes were too big; they were nearly the same height, but Feisal was more muscular and broader in the shoulders which meant that the fabric hung poorly and made Orossy look smaller than he was. Neither were they colors he liked. The dark blue and black looked dashing with Feisal's darker complexion, but they made Orossy's lighter skin look wan. It would have to do until he had something better made.

A quick breakfast of steamed rice and soup, and they were off toward the market district. "Shall we ride?" Feisal asked. Before Orossy could answer, Feisal hailed a passing rickshaw. Orossy climbed in after the Healer, stifling the urge to protest the expense. Feisal had never had to worry about such things.

The runner pulled them at a steady clip through the outer districts, then wove his way expertly around horses, carts, and pedestrians. Orossy clung to his lover, finding it strange that he'd waited for years for the chance to do just this, to be able to choose his own clothing and accessories. So far, he hadn't had time. The Infirmary had given him the pale blue uniform of a student, and Feisal had ordered more clothing for him and had it delivered. None of it had been overtly masculine, hence the need to borrow Feisal's clothes. Wearing them to market would be his trial run. If he could act masculine enough among the crowd, then doing so before the Lord Governor shouldn't be hard.

The runner dropped them off at the edge of the market district, which was closed to horse and cart traffic during the day. Feisal paid him and took Orossy's arm to lead him toward the merchants. The early morning sunlight gave the street an exotic look. Brightly-colored paper lanterns hung from the eaves as decoration. Streamers and incense drifted in the slight breeze.

They walked past shops offering every food or household accessory Orossy could imagine. A potter threw clay on a wheel outside of his store, enticing people inside with his craft. People swarmed the fruit stalls, eager for the freshest products and best bargains. Guards in violet livery patrolled the street, sharp eyes watching for thieves and cutpurses. The scent of fresh bread and roasting meat wafted on the air. Somewhere beyond the crowd, horses whinnied, accompanied by the lowing of cattle.

Feisal wandered from shop to shop, chatting with one merchant after another. Orossy gazed at the goods with childish delight. Knives. Blown glass. Fresh fruit and vegetables. Bouquets of flowers. Rings and other trinkets, leather shoes and boots, vials of oil and incense. A store with brightly-colored fabrics in the window caught his attention.

Inside, bolts of fabric were piled high. Linen, wool and fine silks in every color imaginable filled shelves that went straight to the ceiling. Dummies wore examples of the merchant's work, a green jacket and pants set such as Orossy had in mind and a dress of midnight blue silk overlaid with a gold floral pattern. Orossy looked at the latter for too long before he caught himself. *Men's* clothes. That's what he was here for.

"Welcome, young sir," the merchant said from behind the counter. An outlander, by his looks and his northern accent. Rotund and pale-skinned, chin peppered with stubble, he gestured at the array of fabrics lining the walls around him. "My best selection, gathered from across the continent. And this," he said, patting a bolt on the left of his counter, "is something I think would suit you perfectly."

The soft gold fabric with a pattern of vines drew him until he remembered he'd worn gold the first night he'd met Feisal. That part he didn't mind, but it was the beating from his tavernkeeper afterwards that made him release the fabric. He looked at color after color, trying to find something that didn't trigger a memory. His former patron had liked him in green. As Rossa, he'd worn a dress of blood red the night he'd run away.

The merchant stepped around the counter. "My lord? See anything you'd like? I'd be more than happy to have something made up for you. If you'd just step this way so I can take your measurements?"

A tempting offer—except his eyes kept returning to the blue dress, wondering how it would look in gold. "Perhaps. I'll have to ask my lov—my friend his opinion first."

"Of course, young sir, of course, but keep in mind that many of these fabrics are rare, and sure to be spoken for by day's end."

Orossy ignored the rest of the merchant's attempts to bargain. He excused himself and stepped back outside, looking for Feisal. The Healer wasn't anywhere to be seen. Nor could Orossy sense him through the overwhelming emotions of the crowd.

He fought down panic. It was silly. He was safe enough, and there were plenty of guards around to protect everyone. Even so, he felt suddenly helpless. A man brushed against him, then a woman. Orossy's control cracked. Emotions assailed him; the happiness of a young couple planning a wedding, the frustration of a woman who wanted a lower price for eggs and couldn't get it, a girl child crying for her mother because she'd fallen and skinned her knee. Too much. To his eyes, they stared at him. Imagined whispers penetrated his ears. *Look at him. The freak. Rent girl. Look what he's done to the Lord Governor's son. I'm surprised they let him loose after what happened yesterday.* He had to get out of here, now, before he—

A hand grasped his shoulder. "Orossy?"

The overwhelming presence of the crowd faded. Orossy turned, half relieved, half afraid, to see the familiar face of one of the city guards, Eamon. "Are you here to arrest me again?" he asked as lightly as he could.

"No. Not unless there's something new I should know about." Eamon's smile was kind and genuine. "Is there?"

With a shrug, Orossy said, "Depends on whom you talk to, I suppose." Like those at the Infirmary, but the guard probably knew about that already. Gossip flew fast in a city of mind-readers. "Can I help you, Lieutenant?"

Eamon guided Orossy to a sheltered spot at the corner of the tailor's shop. "The colonel has a job. For Rossa."

Oh, Lady. Uneasiness clenched Orossy's stomach. "She's dead."

"A shame," Eamon said. "Rumor has it that Niklis is up to his tricks again, smuggling in illegal workers."

Once, Orossy had been one of those smuggled workers.

"Niklis knows Rossa, and he's a greedy man. If there's any chance of catching him, we need her—*your*—help. You know the place. You know how he thinks."

"Rossa's dead," Orossy said again. "I can't help you." If he put a dress on again, he might never take it off. Besides, his dresses were gone now. He must get used to wearing men's clothes and acting like a man. Losing Feisal wasn't worth the risk.

"If you change your mind, you need only let us know," Eamon said. "Please consider it. If we catch Niklis with these girls, we can arrest him and put him out of business. Permanently."

It was almost enough to make Orossy concede. Almost.

"I'm sorry, Lieutenant." Hurrying away, Orossy found Feisal bent over a table of silver jewelry.

Feisal looked up. "Are you all right? I turned my back and you were gone."

"I want to go home."

Feisal's smile vanished. "But we just got here, and there's more to show you. One of my favorite clothiers is right over—"

"Please. Take me home, or at least get me out of the market so I can find my own way back."

"All right." Feisal led him through a crowd picking over bins of fresh fruit. "What's the matter? What happened?"

"Stop it. I don't need to be fussed over. I just need to *leave*." Seeing the end of the street clearly, Orossy broke away from Feisal and walked faster, sidestepping a small child running from its mother.

Feisal ran a few paces to catch up. "I'm sorry. Why don't we—"

Orossy stopped and turned. Palms flat against Feisal's chest, he said, "There are too many people here. That's all. Go back and enjoy yourself. Pick something nice for me."

Feisal looked a little sad. "I thought you would enjoy being able to choose things for yourself, and maybe get something new for tonight."

Lady's grace. Now he'd gone and ruined everything. This was supposed to be a special day. "Thank you. I do want to. Just not right now." The thought of going back into that crowd made him feel sick.

"You're sure you're all right?"

"I'm sure. Now go on." He gave Feisal a little shove for emphasis, and finally the Healer went.

Rickshaws waited just outside the district, but Orossy walked home, unable to justify the expense. In the safety of his room, he slid the door shut, thankful for the familiar, comfortable surroundings. The soft, clean mattress on the floor, the cabinet free of scratches and stains, one of Feisal's silk robes in a heap on the floor. Books. Dozens of them, and more if he asked. He'd never felt so utterly grateful to have such wonders in his life, especially now that he was so close to having them all taken away.

He had enough to worry about without the girls adding to it. He couldn't help them, no matter what Eamon said. "I'm not Rossa anymore. I'm not!"

He refused to look in the mirror. If he did, he would see her there, waiting, eager to rebuke him for his lies.

⊰❦⊱

Feisal had missed the midday meal. Orossy had tried not to worry, and instead spent the rest of the afternoon in his room attempting to read through his textbook. It wasn't working. He couldn't concentrate. His thoughts kept returning to the girls. Just like him, they had been promised honest work. Just like him, they would end up in a tavern. They didn't deserve it. His conscience nagged at him, but Rossa was dead, and Orossy couldn't go there as himself. The girls wouldn't trust a man, and as Orossy he would be too vulnerable to Niklis's manipulations.

Rossa had been the one with the power. She was the survivor, the one that had dealt with the men, but she could be just as cruel and unforgiving as Niklis himself. Look at what she'd done to Hannik.

Orossy punched a pillow in frustration. Not her. Him. Look at what *he'd* done to Hannik. He didn't want to be that angry, distant part of himself ever again. The truth was, Orossy dared not go after the girls for fear of what he'd unleash if he lost control. If he hurt anyone else, he'd lose Feisal for sure.

No. He couldn't go. And that was that. Firm in his decision, Orossy turned back to his book but found it no easier to read than before.

Just before sunset, the door slid open. Feisal entered, dashing and handsome in a new silk shirt and pants nearly the same dark blue as his Healer's uniform. It fit him perfectly, showing off every angle of his body. He carried a paper-wrapped parcel under his arm. "Here. I got you something."

Orossy opened it. Inside was a man's jacket and pants of the ivy-patterned silk he'd admired that morning. His throat tightened. He didn't know what to say. The garments were finer than anything he'd owned, and he appreciated Feisal's gesture, but if only . . .

If only it were a dress instead.

"The merchant remembered you. Luckily, he had them half done, so I persuaded him to finish. That's what took so long. Do you like them?"

Orossy swallowed. "They're lovely." They truly were. The neck and sleeves were trimmed in forest green. Exactly his colors.

"Try them on. I want to see how they look."

"All right, all right. But go away . . . unless you want to help me dress." He cocked his head, pleased to see the lustful look in Feisal's eyes. Now *that* would be a way to get rid of all of his tension. "How much time do we have before your father gets home?"

"Long enough," Feisal said. Two steps, and Orossy was in his arms. Feisal laughed. "I should know better than to flirt with a tavern brat."

"You can't win," Orossy said. "One look and you're mine." What a shame to muss Feisal's perfect clothes.

Feisal held him tight. "You're so tense."

Orossy didn't answer. Instead, he pressed his lips against Feisal's, wishing that this moment would last forever, that nothing and no one could ever come between them.

ಜಣ಼ಀ಼

Dressed, flushed, and only slightly rumpled, they reached the front porch in time to hear hoofbeats on the cobbled driveway. Orossy hung back in the shadows, gripping the railing with white-knuckled hands. The sky had turned orange and pink as the sun set. The air was still. Crickets chirped their greeting to the evening. Orossy would have enjoyed the beauty of his surroundings if he hadn't been so nervous.

He knew he was being an idiot. He'd met powerful men before, taken them to bed and usually had received a fat purse to show for it. But none of them had been his lover's father.

A large dappled-gray stallion stopped a short distance from the house. Feisal didn't wait; he ran out barefoot to greet his father before the Lord Governor had even dismounted. Jussi went out more sedately to take care of the horse.

Orossy kept his eyes downcast, seeing only a tall figure dressed in riding leathers, his braided hair silvered from age. He had no idea how old Maddren was, but the Lord Governor was fit and moved with deliberate grace. A moment later, all but the silver hair was blocked by Feisal's eager embrace.

Orossy felt a lump in his throat. Tears stung his eyes at seeing two family members so obviously happy to see each other.

Feisal ran back to grab his hand. "'Rossy. Come here."

Orossy stumbled down the porch stairs, suddenly angry at Feisal for putting him through this. Out of instinct, he groped for Rossa's strength and pulled himself upright. The old, familiar attitude returned. He bowed in greeting. "Welcome home, my lord. It's a pleasure to meet you." He lifted the Lord Governor's hand to his lips. Lord Maddren smelled of horse and dust and leather. Orossy focused on the callused hand to avoid looking in his eyes.

"The pleasure is mine, Master Orossy," the Lord Governor said. "Especially since I have you to thank for saving my son's life."

That was how they'd met; Feisal had wandered into the tavern, drugged by someone who meant him ill, and Orossy had nursed him. Surprised by the sincerity in Maddren's voice, Orossy looked up and found himself caught by a pair of silver-gray eyes. He had the eerie feeling that Maddren was looking *through* him in an intimate and almost disturbing way.

"I love him. I'd never hurt him," Orossy said, too quietly for Feisal to hear.

"I know." Maddren's low voice was no less powerful for its subtlety. "You are not what I expected. I would speak with you later."

The Lord Governor bent to remove his boots just as Orossy felt a spike of fear in his belly. If Maddren sensed it, he gave no sign. Lady have mercy. He was in trouble. He knew it. The Lord Governor disliked him already.

Feisal, who could have no idea of what had just passed, still stood nearby, radiating happiness. "Dinner is waiting."

"Good. I look forward to it. *After* I rid myself of the grime from the road." Maddren embraced Feisal again. Orossy turned his head. No one had ever cared about him like this.

"Go on," Feisal said, finally letting go. "Orossy and I will wait for you, won't we, 'Rossy?"

Caught, Orossy retreated behind his façade without thinking. "Take your time, my lord. I hope everything will be to your pleasure."

Feisal glared at him. Maddren's face remained impassive. "I am sure it will be," he said, and to Feisal, "I will not be long. And then I wish to hear of your adventures in your own words."

As soon as Maddren went inside, Feisal rounded on his lover. "What in the Lady's name was that? He's my *father*, not one of your customers! You don't have to do that anymore, you know."

Lady's grace, he was getting annoying. "Do what?" Orossy had a fair idea of what Feisal meant; he was already angry at himself.

Orossy headed toward the formal dining room, its sliding walls opened wide for a view of the garden and darkening sky. The low table was already set with the leaf-shaped dishes, two bowls and three small plates at each setting along with pairs of wooden eating sticks resting on holders. Caddies of tea and wine stood waiting. He wasn't hungry.

Feisal followed, emanating irritation. "Play the rent girl. Just be yourself."

"Which is what?" Orossy kicked one of the floor cushions so hard it struck the far wall. "It's easy for you. You're a Healer. You always have been. I used to be a rent girl and a gutter rat, but the Lady knows what I am now."

"What do you *want* to be?"

"I hate that question." He retrieved the cushion, not wanting the Lord Governor to see the room in disarray. Dinner had to be perfect. "I have everything I wanted. Safety. Someone who loves me. A chance to learn. So why doesn't it feel like enough?" He dropped the cushion to the floor and sat on it. "He wants to talk to me."

Feisal took the cushion next to him. He rubbed slow circles on Orossy's back. "So? He just wants to get to know you."

"I don't feel like dinner. Tell him I'm sick."

"That's not a feasible excuse."

"Then make me sick."

"How could you even suggest such a thing?" Feisal's face reflected the same disgust Orossy could sense with his dennar. The hand moved up to Orossy's shoulder and squeezed. "Don't do this. Not tonight. I'm not mind-reader enough to figure out what's bothering you these past two days. So tell me."

"I'm a half-breed tavern brat who can't decide which sex I prefer. You're the Lord Governor's son."

"So?"

"'So?' You bastard."

"Stop it, 'Rossy. Stop. I don't care where you came from so long as you're *here*. I love you. Isn't that enough?"

He waved his arm, frustrated. "No, it's not. I—"

His arm collided with one of the tea caddies. Steaming liquid splashed right down the front of his new clothes.

Feisal's face turned to alarm. "'Rossy! Are you all right?"

His skin burned, but not as much as his pride. "Leave me alone. I'll go change."

"I'll come with you."

"Stay. Be with your father. I'll be down soon enough." He left before Feisal could do anything but stare after him. Gods. He ruined everything from the new clothes Feisal had bought him to Feisal himself. *You're not what I expected.* The Lord Governor's words stung.

In his room, Orossy stripped off the sodden garments and threw them in the corner. Thanks to his own carelessness, he didn't have anything to wear. If only that could be a reasonable excuse to not go to dinner.

The door slid open behind him. Lady's grace, why couldn't Feisal leave him alone? "I don't care what you say. I'm not hungry, and you'll have to drag me down naked because I don't have—" He turned mid-sentence to see not Feisal, but Jussi standing in the doorway.

"Perhaps you might wear this?" Orossy's favorite red dress, a gift from Feisal, was draped over Jussi's arm.

Orossy took a step back. "I told you to get rid of that."

"I thought you meant the tear on the side. I mended it. Good as new." Jussi laid the dress over Orossy's arms as if it were a blessing. "He wants you to be as you are, as he's been telling you all along. Him and Lord Maddren both."

"I'm not good enough for either of them."

"Only because you feel you aren't good enough for yourself." The steward smiled. "Yet." He deposited the rest of Orossy's accessories on the bed and left.

Orossy stood there a long time, dress in his arms, torn between throwing it away and putting it on. The soft fabric taunted him, called out to him. He'd always enjoyed the way he looked in a dress, part of his craving for the female body he'd never had. Rossa had been a mask, but one he'd worn more easily than some of the others at the tavern. To him, playing female had never felt wrong; the wrongness came from being exploited by Niklis and his customers.

Feisal loved men. Orossy didn't always want to be one, and therein lay the crux of his difficulties. He wanted, more than anything, to make Feisal happy, but giving in to his lover's desires only made him more miserable. And if he was upset, so was Feisal, more often than not.

"I can't pretend anymore," he said, thinking of Feisal. "I can't be what you want, love. I'm sorry."

Feisal's disappointment was a risk he'd have to take. In a short amount of time, Orossy had donned the dress along with his other accoutrements, the cincher for his waist and the specially-made undershorts to disguise his masculine contours. His cosmetics were still in the top drawer, and in moments he'd applied the basics for his face. Dark lines curved around his eyes, bringing out the wildness within.

And there she was in the mirror. Rossa. His altered self, his better, more powerful half. She felt *right*. The old habits of movement and voice returned naturally, as if he'd never tried to discard them. She smiled, sly and pitiless. It was as if she were there, an entity separate from Orossy, waiting to accompany him on his task.

She couldn't come. Not this time. "Thank you," Orossy told her, "for being there when I needed you. For helping me to survive. But I need you as part of me now." He put his palm to hers on the mirror. Brown eyes met his, curious. "Be with me. Give me your strength, and—and your anger."

Anger frightened him, but Rossa had kept it for a reason. Better to embrace it than to keep fighting it. "I won't let you control me any more. I'm in charge. *I* am."

She nodded, impatient as if she'd been waiting a long time for Orossy to ask. Her overwhelming presence faded, and there . . . there was the real Orossy, without masks or pretense. The gods had made him a man, yes, but taking a woman's form brought him inner peace and calmness.

He'd told Eamon the truth. Rossa was dead, and with her, the fear and guilt over his past. In their place was a simmering, justified anger. This new Orossy wouldn't let innocents suffer his fate if he could help it. He left the house with the surety that he wouldn't need to find Eamon. Eamon would find him.

ଓଜ୍ରେ୪୦

Orossy kept his arm threaded through Eamon's as they approached the tavern, feeling more confident than he would have thought. The guard had exchanged his uniform for the clothes of a respectable, if not wealthy, merchant. They paused at the tavern's entrance. Light shone from nearly every window of the two-story building. Incense and loud conversation drifted into the street.

"Are you sure?" Eamon asked.

"I'm sure."

Even so, it was far too easy to remember how he'd been one of those girls, wandering from table to table with trays of food, chatting softly with potential customers, pretending to enjoy the inevitable fondling. Orossy shook that thought away and took a step forward. He didn't belong here anymore.

They left their shoes with a girl at the door. Since he'd last been here, Orossy had learned to control his dennar. The onslaught of thoughts and emotions didn't bother him as much as it used to. They threaded their way between the customers lounging on cushions around low tables. A few of the serving girls recognized him, staring in disbelief for a moment before returning to their work.

His eyes fixed on the tavernkeeper pouring drinks from behind the bar. Seeing him there, knowing what he'd done, was like a fist to Orossy's gut. Orossy's nails dug into Eamon's arm.

"Easy," the guard leaned over to murmur. "We can't make a scene here. Too many people."

Orossy knew that, but it was the hardest thing he'd ever done to walk to the bar and act pleasant. He would have happily used his dennar to castrate the bastard. Niklis said nothing as Orossy and Eamon sat on a pair of tall stools, concessions to outlanders who didn't like to sit on the floor. "Hello, Nik."

"Rossa." Eyes flicked to Eamon. "Back to work, I see."

Niklis knew Orossy too well. He'd closed his mind off so Orossy couldn't sense his intentions. Orossy had already done likewise lest he give anything away. "My friend here wanted something special, and I knew just the place." Orossy leaned conspiratorially over the counter.

Niklis snorted. "Special? And just what does my lowly tavern have to offer?" He jerked his head toward a bored-looking Eamon. "I thought you were with the Lord Governor's son."

"And what's wrong with having more than one? You never seemed to have a problem with it." His laugh was just shy of Rossa's mocking one. "Feisal knows I go out. He doesn't mind. My friend here is looking for something . . . fresh. Something new. And I *know* you do whatever you can to make your customers happy."

Niklis began wiping down the worn wood of the bar, a gesture he always used when bargaining. "I'm listening."

Eamon dropped a pouch of coins on the bar with a *thunk*. "That enough to get me a look?"

The tavernkeeper laughed. He gestured to the girls in the room. "These aren't enough to look at?"

"They're pretty enough, but I want something new. Unsullied." Eamon brought out another pouch but did not set it down.

Greed seemingly won Niklis over, but Orossy knew better than to trust him. Getting to the girls couldn't be this easy. He would have taken Eamon himself, but new arrivals were sequestered in a hidden, locked room. Niklis possessed the only key.

The tavernkeeper looked from Orossy to Eamon, his gaze lingering a little too long on the guard. "All right," he said to Orossy. "But you come with me to choose. Your friend stays here."

Orossy barely managed to keep his face emotionless. Fear curdled in his belly. Eamon's hand clenched his shoulder, a gesture of support. "It's all right, love," Orossy said, putting his hand over Eamon's. "Niklis and I are old friends."

Eamon didn't let go. For Orossy to be alone with the man hadn't been part of their plan, but Orossy couldn't see another way to deal with him.

"Don't take too long," Eamon said. "I'm a very impatient man." Meaning he would come after Orossy if need be.

Orossy nodded. Niklis snatched the second pouch from Eamon's hand. "Come on, then." He led Orossy to the back of the main room and down a hallway. The rooms here were less extravagant than those upstairs, used by customers with little money to spare. Orossy shuddered at the muffled sounds behind some of the closed doors. He'd rarely had to use these, and he was grateful.

The rooms all looked alike. Orossy couldn't remember which one the girls were supposed to be in. Halfway down, Niklis slid open the door on the right. "After you."

As soon as Orossy peeked inside, he knew it wasn't the right room. It looked like any of the others here, bare except for a mattress on the floor, a low table and cabinet nearby and a washroom at the opposite end. This one appeared too well-used. The furniture was scuffed and there were stains on the matted floor. Niklis didn't rent out the one he kept the girls in. Orossy shook his head. "Sorry, Nik, but this isn't—"

Before Orossy could finish, Niklis wrapped one strong hand around Orossy's throat and thrust him inside. A brutal shove landed Orossy on the floor, gasping for air. Niklis jammed an angled chunk of wood beneath the door so it couldn't slide open.

Fear paralyzed Orossy. Just like before. He recognized the twisted, leering face remembered the beatings and what came after. Eamon wouldn't reach him in time.

The tavernkeeper smiled. "What are you playing at, my dear Rossa? Don't you think I know that man with you is a guard?" He held Orossy's chin in a bruising grip. With his other hand, he caressed Orossy's cheek and neck. Orossy shivered in revulsion. "Did you think you were going to fool me into showing him my secrets? You ought to know better." He laughed softly. "I missed you. And you must feel the same, since you came back to visit me." Cocking his head, he leaned in for a kiss.

No. *No!*

Rossa, the memory of her, surged forward. Orossy was no longer helpless. He could fight back. He *had* to fight back. Palms squarely on Niklis's chest, he said, "I'm not one of your girls. Not anymore."

He raised one foot to aim it at Niklis's unprotected groin, but the tavernkeeper was too quick. Grunting, Niklis used his weight to slam Orossy to the ground. Orossy's vision sparkled. And then Niklis was there, on top of him, hands around his neck.

Flailing, Orossy found Niklis's arm and gripped it hard. Dennar rushed from him. Not enough to kill, but enough to make the tavernkeeper shriek in pain and let go. Orossy rolled over and tried to use the cabinet to stand, but Niklis leapt after him. Orossy slammed into the cabinet as he fell. Pain blossomed in his shoulder.

"Little bitch!" Niklis snarled. "I'll teach you to fight back." One hand tangled in Orossy's hair to wrench his head back while the other pressed a deadly sharpness to his neck. "Your choice, Rossa. Come back to work for me, or I'll cut you so badly even a Healer won't be able to save you."

Orossy closed his eyes, reaching within himself to touch newfound strength. His neck ached from the awkward angle, and he still hadn't quite caught his breath, but he refused to give in to fear. If Niklis truly wanted Orossy back at the tavern, he wouldn't do anything to ruin one of his girls—or so Orossy hoped. "Give me the keys, Nik. It's over. The girls don't belong here."

Niklis gave a vicious jerk. Orossy's throat burned where the knife dug in. "They were abandoned! I took them in, gave them a place to live and a job—" The tavernkeeper broke off, panting. "Like you, you little freak! Who else would have given you work? This is the thanks I get? Gutter brat!" He ground one knee into Orossy's lower back.

"Rossa!" Eamon's muffled voice came from the other side of the door. Orossy didn't answer, not trusting Niklis. Eamon's fist pounded on the door, followed by a short, sharp kick. The door bent, but didn't give.

The tavernkeeper bent close to whisper, his rancid, beer-laden breath suffocating. "Once a rent girl, always a rent girl, *Rossa*. You'll never get free of it, and the city will never forgive you."

Four months ago, Orossy would have been cowed. Not now. "I don't need the city's forgiveness. Only my own. And I have it." Out of spite, he laughed. One arm groped behind him until he found Niklis's leg. Orossy sent another thread of dennar to wrap Niklis's gut in agony. The tavernkeeper howled.

Niklis jerked backwards, careless with the blade. The sleeve of the dress split open as a blaze of pain traveled down Orossy's neck and shoulder. Orossy ignored it, scrabbling on the bed until he could lurch to his feet away from the writhing tavernkeeper. He couldn't go far in the tiny room, and Niklis and his blade were between him and the door.

"Bitch," Niklis said again, followed by a string of other epithets.

Another round of kicks failed to damage the door. Niklis ignored it, intent on his prey. Orossy barely had time to move before Niklis's knife screamed through the air and embedded itself into the wall where Orossy's shoulder had been. As Niklis pulled it out, Orossy clasped his hands together and struck the tavernkeeper hard in the small of his exposed back. Niklis collapsed, groaning, but he held fast to the knife.

Orossy grabbed one of the pillows and used all of his weight to hold it over Niklis's face. The tavernkeeper wriggled, striking aimlessly with the knife. Orossy straddled Niklis's chest, his knees pinning the tavernkeeper's arms to the ground. He caught Niklis's wrist and dug in his nails so that the tavernkeeper had no choice but to let go of the knife. It thudded to the ground. Orossy shoved it under the table, safely out of reach.

The cushion slid aside. Niklis spat. The warm globule hit Orossy's cheek. "You'll pay for this," Niklis said.

"How does it feel to be the one on the bottom, Nik?" Orossy laughed. For the first time, Niklis was at *his* mercy, not the other way around. Pinned beneath him, Niklis was only a man, small and angry and helpless, hardly worthy of Orossy's attention, let alone his fear.

Orossy's dennar screamed, *Kill him.*

It would be easy, so easy to stop his heart or lungs, or to pick him apart from the inside out. The little bursts of pain he'd given the tavernkeeper were nothing compared to what he *could* do.

"Do it," Niklis said. "I took you in. I taught you. Do you think I don't know what you're capable of?"

Kill him.

Rossa would, without hesitation. Orossy wanted to. Some dark part of him craved to treat the tavernkeeper exactly the way he'd been treated.

Niklis grinned. "I taught you well. Like a dog. Every time you tried to bite, I beat it out of you. You can't do it, even now. You're too weak."

The pounding at the door came sharper and harder. Eamon must have found something heavy to use.

"Am I?" Orossy asked. "I could take you apart, piece by piece. One little thought, and I could leave you in agony for the rest of your life. You know I can. Just as you know your words can't hurt me now."

He wanted more than anything to send his dennar cascading into Niklis, loosing all the hatred and rage he'd long kept buried. To pound Niklis's mind as the tavernkeeper had thrashed him in body.

But he didn't. That wasn't Orossy, to beat his victims into submission. Much as he wanted to make Niklis suffer, he knew that torturing someone deliberately would be the one thing Feisal would never forgive him for. Now that his rage had lessened, he found the idea despicable.

Strength came from knowing when to use his dennar—and when not to. Ironically, he now had a subject for the essay Deverrin had assigned him, although he doubted he'd ever get a chance to write it.

"You lose, Nik. I'm not like you. And I'm not one of your girls anymore. You can't control me, and I . . . I will be merciful enough to let you live unscathed."

A twist of dennar and Niklis went limp beneath him. Orossy stayed where he was for a moment, panting with exertion. Then, taut with the thrill of victory, he eased away to sit with his back against the wall.

Another sharp crack, and the door splintered inward. Eamon, holding an erotic stone statue swiped from the common room, looked down at the unconscious tavernkeeper. He let the statue fall to the ground with a heavy thud. "I see you didn't need me after all. Is he—?"

"I knocked him out. Feisal showed me the trick." Now that he wasn't afraid for his life, he felt giddy.

Niklis was gone. Forever.

Eamon crouched beside him. "You're bleeding."

The cuts on Orossy's neck and shoulder burned anew. "I'm fine." Orossy stared past him at the unmoving form. "I almost killed him."

"Almost." Eamon rifled through Niklis's pockets and drew out a set of keys. At Orossy's nod, he tossed them over. "Go on. Get the girls out. I'll see that he doesn't go anywhere."

Happy to be away, Orossy went into the room across the hall, identical to the one he'd just been in, except for the cleanliness and the nearly invisible outline of a door embedded into the stones at the rear of the washroom. Using his fingers more than his eyes, Orossy found the keyhole. A little fumbling for the right key and he finally got the door open. The windowless room was lit by a single oil lamp and fitted with four mattresses and two worn cabinets. In the corner, huddled in wide-eyed fear atop one of the mattresses, were two half-breed girls and a dark, exotic-looking boy.

Orossy stared at the latter, stunned. No doubt the slight, feminine-looking young man had been picked to be his replacement. The boy's gaze darted over Orossy, taking in his bloody, disheveled appearance, the ripped dress that exposed his chest enough to prove he wasn't a girl. Shocked, tear-stained eyes met Orossy's.

In that moment, the boy saw what he might have become; Orossy, what he might have been, had someone helped him in time.

Orossy held out his hand to the nearest girl. Shivering with fear and relief, she let herself be enveloped in his arms. Dennari, he sensed, with a bit of empathy so she knew who to trust. Poor thing.

"It's all right," he told them all. "It's over."

ೞେଛେ

"... and Eamon took Niklis off to the prison. The girls are orphans. The boy was sold by his uncle. One of the female guards is looking after them until they decide what to do." Orossy sipped the cup of tea Jussi had handed him after they'd gathered in the kitchen. Feisal sat on a stool behind Orossy, using bits of dennar to heal every cut and bruise, however minor. The Lord Governor sat next to him, relaxed, leaning on the table with one arm.

"As they were tricked and harmed within my territory, we must make reparations," the Lord Governor said. "Their future will not be left uncertain for long."

"Good," Orossy said abruptly before he remembered who he was talking to. "Thank you, my lord."

"And thank you, Master Orossy, for your services."

The gratitude surprised Orossy. He met the penetrating silver eyes. "Even if I'm not what you'd hoped?" He gestured to his torn dress. "Forgive me, my lord, for being less than you expected, but you see me as I am. I cannot change for anyone's sake but my own."

The Lord Governor held up a hand. "I said that you were not what I expected," he replied, "but I regret that you misunderstood. You are all I expected from someone my son would love, and much more, as you have proven tonight. I am proud to accept you into my home and family." He inclined his head and gave Orossy a slight bow. "Now, if you will excuse me, the fatigue from my travels has caught up to me. I will see you both in the morning." He stood and bent to kiss his son on the forehead before leaving.

Feisal used one last touch of dennar on Orossy's cheek. "Good as new." He kissed it for emphasis. "I told you. He likes you, dress and all."

Orossy held his breath, suddenly nervous. "What about you? I know you love men, but—"

"I love *you*, whether you decide to be male or female. Or if you wear dresses or rags or nothing at all." Feisal framed Orossy's face in his hand and kissed him, hard.

Orossy let Feisal take his time, enjoying himself, and then drew back to watch Feisal's face. "Even if I got myself kicked out of the Infirmary?"

Feisal's expression saddened. "Ah. That. Rewenna sent word. You'll have to appear before the senior Healers and explain yourself. There's a chance they'll reconsider your expulsion, but it won't be easy to convince them. Even then, it's likely you'll be put on probation until they trust you not to misuse your dennar again."

"That's fair," Orossy said. His next words were harder. "I'm going to apologize to Hannik. Maybe talk to him a little more rationally."

"Good. That will help. Just promise me one thing," Feisal said, wagging a finger. "Don't *ever* run away like that again. You worried me."

"I didn't mean to," Orossy said, filled with another surge of love for Feisal. "I only wanted to be worthy of you and your father."

"Oh, 'Rossy." Feisal embraced him so tightly that Orossy found it hard to breathe. "You were always worthy. You never had to prove anything to me. I don't care where you came from, only that you're here, with me, right now."

"I had to prove it to *myself*, though," Orossy said. Jussi had been right. "And I had to stop being afraid. I thought I was going to lose you. It scared me more than Niklis ever did."

Feisal eased back to meet his eyes. "Are you still afraid?"

"No," Orossy said. "Not anymore."

That night, Orossy lay curled in his lover's arms, warm and happy, dreaming not of loneliness, but love.

THE BARONESS' BALL

by Pauline Zed

Pauline Zed studied film, English and astrophysics at the University of Toronto. She spent two years in the wilds of Madison, Wisconsin doing an M.A. in film before returning to Canada. She has a blue belt in Hap Ki Do, is a sometime student of Tai Chi, and was on the U of T varsity fencing team at the grand old age of thirty. Her first job was as a book store clerk, which turned out to be not nearly as glamorous as she'd hoped, and has since worked as a short order cook, a bank teller, an editor, a teacher, an SGML analyst, and a cashier at a racetrack. When not writing, she is the one-woman technical training department at a law book publisher. She has studied Cantonese and Mandarin, attended film festivals on three continents and lives in Toronto with her husband and young daughter, one cat, three swords, and far too many books. Her blog can be found at paulinezed.livejournal.com.

"The Baroness' Ball" is Pauline's first published story. The setting for the story arose from the Latvian heritage of her father, who bestowed upon her both a spirit of independence and an unusual last name that begins with, yes, zed.

The summer ball of the Baroness Ulmanis was not the high point of any social season. The baroness was of a respected but faded line, and both her ballroom and her guests reflected that fact. The room's furniture was just a little worn, its wall coverings just a little frayed, its chandeliers just a little dimmed. There were no famous beauties or infamous rakes amongst the young women and men who paraded on the dance floor and preened around the banquet tables. Those in attendance were of good families, but not the very best, which is no doubt how my aunt had managed to obtain invitations for us at all.

As I had done for the past two months at any such function, I lurked at the edges of the dance floor, ignoring the not-quite-whispered comments about how out of fashion my dress was, and avoiding the sight of the many mirrors in the ballroom. I am no gargoyle, but neither am I a great beauty, and I never catch sight of a looking glass without the voices of my mother and sisters enumerating my many faults sounding in my ears: the unruliness of my too-wild hair, the commonness of my too-tanned skin, the stature of my too-tall frame. My one point of pride was the necklace my father had given me before we set out for the capital, delicate drops of amber strung on silver threads, an ornament I would not have surrendered for a cascade of diamonds.

Unlike my sisters, I was not made for garden parties or fêtes, preferring the cool comfort of my father's library or the exhilaration of a stolen afternoon spent on horseback in the woods of our estate. In such a room as this, with an atmosphere as airless and stifling as the people within it, all I could think of was the insistence of my mother that I find a husband I did not want, and the resolve of my aunt to find a candidate that would suit the family, if not me. I looked across the room and saw a gaunt young noble that my aunt had declared "an unpleasant young man from a family of no great reputation." An unease prickled my skin as I wondered if he was the manner of man I was destined to marry, and I cast about for an illness I could feign to convince my father, the Baron Arkadijs Rozkalni, and my aunt, the widowed Countess Ilze Berzins, to leave the ball early.

And then two men strode into the stuffy ballroom, and it was as if a cool, autumn breeze had caressed my face and stirred my blood.

They were clearly not nobility, not fashionable young men searching for wives to please their families. There was their age for a start. Though they were by no means infirm, they were past the age at which young nobles seek wives, perhaps as old as thirty. Then there were the circumstances of their attire.

The first man was handsome. His hair was, against the current mode, close-cropped and jet black, encumbered by neither powder nor wig. His eyes were framed by the longest lashes I'd seen on any person, man or woman. His expression had a haughty turn, but I fancied I could see a tendency to wry humor in the corner of his mouth. His frame was tall and muscular, his clothes well-tailored, if not entirely in fashion, and his sword, a simple rapier in the Frankish style, was clearly meant more for fighting than decoration.

The second man was breathtaking. More in keeping with current men's styles, he had longer hair, but such hair as I had never seen on any person. It ran riot with chestnut curls and was kept in the barest control by a thin emerald ribbon. His eyes were almond-shaped and feline, his mouth full. A dueling scar ran down one cheek, a mark that heightened his beauty rather than marred it. The sword at his side was even more common than his companion's, and clearly forged by a local smith rather than a more stylish foreign weapons master. Its scabbard was battered, its hilt wound in simple leather rather than silver wire. His clothes, however, were spectacular. Not the sort of attire this assembly of social climbers in imported silks would appreciate, but stunning, all lace and leather and linen, thrown together in a way that suggested the capital's bohemian quarter rather than the drawing room.

My curiosity piqued, I sought out my father to learn what he knew of the baroness' extraordinary new guests. I found him drinking punch with my Aunt Ilze.

"Perhaps they are entertainers?" he suggested, a possibility even he seemed to think unlikely.

"Bodyguards," Aunt Ilze pronounced with a definite sniff. "And rather common, by the look of them." Her assessment of the men reminded me yet again why I considered her one of my most disagreeable relatives.

Neither answer seemed to hit the truth. The pair of them projected a sense of danger beyond the artifice of mere acting, and they had a look that contained more of the hunter than usually found in those hired to defend the softer members of the aristocracy.

Then one of my father's more pleasant acquaintances, the Count Klavina, appeared and solved the mystery.

"They belong to the prince's Kavalieri, I believe."

"Soldiers, then," my father said.

"Ruffians," my aunt said with a sneer.

I said not a word, but I observed these two interlopers at the baroness' ball with even more interest.

The Kavalieri had been created by our ruler, the Prince Andris, in response to increasing threats on our realm and on the prince's life. It was a new sort of elite corps, one that relied on subtlety rather than brute force. Members of their ranks, men and an increasing number of women, were not only trained in the disciplines of both war and diplomacy, but also instructed in the ancient art of espionage. There were even murmurs that certain individuals in their ranks possessed a thread of the old, wild magic that even now was only spoken of in whispers. Magic that, if discovered, would have resulted in their deaths in earlier times.

What was more, it was said the Kavalieri were only seen when there was danger in the air, danger of the sort that I had read about in a few dusty tomes found in dark corners of our

THE BARONESS' BALL

library, but never encountered. Looking around a room filled with shallow girls and insincere men, none of whom seemed capable of formulating a plan of any sort, let alone one it would take the Kavalieri to combat, I could only think that they must be here on some entirely ceremonial mission.

Whatever the reason for their visit to the ballroom of the Baroness Ulmanis, I could not help but stare at them, trespassers on genteel respectability. I had never before seen a member of the Kavalieri, but rumors of their exploits had penetrated even our obscure corner of the country. I wondered which of them was the better fighter, wondered if one or both of them possessed the old magic. Not for the first time, I wished I'd been born in different circumstances, free to choose my own path instead of bowing to family pressure to marry, free to petition the prince to join the ranks of the Kavalieri as my brother, Edvards, had been alowed to join the prince's cavalry.

But if I couldn't join their ranks, at least I could talk with a member of the Kavalieri.

Knowing neither my father nor my aunt would condone such social intercourse, I simply left their company and made my way to the second man by the most circuitous route I could devise. He was standing at the periphery of the dance floor, his cat's eyes scanning the crowd as if examining the perfumed dancers for deadly threat. His companion had stationed himself at the banquet table across the room, his stance similarly vigilant, though I did notice him cast a longing eye at the heaped plates of pîrâgi and platters of herring and pickled mushrooms laid out for the guests.

I reached his side, and curtsied to gain his attention.

"Lady Astrida Rozkalni," I said, introducing myself, since I knew no other would be willing to do so. I began an internal calculation of how long it would take my aunt to notice my inappropriate behavior and drag me away before my reputation was damaged beyond repair.

"Shouldn't you have waited for a formal introduction?" he asked, though the sparkle in his eyes spoke more of amusement than censure.

"I should have waited forever, and then I would have been deprived of your charming company," I said, mischief making me bold.

"Then I am pleased at your initiative, Lady Astrida." His voice was a charming baritone with a hint of pleasing roughness; his accent seemed to belong neither to the upper classes nor the lower. He was, of course, no fit candidate for a husband, but I began to wonder with a delicious thrill what it would be like to lose my maidenhead to such a man as this, hoping no such thoughts were visible on my features. "I am Pavil Holte," he said with a bow.

"A delight to make your acquaintance, Lord Pavil." I tilted my head at the exact angle that my oldest sister, Elizabete, used when she wanted to drive one of her many suitors mad with desire, and batted my eyelashes. "I don't suppose you would care to fetch me a glass of champagne?"

"Pavil will do," he said with a laugh, a delicious sound that carried straight down to my toes. "You're an impertinent youngster, make no doubt."

"I am neither impertinent nor a youngster." I rallied my indignation around me. Bad enough to be condescended to at any time. It hurt worse coming from this man, one whose good opinion I suddenly and inexplicably craved.

"I meant no disrespect, Lady." He bowed once again, his face serious, but with traces of humor still dancing in his eyes. "My usual companions would have recognized that as a rather poor joke."

"Is he one of your usual companions?" I asked, looking across at the dark-haired man, who was even now aiming a suspicious look in our direction.

"Talis is more than a companion. He is my partner." He smiled at this Talis, who only scowled back. "If I went about fetching champagne for striking young ladies such as you, it would only make him jealous."

I laughed at his comment and tried not to blush at his compliment, but noted with interest that he seemed quite serious. I looked back at Talis, his expression as dark as his hair, and wondered if Pavil was jesting, or if the rumors about the nature of the bond that sometimes formed between members of the Kavalieri might have a basis in fact.

"Would your partner be jealous if you honored me with a dance?" Amongst my class, it was scandalous for a young woman to ask a man of any age for a dance, but I didn't care. I was willing to breach all laws of etiquette to spend more time with this captivating man, partner or no.

"Intensely jealous," he said with feeling. "But once my duty here is done, I might convince him he has nothing to be jealous of."

"I think I might have much to be jealous of in him," I said, but my words were swallowed in a tumult that engulfed the ballroom, and any response he might have made was lost in the commotion.

As I watched, Prince Andris himself was announced and entered the salon. Suddenly the presence of two members of the Kavalieri at this most ordinary of balls was explained. As displaced from court as I was, I had still heard of threats to our prince's life, rumors of dissatisfied nobles intent on taking his place, mutterings of the Frankish realm to our south preparing to invade our land. Pavil and his partner scanned the room, their stance wary, huntsmen heedful of any threat to their master. As the prince strolled through the room, charming his subjects and sending more than one pretty, silk-clad girl into a paroxysm of giggles, I stood back from the throng surrounding our ruler. I put myself in the place of a member of the Kavalieri, tried to see the room as Pavil and his partner must, a throng of people that might hold a possible threat.

But then I caught a flicker of movement across the dance floor and suddenly my game was no longer simply an amusing diversion. I turned toward the movement to see that strange young man moving in the direction of the prince. The unease I'd felt when I'd observed him before grew now to a crawling across my skin, the same sort of feeling I'd had once as a young girl, when I had been too close to a tree struck by lightning. Only this time the lightning came not from the sky, but from deep inside me, a red lit, pulsing core I had never before suspected lurked in my breast.

I looked over at Pavil in panic, wanting someone to tell me I was imagining it all, that everything was as it should be, but what I saw was far from comforting. The lighthearted expression had vanished from Pavil's features and I saw the beginnings of a pale blue light suffusing his skin, creating an aura of power surrounding him, an aura that seemed to call to the power building within me.

I opened my mouth, whether in horror or confusion or simply in awe I'll never know, because a tug at the pulsing core within me drew my attention back to the dance floor. I turned to see a writhing purple coil of otherworldly energy rise up from Aunt Ilze's "unpleasant young man" and form into the shape of a ravening wolf, its sneering muzzle straining toward the prince. From where I stood, I could hear a crackling in the air, could smell a burning that had nothing to do with the candles in their chandeliers. What astounded me most was that no one else seemed to see the danger, not even the prince himself. They were all laughing and chatting and simpering as if their evening's entertainment had not been visited by such a nightmarish vision.

I turned back to Pavil, hoping he, at least, could see the peril that threatened our ruler. He was staring at the dance floor with a frown, as if straining to see something hovering at the edge of his vision. In frustration, and out of all propriety, I grabbed his wrist and pushed at his mind with my own, willing him to see the terror in our midst.

See, he did. He drew in a great hissing breath, and I could feel his muscles go taut in my grasp.

"Talis," he bellowed, his voice cutting through the din surrounding the prince. All music and chatter halted abruptly and all eyes drew toward him. All eyes but those of the young man whose strange powers threatened the prince and whose eyes remained fixed on his target.

Whether he could see the spectral wolf or not, at least Pavil's partner recognized from whom the peril sprang, and moved toward him. The young man ignored Talis, ignored the disconcerted crowd, ignored everyone but the prince. But then after a few seconds that seemed an eternity to me, the young man did finally turn from the prince. Whether he felt a stirring in the power he drew upon or simply felt our gaze upon him, I do not know, but he shifted his attention to us.

His gaze settled upon me first, and that nearly undid me. I had never before felt such malevolence in a simple look. As I watched, the wolf of writhing purple energy snarled and turned toward me. I would have screamed, but I found myself without any breath at all. The wolf began to leap, and I braced myself for the worst, but then Pavil shook off my grip and stepped in front of the beast. The wolf crashed into the Kavalieri, shaking him as if he were a small child before tossing him to the ground.

I do not understand how I knew what to do—perhaps the contact with Pavil opened up the channels of my power—but know I did. I stood my ground, shut out awareness of anyone but my opponent and focused my thoughts. The red energy within me churned and roiled and flowed through my fingertips, my hair, the very pores of my skin, to form a red, taloned eagle that faced down the growling wolf. Drawing in a breath, I concentrated, and the eagle swooped down on the wolf, raking the beast's back with its claws. I was working on pure instinct, hoping to draw the attention of the wolf and his master from both Pavil and the prince. My strategy worked, if such an unsophisticated ploy can be called a strategy, and the man's malevolent glare returned to me. Inside, I quailed, but I did not retreat, and the manifestations of our magic—for how else to explain those unearthly creatures?—joined battle. I struggled to overpower my opponent, to rend his wolf and put its master on his knees, but he was at least as powerful as I, and experienced in wielding this weapon I had only just discovered within myself. I felt a sharp pain as the wolf's teeth caught at my eagle's wing, felt my initial confidence fade and a panic at what my defeat might mean well up inside me. But just as I thought I might fall, I felt a presence at my side and Pavil took my hand in a cool, firm grasp.

As power and knowledge flowed between us, the faint blue of Pavil's aura grew and rose into a great column, a column that resolved itself into a fierce fighting cat. Together we brandished our power, my eagle's claws raking the wolf's muzzle, her beak pecking at his eyes, while Pavil's cat tore into his flank. Together we fought, until the wolf was brought to the ground and the young man staggered. One last push from Pavil, one last swipe of his cat's paw, and the wolf dissolved into nothing and our adversary collapsed insensible on the parquet floor.

Breaking free from the confused and milling crowd, Talis reached the young man's side and bound his hands with a strange silken cord. A brief consultation with Prince Andris, and then he was running in our direction, pushing through young nobles who only began to panic now that the danger was past. But before he could reach us, Pavil released his hold on my hand and dropped to the floor himself.

If I'd wondered at the extent of Talis' relationship with Pavil before, I wondered no longer. He was at Pavil's side in an instant, checking the barely conscious man for injury and murmuring quietly to him as he stroked his brow.

THE BARONESS' BALL

"What am I going to do with you?" Talis said, affection warring with frustration in his voice. "Facing a mage beast without setting your guards."

"I couldn't see the danger." Pavil said, and though his face was strained, his voice showed a strength that boded well for his recovery. "Not until it was too late."

"So you let a slip of a girl save your life."

"That slip of a girl has more raw power than I have. More than I've seen in any of our recruits."

"You magic users," Talis said with what I recognized was fond exasperation. "You'll all be the death of me."

I was just about to step in and argue that I was not a slip of a girl, and to demand that Pavil explain exactly what this power was that I possessed, when my hand was seized in an iron grasp that could only have belonged to my aunt.

"Astrida Rozkalni, what have you done?" Aunt Ilze's tone was the one she usually reserved for female relatives who had the bad manners to produce a child out of wedlock, though there was a thread of fear running through it as well. "You will come with us at once." She pulled me in the direction of my father, surrounded by a crowd whose attention focused increasingly and uncomfortably in my direction.

Just as I'd known how to access my powers, I knew without a doubt that I was at a crossroads. Accede to my aunt's will, and I would be transported to the country and married off to the first suitable male who would have me, what little choice I'd had in the matter disappearing entirely. Oppose that will, and my life would take a path I had never even seen on the map. A path that might just be the one I had been searching for all my life. So I set my shoulders, planted my feet, and retrieved my hand from my aunt's clutches with a swift tug.

"No, Aunt Ilze." Judging by the look on her face, this was the first time she'd ever been contradicted by anyone in the family, let alone an insignificant niece. Her face took on the reddened hue that usually presaged an outburst of epic proportions, but any eruption was diverted by the appearance of a new figure out of the murmuring crowd.

"Countess Berzins," Prince Andris said with a bow before turning to me. "Lady Astrida, I believe I have you to thank for my life. The eagle was yours, was it not?"

"Yes," I said, nodding and struggling not to stutter. "You could see it, your highness?" At the time, it hadn't seemed that anyone, outside of Pavil, myself and perhaps Talis, had seen the magical beasts.

"Only at the end. The magic does not run as strongly in my blood as it does in yours."

"Nonsense," my aunt blurted out, her contradictory nature overcoming even her diffidence toward her ruler. "There is no magical taint in my family's blood. I am certain of it."

"A gift rather than a taint, Countess. Had your niece not intervened when she did, I would not have survived that traitor's attack. Nor would my men have." He nodded to where Talis supported Pavil.

"But—" my aunt began, then broke off in frustration, clearly not wanting to contradict the prince further, even as she wanted to give me the firmest rebuke possible.

"Baron Rozkalni," the prince said, motioning my father over to join him. "We must arrange a meeting tomorrow to confer about your daughter's future."

"My daughter's future?" My father was recovering his color, but had obviously not fully comprehended what I had done. Which was understandable. I wasn't sure I comprehended it myself. In fact, now that the danger had passed, my whole body was trembling and I felt in imminent danger of the sort of fainting attack that my sisters often indulged in and I had always scorned.

"She has the sort of power that is rare in our realm today. The sort that is badly needed within the Kavalieri." If nothing else did, Prince Andris' confidence in me stopped the panic in my breast and made me stand just a bit taller.

THE BARONESS' BALL

"But she's a girl," my aunt blurted out, outrage winning out over the required respect for her ruler. "She should be getting married and having children, not consorting with a horde of ruffians."

"My Kavalieri are not ruffians, though many were born of the common folk." The steel in the prince's voice caused my aunt to cower, however slightly, and made me hopeful that I might yet evade the future my mother and aunt would have for me. "It is considered an honor to join their ranks."

"An honor we will be pleased to discuss with your highness," my father said with a bow, shooting his sister a quelling look. I had never been so grateful for the quiet determination my father possesses than at that moment. He might acquiesce to his wife and sister more than he should, but he had never done so on matters of import.

"I will send for you and your daughter on the morrow. And now, if you will excuse me I must see to my fellows." Prince Andris gracefully turned and strode over to where Pavil was struggling to regain his feet and Talis was firmly trying to restrain him. Pavil won the battle as the prince appeared at his side, though he did not shun the support of his companion.

My concentration was all for the three men, though around me a tumult was breaking out, my father and aunt being the least of it. The evening's events and our prince's regard had gained me attention that two months' presence in the capital had not, and I was beset by young men and women claiming my acquaintance. I ignored them all, not wishing to be this week's notorious wonder, and strained unsuccessfully to hear what Pavil and the others were saying.

I nearly groaned in disappointment as two newly arrived men, no doubt also members of the Kavalieri, escorted the prince, Talis, and a still shaking Pavil from the ballroom.

If Prince Andris were serious, if he truly wanted me for the Kavalieri, if my family allowed it, it was likely I would see Pavil and his dark companion again. But if the prince had only jested, if my family opposed my choice, this would be my only opportunity to speak with him once more. The thought of never seeing Pavil again caused me a pain such as I'd never felt before. It was as if we were joined together by some remnant of the magic we had wrought, thin as spider's silk and just as strong. Heedless of the protests of my aunt and the confusion of my father, I spun and ran to the door through which the Kavalieri had disappeared.

The prince and the other two men had vanished, but I found Pavil and Talis in the grand hall of the baroness' mansion. Pavil, his face a ghastly ashen color, was leaning against a marble column. Talis supported his partner around the waist, his mouth drawn into a tight, severe line. As I took a step toward them, the most extraordinary thing happened. Talis' expression transformed from one of the utmost harshness to one of the gentlest affection. He leaned forward and rested his forehead against Pavil's, a gesture of remarkable intimacy and trust.

My feet froze where they were and I felt a flush hasten up my neck to flame my cheeks, my foolish, half-formed dreams of a life with Pavil evaporating like morning dew under the summer sun. I did not know then, as I know now, how very deep the connection went between them, but I did know without question that even the magic we had performed together could not surpass the ties between these two men.

Swallowing my disappointment, I withdrew into the ballroom, hiding behind a tall fern until I once again felt ready to face the room.

When I finally rejoined my family, my aunt swept the three of us out of the ballroom almost immediately. It is one of the few acts of kindness she has ever done me, however inadvertently. I spent the night sitting cross-legged on my bed, listening to my father and my aunt argue over my fate, and wondering with both hope and fear what was to become of me.

I must have fallen asleep just before dawn, as the starlight faded into the lightening sky, and awoke with the late morning sun streaming through the window and the sounds of the city penetrating the room.

Astonished that I had not been disturbed earlier, I hastily dressed myself and hurried down to the breakfast room. There I found my father dining heartily on cheese crepes and a salmon omelet, with my Aunt Ilze nowhere to be found.

Neither of us spoke of the previous night's happenings, nor did we comment on the absence of my aunt, but instead we passed a most pleasant hour. I talked more openly with my father in that brief time than I had since I was a youngster and he had taught me, against my mother's wishes, to ride.

As the hall clock struck one, there was a knock on the door, and a servant appeared to tell us a carriage had arrived from the prince to take us to his grand palace. I traveled to the meeting to decide my future in a state of serene unreality, my father sitting calmly at my side.

I had harbored a faint hope that Pavil might be in attendance at my meeting with the prince, but any disappointment I might have felt that Pavil was not with the prince was more than overcome by the attentiveness and consideration our ruler showed my father and me. He explained the training members of the Kavalieri received and some of the duties for which they are responsible. And he offered me a place in their ranks. With my father's blessing, I accepted immediately.

My father was remarkably understanding of my decision to join the Kavalieri. My mother's reaction, when we arrived home at our estate a few days later, was more complicated. Though she was outwardly distraught, I suspect she was secretly relieved at the prospect of having a difficult daughter taken from her hands. My aunt, however, has never retreated from her initial outrage, and arranges not to be available for visits when I am on leave.

I have been a cadet in the Kavalieri for nearly a year, and never once in that time have I ever regretted the events that occurred in that ballroom or the choice that I made in Prince Andris' salon. I have experienced more elation in this year than in the seventeen that preceded it, though it is sometimes mixed with a faint disappointment that real adventures are never quite as wondrous as they sound in books. I am nearing the end of my training, having learned enough of the disciplines of sword and intellect to perform my duties, though I have discovered to my delight that for a member of the Kavalieri, learning is a lifelong pursuit.

In spite of the regulations of the barracks, I enjoy a freedom of the sort I could never have imagined in my old life. I never attend garden parties or balls unless it is part of an assignment, and then I am always happy to be wearing breeches rather than a ball gown. I am under no obligation to marry, and indeed am encouraged to follow my own heart. And I am pleased to see Pavil nearly every day.

Not that I have the slightest illusion that he would ever return the romantic feelings I harbored for him on our first meeting. More than ever, I'm aware of the deep bond he has with Talis, a bond I would never want to sever. He has become a trusted mentor, offering instruction in the uses of the old power we both share. Even more, he and Talis have become my friends.

The future lies before me, limitless and exhilarating, and I owe it all to the baroness' ball.

THE SIXTH STRING

by Elisabeth Waters

Elisabeth Waters sold her first short story in 1980 to Marion Zimmer Bradley for *The Keeper's Price*, the first of the Darkover anthologies. She then went on to sell short stories to a variety of other anthologies. Her first novel, a fantasy called *Changing Fate*, was awarded the 1989 Gryphon Award. She is now working on a sequel to it, in addition to her short story writing and anthology editing. She has just turned in *Sword & Sorceress 23*, to be published by Norilana Books in November 2008. For more information, see her website at www.elisabethwaters.com.

    About "The Sixth String," Elisabeth writes, "The *qin* (Chinese for "musical instrument"), also called the *guqin* (Chinese for "ancient musical instrument"), has been played in China for thousands of years; there are paintings of Confucius playing it 2500 years ago. A well-educated scholar was expected to be able to play it skillfully, and a person who couldn't play it frequently hung either an instrument or a replica on the wall of his study so as to appear cultured.

    "When Voyager was launched in 1977, the classic *qin* composition, "Flowing Water," was included on a CD of Earth's music. (Now if Voyager can just find aliens who can work a CD player . . .) The *guqin* was also played in the Opening Ceremonies for the 2008 Olympics in Beijing.

"There is a great deal of symbolism associated with the *qin*: it measures 3' 6.5" (Chinese feet and inches) to symbolize the 365 days in the year, and it has 13 inlays representing the 13 lunar months. The upper surface is rounded, representing the sky; the bottom is flat and represents the earth. The *qin* was traditionally played in small gatherings of close friends, for a *qin* strung with silk strings is a very quiet instrument. Most musicians playing it today use metal strings, along with amplification."

On a more personal note, she adds, "The *guqin* is taught orally from master to student (traditional *guqin* tablature does not include anything that tells how long a note is held or what the tempo of the piece should be). I would like to thank Wang Fei, who taught me everything I know about the *guqin*, her teacher Li Xiangting, his teachers Zha Fuxi and Wu Jinglue, and all of their teachers back through the centuries. Knowledge is a most precious gift."

"He said that he loved me above all else in the world. He said if I agreed to marry him, he would build me a palace of gold." Jia looked at around her reception room. Walls hung with yellow silk were interspersed with polished hardwood pillars. She paced across the carpet, ignoring both its softness and the beauty of its design, to the window. It was raining outside, and the water dripping off the points of the tiles that edged the roof formed a beaded curtain. The wooden latticework in the window prevented anyone outside from seeing her, but it did not obstruct her view of the palace grounds—or the other portion of the women's quarters.

"He did not," she snapped, "say anything about becoming Emperor and taking three thousand concubines!" She ran her hand along the smooth wood of the pillar next to the window. Wood was her element, and touching it usually soothed her, but at the moment she was feeling much too frustrated.

"Does he really have three thousand of them?" her maid Li asked. "He's been Emperor for only six years!"

"Three-thousand-fourteen," Jia replied, "with more coming in every month." She stopped pacing to sit on a barrel-shaped sandalwood stool and stroked the wooden body of the *qin* on the matching table before her. "I've been keeping track."

Jia played a soft ripple of notes on the silk strings strung the length of the instrument. She was small with a deceptively fragile appearance, which she wielded—along with her beauty—as a weapon in the undeclared warfare of the harem. She regretted, however, that her small hands gave her trouble with the fingering of some of the classic repertoire for the *qin*.

"But it would take him more than eight years—assuming a rate of one concubine per day—to go through them!" Li protested.

"It's supposed to be more than one each day, but you're forgetting the 'more of them every month' part." Jia sighed. "I'm twenty-eight years old. I haven't been with him often enough even to conceive, let alone bear the son he needs. And I do want at least *one* child of my own."

Li paused, obviously trying to find a delicate way to phrase her next question. "How many children does he have?"

"Fewer than one would suppose, given the number of concubines," Jia replied. "Also, all his children are daughters. Sooner or later, he *is* going to need a son."

"*All* of his children are daughters?" Li thought about it for a moment. "You must be correct; we would have heard had anyone borne him a son. But surely the odds . . ." Her voice trailed off as she looked suspiciously at the *qin*. "What did you do?"

"Almost nothing," Jia shrugged. "I invite them to my little gatherings, and I play the *qin*. Concubines are chosen for their youth and their yin essence. All I have done," she played a series of notes, plucking delicately at the strings, "is to enhance their yin. Perhaps that results in their having so much female energy that they give birth only to daughters. Who can say?"

"Who indeed?" Li agreed, smiling. "Certainly not I." She contemplated the *qin*. "Are certain strings more yin than others?"

"Not really. The *qin* originally had only five strings: one for each of the five elements—which have both yin and yang aspects. The sixth string was added by the first Zhou Emperor to mourn the death of his son, so it is sorrowful. The second Zhou Emperor added the last string to inspire his soldiers, so the seventh string is strong."

Li chuckled. "That would be your string, then. You are definitely the strongest person I've ever met."

Jia smiled wistfully. "Would that make the sixth string— the childless Emperor—my husband? At least, the first Zhou Emperor *had* a son to lose."

"Who can say?" Li said, echoing Jia's earlier remark. She rose to her feet and bowed. "By your leave. May the Emperor soon tire of his concubines and return to you, and may Heaven grant you a son."

After Li was gone, Jia bent her head over the *qin*, trying different fingerings on the sixth string. "Help yourself, and Heaven will help you," she murmured.

She rose and moved to her writing desk, where she took out her ink-stone, brushes, ink, and paper. Using her best calligraphy, she composed an invitation to the Emperor to join her for an evening of poetry and music, carefully scheduled for three days hence: the night she was most likely to conceive.

ॐॐॐ

The next day the *nü-shih* returned to court, bringing another group of concubines with her.

"How many does she have this time?" Jia asked Li, who had brought her the news.

"Only five." Li was obviously trying to be optimistic about the matter.

"That brings the total to three-thousand-nineteen," Jia remarked, "although I suppose that at this point, five more doesn't make much difference."

"It *is* her job to arrange the Emperor's sex life," Li pointed out.

"True. And she is so *good* at it—such enthusiasm . . . such dedication. . . ."

"Such desperation?" Li asked archly. "I hear their ages range from nine to twelve."

"That young? Really?"

Li nodded.

"Has she already collected every maiden in the Empire old enough to have sex? I know that in theory the younger a virgin is, the better her yin will nourish the Emperor, but these won't be old enough to do him any good for years." Jia frowned. "Considering the number of concubines gathered for the previous Emperor—I don't think the man ever did anything but search for immortality in the bedroom—not that it did him any good. . . ."

"And all of them were sent to monasteries after his death," Li pointed out. "Concubines are not allowed to go from the harem of one Emperor to the next."

"She needed to start all over for the new Emperor." Jia had not taken that into account in her calculations. "Maybe she actually *has* collected every suitable maiden and is now reduced to gathering children for the future."

Li didn't even try to answer that. She picked up a brush and ran it through Jia's hair, and Jia sat silently, beginning to relax under the rhythmic strokes—at least until the *nü-shih* was announced.

The *nü-shih* bowed upon entering, for technically the Empress outranked her. But rank did not overawe the woman in charge of the Emperor's—and by default the Empress's—sex life.

"I hear that you have plans for the Emperor tomorrow night," she began.

"The Emperor and I have plans for an evening of poetry and music," Jia said. "I do not believe that simple poetry and music fall within the scope of your duties."

"As long as he confines himself to poetry," the *nü-shih* said. She scowled at the scroll hanging in the place of honor on the wall. It was the first poem the Emperor had written for Jia, and she displayed it to remind everyone, including herself, that of all the women in the harem she was the only one the Emperor had chosen himself.

"Always remember," the *nü-shih* said firmly, "that young virgins give him their yin energy and make him stronger, while *you* take his yang energy and weaken him."

"That *is* the only way he will ever get a son to succeed him," Jia pointed out.

"You could adopt a son for him." The *nü-shih* smiled sweetly. Jia knew that the woman would really prefer that the Emperor divorce her for childlessness—as if *that* were Jia's fault! The *nü-shih* had firm control over the concubines; if one of them replaced Jia, the *nü-shih* would have much more influence.

"Adopt? From what pool of candidates?" Jia asked. "It's not as if he has a son by another woman. Nor does he have siblings to give him nephews. In any case, now is not the time to speak of it—I hear that you have a group of children to settle in." Jia gave a smile as sweet—and as false—as the other woman's, and dismissed her.

ଷଔଷଡ଼

Jia spent most of the day resting. Her plan, born from Li's remark about the strings, would take a great deal of energy. She couldn't do anything during the daytime while there were people about and she would certainly be interrupted, but once she had supposedly retired for the night, she would be undisturbed.

Alone in her bedroom, she worked far into the night, composing a piece that brought out the energy of the sixth string, while using the audible music to hide the imbalance. When tears for the son she had never borne welled up in her eyes, she knew that she had succeeded.

"It's not enough for the Emperor to want a son," she said softly to herself. "He must want to have a son with *me*."

She carefully removed the string from the *qin*. This particular string, she recalled, was approximately two years old and had broken only once so far, so there was plenty of length remaining. She took a ceramic teacup, filled it almost full with hot water, then took an embroidery needle, passed it through a candle-flame, and pricked the fourth finger of her left hand. She squeezed six drops of her blood into the water, and then dipped both ends of the string into the cup. As the ends of the silk soaked up the water and her blood, she prayed to Heaven. When she removed the string from the cup, the ends were a pale pink, but the color became indiscernible a thumb's length from the ends. By the time she had replaced the string on the *qin*, there was no visible difference between it and the other strings, save for the usual variation in diameter.

෴

Privacy was almost impossible anywhere in the Imperial Palace, but the Emperor sent his guards to await him at the end of the hallway—after they had inspected Jia's rooms, of course—and Jia dismissed Li after she had brought in the tea and spice cakes.

"I have a new poem, if you would like to hear it," he said once they were alone.

"I would love to hear it," Jia said promptly. His skill with poetry was one of the things that had won her heart when he first courted her. She listened appreciatively to his newest poem, and countered with one of his old favorites, accompanied by the soft sound of the *qin*. He picked another of his poems and asked her to play accompaniment to it; while he could play the *qin*—a man with any pretense to education was expected to play it—her playing was superior to his. Of course, she did get more time to practice.

They shared music and poetry for several hours before she said diffidently, "I have a new piece for the *qin*, if you would care to hear it."

"By all means," he said.

She bowed her head over the instrument and played, concentrating only on the music, not daring to look up until the very end. She blinked the tears from her eyes and saw that his eyes held tears as well.

He walked to her side, took her hand, and led her to her bed.

⋘⋙

Nine months later Jia held the newborn Crown Prince in her arms. "Help yourself, and Heaven will help you," she whispered to him.

COMFORT AND DESPAIR

by Tanith Lee

Tanith Lee is the author of almost 100 books, over 270 short stories, 4 radio plays, 2 TV scripts, several (mostly closet) poems—but not a partridge in a pear tree. Her work includes fantasy, SF, horror, historical, YA, contemporary—and even the detective genre—plus endless combinations and crossovers of all of the above. She writes longhand, then types the results, in a blue and yellow room, through whose windows tall trees, squirrels, doves, pigeons and magpies stare, (naturally with appropriate disbelieving amusement).

"In childhood I wanted to be an actress," Lee recalls, "but what I was, and am, is a writer. Acting on paper is my trade—the only thing I can really do well. The most important part of me."

ඏෙ 1. Grey ෨෬

Everyone said she was the perfect wife.

Perfect, that was, in her demeanour and her constancy. For example, she was never seen to look at another man, even should he be glamorous, except in the most friendly, indeed almost *maternal* way. She never flirted with him either, was only courteous, sympathetic and, when occasion called for it, amusing. It would seem, they said, Monsieur Carmineau must have more to him than met the eye. He must be an ardent and accomplished lover, a vigorous and entertaining partner in all the dual occupations of a marriage. They would not normally have suspected this of him. He was in his later fifties, and though as a youth not unattractive, now he had grown grey, jowly and corpulent. His own wit was rather slow. Nor was he either a poet or a dazzling intellectual, the sort that might despite all else still sweep a young woman into adoration. He did, however, own the big house, the Little Chateau, and its park. He was rich. And *she*. Madame Carmineau—well, she came, one heard, from very humble beginnings, a dead scholar's daughter, who had been teaching ungrateful brats in the town, and they more likely to put a rotten cabbage or a dead mouse in her lap than to learn a single lesson. Probably she was grateful to be rescued. Probably she knew when her luck changed, and wanted to risk no new loss of it. And yet, Madame never appeared caught in a union of that order. She seemed—if not in *love* with her husband—yet raptly fond of him, sensitive only to his welfare. While there was about her the blissful inner vivacity, the hint of melancholy and unease, the *absorption*, that only those in love ever demonstrate. More, she seemed *happy*. Fulfilled. And true happiness and fulfillment are so rare, one must always doubt them, in oneself and others. For surely there is always something behind the densest and most sparkling veil that may give the lie to both.

ଔଋଌଈ

At seven o'clock, rather late in fact, certain business confrères of Monsieur were to dine at the Little Chateau.

Jeanne had spent an afternoon supervising the bevy of cooks and kitchen staff; thereafter, another two hours in self-preparation.

While she did this, she mentally reviewed the dinner guests. There was faddy Monsieur Belart, and didactic Monsieur Devalle, each with his wife. Besides there was the old actor Ronesset, whom Jeanne had privately christened the Wasp, for his verbal sting. Monsieur Ronesset brought no wife. He preferred himself to eat for two. To make up the extra female at table, Jeanne's husband, Monsieur Carmineau, had asked the insane widow of a dog-breeder, Madame Tupe. She would come with her current 'husband' naturally, a hound by the name of Petit, a creature almost as tall as a horse and covered in thick black fur.

Did Jeanne sigh over these guests? Not at all. She did not mind them. She always made sure Belart's food was exact, listened respectfully to Devalle, subtly commiserated with both their spouses, laughed at Ronesset's stings, and agreed with every word uttered by La Tupe. And when the English custom was observed, and the ladies withdrew to leave the men to their brandy, pipes and cigars, (Mme Tupe would always remain) fed the two wives and the big dog called *Small*, who usually left with the retiring ladies, treats and dessert wines in the hothouse.

It tickled Jeanne slightly, the way in which the other women always puzzled over her. Each time, even as they pecked the sweets and fruits, they would try to tease out of her some confession of regret. They failed. They, on the other hand, (around the second glass of Armagnac au Framboise) were soon openly regretful on their own accounts. "Oh, Devalle can be such a beast!" "Oh, Monsieur Bel drives me into madness with his carping—I have lost our third cook only this month, due to his foolishness!" "Woof," said Petit softly, gnawing a honey-glazed meat-bone under the ferns. As if to add, "And none of you knows what I have to put up with from that Tupe woman."

This evening, things went as always.

Jeanne, in her pale silk gown, oversaw the candles and flowers and the impeccable service of a tasty, greedy dinner. Now and then, between her attentiveness to his guests, she glanced at her old husband. Tonight he had a glow from the wine, and when their eyes met they smiled at each other, assured, content. If she had been twenty-five years older, even so some might have remarked on it, for contemporaneously aging couples do not always like each other, either.

Next in the hothouse among the orange trees, Jeanne commiserated as ever with the wives, yet contrived also to spare the erring husbands. "How aggravating for you, Sophie—" this to Mme Belart. "Your *fourth* cook to leave. Dreadful! He is so fortunate you are so kind. And I suppose poor Monsieur does suffer with his stomach. But you are so understanding and clever, why he'd be lost without you, wouldn't he?" Or: "Poor Monsieur Devalle must be so tired after his work at the university. Yet how exhausting for *you*, Annette, with everything else you must deal with." To the dog luckily she need only slip a candied alcoholic cherry to soothe his nerves.

Eventually in great gladness they were able to unite en masse in the wish that Monsieur Ronesset should be flogged and drowned. While they were, when with him, his merciless target, he became theirs once they were out of his hearing. Soon the hothouse rang with pitiless laughter as they pictured him hung up for crows to peck—let him try his stinging remarks on *them*.

Petit meanwhile slept. Jeanne stroked his huge sleeping forehead, which frowned somewhat in slumber. Had he been a cat, she thought, he would be purring. But he led the life of a slave with his mistress, this extraordinary animal. Walked once every day or so, by one of La Tupe's reluctant and scared servants, but only around the paved paths of the town's public gardens. Meagrely fed on 'healthful' foods that left him hungry. Expected to attend his owner in virtual silence and to behave like a well-trained lap-dog. When all the while he should be romping over fields and through woods, terrifying innocent rabbits and barking at sun, moon and stars. Jeanne felt she respected Petit. She sensed that he acted as well as he did less from coercion than out of his compassionate nature and good manners.

The party concluded around eleven. The church clock was striking from the village, clearly heard across the summer night.

The guests climbed, most of them heavily, (the dog included) into their carriages. Only Ronesset sprang like an elderly and over-athletic weasel into his equipage, and sat there picking his pointed fangs with a silver toothpick filched from the table. "Won't miss this gew-gaw, will you, Carmineau? No, I shouldn't think so. I've seen better on a stage. But the food was not so bad. Even if your cook can't tell a flambé from a flambeau."

Off they all presently rattled, into the darkness under the trees.

A huge golden moon stood high in the east, calling the earth to wake for day-in-night. But yawning, Jeanne's husband led her back towards the house. Below the servants were dousing the lights.

Husband and wife climbed the stair, he commenting on the dinner in a mild and satisfied manner. He thanked Jeanne, as he always did, for her stewardship of house and table, and complimented her on her charming looks, the way her fine brown hair shone in candlelight, the luminous whiteness of her skin. Despite that, she knew he would be too drained by the pleasures of the evening to ask, polite as he always was, and more so when asking this, if he might visit her in half an hour in her bedroom. She never of course refused such a visit. She had no reason to. She had guessed from the first, and been proved right, that Monsieur Carminaeu was a gentle and undemanding lover, dull but in no way unwholesome or offensive. The transaction was on every occasion swiftly accomplished. Nor did he expect lies and raptures from Jeanne, only that she did not mind, and she demonstrated freely that she did not. The other aspect of the arrangement which pleased her besides was that she suspected her husband was sterile, and this far had found him so. She had no wish to bear a child, having had more than enough of them when forced to teach.

At the top of the gracious stairway, they graciously kissed each other on the lips. He said to her the one sweet and romantic thing then of which he felt able to deliver himself. "Sleep well, my beauty. You are the jewel of my life." He meant these words, and sometimes when he said them, (as he had, almost every week of their four-year life together) his eyes filled briefly with the tears of truth and joy. Because of this also, Jeanne loved him. For love him she did, as he loved her. The ideal couple, in their own fashion. They parted quietly, each going to their own chamber.

Now risen so high, the golden plate of the moon blazed on the roof of the Little Chateau, screaming and hammering to be felt and answered.

But every light had faded from the house.

Beneath heaven's fire, even the black woods seemed sleeping.

ങ‌ര 2. Gold ഇള

Just after midnight, Jeanne woke up. The distant pangs of the church clock might have roused her, but she doubted they had. She left the bed and dressed hurriedly. Her hair, plaited for the night, she undid. It fell around her to her waist. Quickly she threw on a cloak, hooding herself within.

Like a phantom she went through the house and down by a lesser stair. She had the key to every door. To unlock the narrow one between the lower rooms was simple. She crossed the open ground beyond unseen, save by a low-flying owl, a spider on the wall. Their witness proved, however, that not everything else lay asleep.

Passing over the rough lawns below the garden and into the avenue where the wild trees began, Jeanne was conscious of the symphonies of crickets in the grass, hesitating their orchestra only to be sure of her, then resuming. A spray of fireflies made jewelry in sweeps of branches. Something squealed malevolently amid the undergrowth. But it was the voice of sex, not violence.

Jeanne entered the woods.

She knew the way, had taken it so often since living in the chateau, now and then by day, usually nocturnally. Yet long before she lived with her husband, Jeanne had known the way, even in the town, those nights after her father died, or the children at the school tormented her. She had known the way since her fifteenth year, when first *he* had shown her—but that was at their second meeting.

Their *first* meeting had been momentary—his face suddenly at her midnight window, where the old tree craned outside the small crumbling apartment in which she and her ailing father lived. The moon had been slender then, and ivory white. Yet it gave enough illumination to show him, a boy perhaps three years her elder. He was thin and strong as a figure of burnished oak, tall for his young age, his face arresting as a note of music heard in silence. His eyes were the green gold of pirate coins in the museum, his long thick hair the pool-bright gold of newly gilded pages.

Just a glimpse. But the image of him had been emblazoned on her eyes and mind. Then he was gone.

She ran to the window and looked out. Tree, courtyard, street were empty. Then, and even by the morning, still she was certain she had not dreamed him.

And, curiously, she promised herself she would see him again. But by the time she did, which was four years later, when she was fifteen and he, she judged, seventeen, she had lost her faith in him and in most other things, too. As if, while not thinking him a dream, yet his appearance to her could have meant nothing in her life. Or worse, a warning that all marvels, even when so shining, must immediately vanish, not being meant, ever, for her.

Nevertheless, at fifteen the second meeting occurred. It took place at sunfall, when the sky was crimson. Also, it was on the evening she had realized her father must soon die.

Jeanne had been desolate, for although she had really known of this surviving parent only strictness, mendacity and a harsh, cold intellect—cemented soon enough by crotchety and demanding invalidism—her father was all the anchor she had. Already she was schooling various unwilling and often nasty children, but this within inevitable limits. Bereft of any other duties or support, emotional or financial, she understood very well her future. She must throw herself on the adamantine bosom of the world, where tigers of hate and viciousness waited with bared teeth for timorous prey. Mingled in her sorrow and regret for her father was pure fright, and not a little despair.

She was coming home from the chemist's shop, where she had collected the latest tonics and palliatives needed for her father's care. She was worrying as she walked the cobbled lanes, wondering how she could buy bread or milk the next morning, seeing most of the money had now gone on medicine.

She looked up because a shadow fell across her feet, slanting from the royal red sunset.

Raising her eyes, she saw a young man there, not twice her own arm's length from her. He was tall and strong, his shoulders wider now than they had been in his boyhood. His clothes generally were quite good, not rich, but far better than her own. His shirt was very white too, and so close to him as she was, she could scent its cleanness, and his own, and with that, an alluring aroma of masculine youth and health so unlike the odour that now clung about her father's rooms.

Under the deep-dyed sky then, the young man's golden hair burned. His eyes were like embers.

"Good evening, M'mselle," he said to her. "I think we have already met."

She had not heard him speak before. It was a blond tenor voice, itself very musical.

She thought she must hurry past him and away. But she had known him at once. *Knew* him utterly, as if she had seen him every day about this time, at just this spot. And his familiarity was devastating. Her excited heart scrambled and stuttered, so she would barely move.

"May I carry your purchases? You must allow me to, we're such old friends."

She said nothing, and he relieved her of the things quietly, not even glancing to see what they were. Was he a thief? Yes, but only of her unwanted drudgery and boredom. "Will you walk with me?" he asked, and held out his arm.

No respectable woman would accept such an invitation from a stranger, even one who was well-known. She would be a fool to do so. Yet naturally, since he was *not* a stranger, was unlike any other, no human law, however obdurate, could govern such a situation. The street was also empty, as it seldom was at this hour. Above, a woman leaned idly to water some plants on a little balcony. But she took no notice of Jeanne or Jeanne's sudden companion. Jeanne comprehended, with the heady delight of a slave released on holiday, that this woman would never see either of them. That none now *could*. Magic had happened as it always should, easily and fully. Both she and the golden man were invisible to all eyes but their own and each other's.

And so, they did walk together. And presently there came a twist in the lane, and a high wall and open gateway, through which Jeanne beheld a winding track, and on either side pine trees that towered up to mask the rouged sky as if with spiked black fans.

Long after, (and by then she and he met consistently if irregularly) Jeanne perceived that she liked the track and the black trees so very much not solely because, as a rule, they were not to be found in the street, but because they reminded her of vague daydreams she had had for years. Perhaps these had been prompted by some unrecollected print seen in a book. The avenue of pines fascinated and drew her at once. Its balsam flavour was so thick on the evening air, and the track was both mysterious and enticing. It had no look of a primrose path to sin, but of an enchanted way that led to the heart's lifting. It led too, when they took it, to a beautiful old house, of palatial and unusual style, white and pillared, with long, greenish windows. A deserted partial ruin, it had all the mythic quality of a palace under water. It represented not domestic homeliness but perilous romance. Maybe the original of this house had also been viewed formerly in some volume of prints. It was nothing like Jeanne's own wretched dwelling in the yard. (Nor was it anything like the Little Chateau where, four years following, Jeanne would reside.)

Here then they walked, Jeanne and the stranger. And beneath one of the pines at last, the ghastly medical parcel having disappeared from his grasp, (it reappeared later unimpaired in her own) the young man caught her lightly to him and kissed her, kissed her awake, into a new world of hope and ardour, desire and possibility.

When finally she returned to the Scholar's rooms, Jeanne learned she was only a few minutes later than she had planned. But obviously, in a magic realm and in the arms of a daemon prince, an hour might be an instant, a year less than a day.

She did not quite suppose him a daemon. Not quite. Having no name for him—he never employed hers, if it came to that, and there indeed she was not Jeanne, but her own *self*—she *coined* a name for him. A golden coining, with a shadow's edge. *Angeval* was her name for her lover. And for years they met, embraced, lay together and made a glory of love, if never to love-making's fullest extremity. Despite her yearning for this, her demanding existence had made her prudent, which Angeval, daemon though he might be, and without her ever speaking of it, honoured.

Her body then he caused to blossom and her spirit to thrive. Through all the vileness of her father's illness and rage, his grim death and dismal burial; through the horrors of the evil children; through poverty and misery—Angeval was with her, her guardian angel.

And when Monsieur Carmineau appeared, her *earthly* saviour, there was never between Angeval and herself any hesitation or dismay. For their relationship was of another order, a mating made in heaven.

Only five nights after Jeanne had dutifully lain down with her mortal husband, giving herself from kindness and practicality, and only glad to see him content, she left the Little Chateau on a coin-golden afternoon when Carmineau was from home, and met Angeval among the pines. Then, safe from any stricture, she and *he* at last lay down to consummate their union.

Among the multitude of persons in the house, or workers about the park, not one saw this, or saw Jeanne. She had become invisible, as ever, as Angeval was for any but herself. Likewise, her long calls of ecstasy went unmarked. Or they were mistaken for the feral pleasures of the birds and beasts. Love was not blind. *Love* saw it all. And covered itself in a dome of glass, that shone so bright no other might see *through* it.

⋄⋄⋄⋄⋄

Tonight, as Jeanne sped into the labyrinth of the chateau woods, foxes glided in front of her across gold-lit glades, pausing to stare from wolfish faces. Nightingales whirred in the beech trees. Once a large black animal bounded over her path. She had no notion of what it was—absurdly, she was reminded of Petit. Whatever, it had no care for her and she felt no fear of it. Natural things, though, *did* see her—and presumably also Angeval. And it was, besides, as if these creatures would reveal their benighted activities only to ones as clandestine and lawless as themselves.

Presently there came a twist in the woodland. Jeanne saw the high wall, the open gateway. If any other living thing went in and out of that door, she had never known. Certainly, birds sang about the white ruin, sometimes a fish would rise in the pool there, jewelsmithing a silver ring or a golden one, depending on the hour or the light. Once, when she had been lying in Angeval's arms, a leopard-spotted snake had coiled across her outflung hair. She had not feared it.

Next second, he stepped on to the track.

Ever since Jeanne had become wealthy, so had her lover. That was, he was not adverse now to displaying wealth. To his inordinate beauty was therefore added a suit of finest silk, a shirt ruffled and trimmed with lace. The garments came from an earlier era, but so did Jeanne's, as she had found once she entered the pines. She never questioned it, thinking their clothing better fitted to the ruin and its gardens than what either of them had worn before.

She did not run to him but stopped still, transfixed, dazzled, lost. This had never altered, her amazement every time on seeing him.

And so he moved towards her and reaching out, caught her about her waist.

"I look into your eyes," he said, doing so, "and their light puts out the moon."

"It seems a year since we met," she said. "Or only one minute."

"Both. Neither. Come closer. We're only half-met still. Better. Is it better?"

"Yes," she whispered.

She felt the warmth of his hands, the hardness of his body pressed to hers, burning through her dress, filling her with flame. But he was the lamp, she the moth. She wanted no other thing than to dash herself against and *within* his fire, and be consumed.

This too had never—could never change.

When he lifted her off her feet and carried her away, through the pine shadows and the ormolu brilliance of the moon, as if under endlessly alternating pillars of swimming ebony and orichalc, she lay in his arms and gazed up into his leopard's face. Soon he lay her down on a bank of thick turf, where asphodel was blooming, and wild violets, filling the air with an uncanny perfume as her body crushed them.

He was beside her in a moment. His hair brushed her face and neck, her breasts, as he bent to kiss her thirstily. His mouth had the taste of clear water and was of a perfect heat. The scent of him drugged her.

They did not talk now, said nothing. Their mouths, their hands, bodies said all. To the roots of her bones, shores of her blood, she experienced the feather caresses of his fingers and his lips. His unspeaking tongue yet spoke a language, which it wrote in mantras of lust and longing on her skin. The costly and historic garments, real or illusion, were stripped from them. The joining of their flesh became the only sanity. The earth spun through the night, as if it had left its moorings on some sullen coast and now sailed among the oceanic galaxies. It seemed to her as if *they* flew, he and she, one on another, a curious duality, curving and rushing, their outflung fiery wings scattered with stars, while a thousand golden moons shattered at their impact, worlds ended, and again began.

ଔଔଌଔଌ

They did not separate until the moon was down behind the ruined house, and dawn kindling in a cinnamon thread.

By then, they had said over to each other those prayers by which lovers worship. And drunk cold champagne from a bottle lifted out of the pool.

He had wound violets in her hair. She had held his hands away from her and kissed him until he groaned. Their second love-making had been savage and animal, the third tender, the fourth slower than a serpentine dance.

When she went away, she looked back at him only once, and saw him standing in the fading night, a statue of marble, the flawless ashes now of gold. On leaving, she would only ever turn one single time. No need for more. In her mind, his acts and words of love, the sense of him, were fastened firm as vines. Dew was on the grass like splatters of crystal. The sun was rising. But she never doubted it would.

ಚಃ 3. Azure ಃಃ

She had met Monsieur Carmineau one morning in winter.
Oddly, perhaps, it was on the following night she first encountered Lalise.

Two hours after dawn, Jeanne had been crouching over the schoolroom stove, which as ever the caretaker allowed to remain unlit. Clouds of smoke had already doused the area. Coughing, she had drawn back, hands, face and gown blackened, when the door opened.

The school was run by a pair of religiously-minded ladies who had forgotten most of the teachings of Jesus Christ in their wizened and murderous efforts to serve him. Its supposed charitable function, which was to instruct the offspring of the poor, was carried out by six or seven malnourished young women, of whom Jeanne was one. Regularly viperishly berated, and often unpaid by the benefactors, these girls were also simple prey for their charges. Having little to lose, and rating literacy far below the skills of knife and fist, most of the pupils were sly and venal, also violent. The rest were weaklings who preferred, in the interests of self-preservation, to obey their stronger peers.

Jeanne turned to the opened door in misgiving. The children, when they bothered or were forced by their dangerous relatives to attend, seldom arrived before eight o'clock. Now and then, however, one would appear before the hour, generally on some repulsive mission.

To her surprised relief then, Jeanne saw what was, to her, an elderly gentleman standing in the doorway.

Monsieur Carmineau had come to the school only in order to help present a donation. He was one of a party that included the mayor, but had lost his way during a very irksome and unwished-for tour of the premises, fetching up at Jeanne's particular room by sheer accident.

The moment he saw her, nevertheless, as he later informed her through his lawyer, he had been much taken with her delicacy and superiority of person, indicative of her total unfitness for such thankless work. In short, his aging body, (this he did *not* convey) leapt in a (to him) startling flush of enthusiastic sexual resurgence having to do with the female form. He felt twenty again. And though not such a fool as to think anyone *else* thought him twenty again, he set about wooing Jeanne. He used those means common in such cases. Had she not been of a decent if unelevated family, he would have set her up as his mistress. Or perhaps not. For he had a sentimental, large-hearted streak.

At the time, Jeanne had only been further harassed by appearing as a sooty cursing harpy before the poor old fellow, who seemed madly flustered. She privately grieved she had shocked him. Going home, she learned that very evening that she had indeed, if not in the manner imagined. The lawyer had called, on the pretext of a 'patron' who would find her nicer employment.

Jeanne's father was by then, of course, some years underground. No one else was there to bully or advise. She played the game presented as best she could. She knew the game's nature, though did not get so far as to guess her 'patron' might prefer marriage. The lawyer having taken his leave, in a stunned trance she reviewed what her life might become. Better surroundings, enough to eat, warm winter clothes, some luxuries—best of all, an end to her service at the school. But in trade for these, the indenture of her freedom and personality, trammelled though they already were, to an old man. Enslavement, if under different rules, not entirely dissimilar to her serfdom when with her father.

༺☙❧༻

Taking no supper, Jeanne paced the dank apartment, watching icy rain fall beyond the windows. She pondered then if she should go out, invisible as always when on such a quest, and seek her golden lover. Among the pines, it was always summer. But events had exhausted her, and instead she sought sleep. Whatever outcome might ensue from Monsieur Carmineau's attention, tomorrow she must return to hell, (the school).

Angeval had never entered these sordid rooms. The nearest he had ever approached had been the tree outside, and that only on the first occasion.

Near midnight, something woke Jeanne from her gloomy stupor.

She opened her eyes to see only the wall, but someone spoke to her from the bed's foot.

"Get up, you bitch. You're late. I will meet you in the street."

Jeanne flung about. She was unsure if what she had heard had been the tones of a woman or a man. The voice was low and dark.

What she *saw*—and there was only the slightest instant *to* see it—was a slender male form, a tide of dark hair, the glint—surely it was?—of a *sword*. Then the vision had gone.

COMFORT AND DESPAIR

Jeanne propelled herself from the bed. She was alert and fired by independent anger. By a sort of hunger, too, that was unconnected with food.

Hurling herself into her clothes, she found peculiar alterations there, as if suddenly nothing fitted her, despite doing so perfectly well the day before. Then she was opening the door, running down the cranky stair, expelling herself from the outer doorway and yard on to the cobbled thoroughfare to find this was no longer the street she had lived by and been familiar with for so many years.

She stood amazed. (Indeed, the astonishment of a Monsieur Carmineau, confronted by the rising phoenix of his youthful ardour for a pretty woman, was nothing to Jeanne's upon that alien street.)

She had never beheld, either in ordinary reality or a painting, such a place. Yet, to be fair, very likely she might have *read* of one in, say, the translated tomes of Arabia, Greece or Italy.

The byway was itself made of hard-packed earth that baked in the heat of a dry and sultry night. (The rain then was also gone.) All along the way squatted innumerable tiny shops, these mostly like caves, in which mysterious objects sparkled like eyes from the flare of various flambeaux on poles, or clay dishes of oil, each with a single tear of fire. Here and there a canopy, awning or patterned carpet hung down. There was the smell of spice and dust, oil and alcohol, perfume and incense. High above, abnormal constellations lustered in vast quantities, as if a sack of diamond sugar had been spilled all over the sky. The road was additionally full of people. Some idled, others scurried by. Tall horses, caparisoned with tassels and bells, jingled arrogantly past. Their riders, hawk-like faces muffled in hoods or other wrappings, stared with contempt on all and everything.

Directly across from where she stood—which, turning again, Jeanne saw as in an ornately-carved stone gateway, shut by a stout black door—a tavern blared with lamps.

This is no dream—so Jeanne thought to herself. She was by now, after all, familiar with her relocation to otherness. But unlike the pine-grown garden, this place was of a very different other time, and of another culture, too. Even another earth.

At the same moment, she realized her unmanageable garments had adjusted themselves. Without looking down, although soon she felt compelled to do so, she grasped that now she wore the fine silk shirt, breeches and cloak of some well-off male of the environ. All was embroidered. Even the boots had been incised with silver. And at her side, (she was still most definitely a woman, as this escapade had altered her apparel not her gender) hung a light and lissom sword, with what seemed a sapphire in its pommel.

Jeanne engaged herself by swaggering a little. She next crossed to the inn. And when a boy ran out and begged to know what she would have, she tossed him a coin from a pouch handily at her belt, and called for wine.

No sooner had she downed the cup than she heard again behind her that *voice* which had intruded on her bedroom. This time, it was augmented by a sharp tap on her left shoulder.

Sauntering around, Jeanne beheld her new companion.

There was no doubt, this too was a woman. But clad, like Jeanne, in the exquisite garments of a wealthy male, even to boots and sword. The entire costume was of a deep sky blue leavened with more somber tones, and sewn with lapis lazuli. The hue, however, did not give over its theme. It had informed the colouring of the woman herself. Her eyes were the blue of smoke, and quite beautiful. But the lashes and brows which framed them were of a dark indigo shade, while the cascade of hair, that in the earthly room had seemed black, was itself of an even denser blue tint, smalt blue, like the glaze on a priceless plate. Nor was the woman's skin merely pale. It was like dusk reflecting on white snow.

"Well," said the woman, her face cold as her glamorous colour, "what do you want, then?"

"I?" said Jeanne, amused. "It was you yourself that called me here."

"I never called you. What rubbish. Go back to wherever you came from. Some lesser hell, no doubt."

"With you gone from it, it must be hell now," said Jeanne. "But," she added, "not a *lesser* place, if you were ever in it."

"Why do you pursue me in this way?" demanded the woman.

"Oh, as to that—why do you think?"

"You are obsessed by me," replied the woman.

"Body and soul," Jeanne heard herself answer. This, now, did not confound her. She knew it to be true, just as, her initial disorientation over, she knew the woman. As though they had met every day for all the years of Jeanne's young life, played and fought together as children, later dallied, (yes, dallied too when adults—lovers) at least in Jeanne's many feverish dreams.

But at the declaration, the blue woman drew her sword with a practiced air.

Jeanne felt no misgiving. A tide of delirious abandon went over her. (It was comparable, perhaps, even if she did not then compare them, to those times when Angeval had swept her up in his strong arms, spread her before him, mastered her and ridden with her through the golden spasms of exploding moons.) This was surrender of another order. Yet, like the other, it had the most feared, longed-for, bitter-sweet taste in it of death.

"I must kill you, I see," said Jeanne's beloved foe, "to be rid of you."

"Kill me if you wish. That won't do it. I'd rise from any grave to haunt you. But then, naturally, we are pre-supposing you might succeed." And she drew also, her blade with the sapphire.

The street had cleared. Since their meeting, all passers-by seemed to have withdrawn themselves. Maybe they still watched intently from hidden apertures. Or else, the essential privacy of the duel between Jeanne and her opponent conjured its own supernatural exclusivity.

Only the lamps and torches now, to see, the secret gleams that were not eyes, and the many billion stars.

The swords smote on each other, sent up lightnings, crossing and recrossing. Jeanne became aware that both she and the woman fought—seemingly—with lethal intent. As if one of them *must* surely kill the other.

In spite of the prelude, perhaps Jeanne was taken aback. She had discovered herself well-versed in sword-play, which in her ordinary life she had never been. Versatile she, as did her adversary, translated their match into an elegant and *witty* spectacle, which even the stars might be enthralled to spy upon. But in the instant of realizing where it would lead, this choreography, Jeanne lost her concentration. Only a moment. Enough.

She felt the woman's blade pierce all through her with such minimal difficulty, Jeanne's own body must be like a green stem—without bones—though not lacking blood, because now blood sprang from her, copious, like wine.

The world darkened. Stars, lights, fading. The sapphire sword dropped miles off with a tinsel sound. As she sank, the other caught her. Jeanne did not know if she were dying, not even if the blade had struck her heart. There was no pain.

But the woman with blue hair held her; this was all that mattered. She had the scent to her of open skies, of sand dyed blue with evening. "Listen," the dark voice breathed in Jeanne's ear, across the sea-song of faintness or death. "I love you. *I* love *you*. I will always be with you. You're mine."

COMFORT AND DESPAIR

And in Jeanne's last conscious second, she felt the pressure, the divine invasion of this lover's ice-smouldering kiss. Then through the black door in the gateway Jeanne drifted. And fell back, woundless and whole, into the wretched reality of her own world.

༺༒༻

Jeanne named this daemon *Lalise*. Jeanne did not have a reason for the name, did not select it. Like the events of their first meeting, the name *occurred*, and *was*.

To begin with, nevertheless Jeanne believed the first meeting might be the only one. Or would it, as with Jeanne's first sight of Angeval, not be repeated until some years had passed? This was not to be the case. Her female daemon returned only a few nights later, at the end of the very day, in fact, that several gifts arrived from the elderly suitor, Monsieur Carmineau.

Thereafter, Jeanne met as often with Lalise as with Angeval. And her meetings with Lalise never altered in their main component of flirtatious, adoring, delicious dread. Just as the times with Angeval never changed their tumults of fulfilling passion, their glorious and uncomplex joy.

With Angeval she made love. With Lalise she made a loving and lascivious hate. To the heights of ecstasy Jeanne ascended in each scenario, never disappointed, although the dramas, and their *climaxes*, were so unlike each other in content and form. Honey and opium. Kiss and steel. Lace and blade.

A week after her wedding, folded in previously unknown comforts, (and only a night or so after her full consummation with Angeval) Jeanne and Lalise duelled to the death, as so frequently they did. Yet the outcome was not always fixed. It varied. As did the venue, which was sometimes again the street of shops, or inside the tavern, or sometimes in an open square with fountains, on a night road walled by grasslands, in the nave of some huge building like a cathedral. And Lalise might spurn the duel and turn mockingly away—or else seize Jeanne, embrace her with an incinerating flare of desire, only then to push Jeanne from her with, "You? Oh, most others will find you appealing. But to me, you're *nothing*." Even, once or twice, Lalise would appear in female garb, her midnight hair piled intricately on her head with combs of turquoise. And Jeanne, still clad as a man, would woo her as a man would, attempting Lalise's seduction—and agonizingly almost achieve her goal—then lose, lose all, as always she must, since Lalise, in breeches or petticoats, was her master, and Jeanne an abject slave.

With the golden lover, consummation was essential and certain and could never fail.

With the azure lover, resolution must never be reached. As it never would be.

☙❈❧

Approaching the chateau, Jeanne walked slowly. Like a wild beast of the woods, she scented dawn. She was wonderfully tired out from the pleasures of Angeval's attentions, yet vaguely felt a foreshadow of Lalise, even in the dew that coolly startled her feet. Jeanne sighed, replete, but not sated.

And precisely then, she glimpsed the dark animal she had seen earlier, racing across the distant lawns, its coat spangled with dew. What could it be? Some big dog, perhaps, from a neighbouring farm? Her instincts still honed, Jeanne knew it meant her no harm, although she sensed too it saw her, as non-human creatures always did, while her fellow humans, unvisited themselves by daemons, never could.

Reaching the lower door, Jeanne paused. She aligned herself again with her role of wife. And her thoughts turned to her old, naive husband, Carmineau, with great fondness.

She would, she thought, rather suffer on a rack than hurt him. But she never *could* hurt him. There was no one else who could rival what she had. No human lover would ever tempt her.

Jeanne knew, as few are given to know, will and vow and *mean* it as they may, that she would not be unfaithful to her husband. At least, amid the concrete reality of mankind. Which was all that counted, was it not, in the mortal world.

※ ※ ※

> Two loves I have of comfort and despair,
> Which like two spirits do suggest me still;
> The better angel is a man right fair,
> The worser spirit a woman coloured ill.
> —William Shakespeare, *Sonnet 144,* 1609

Epilog. Amethyst

He woke, some faint unusual noise woke him. Leaving his bed, Monsieur Carmineau went to the long window and looked out on his park. He wondered if he would see Jeanne out there, on one of her nocturnal jaunts, and smiled a little, thinking of her, and of that. He did not grudge her, any more than he grudged her the luxuries their marriage afforded. She was a lovely girl, his Jeanne, and he had long wished for a pretty wife to adorn his house. In any event, it was *not* Jeanne he saw, there in the mauve hour before sunrise. It was the dog! By the stars, the black hound of La Tupe, Petit—who had been borne home in the carriage hours back, and doubtless locked indoors as ever. But now Petit was rushing over the lawn towards the woods, with a rabbit in his jaws. Except, of course, the rabbit was abnormally large, and *silvery*, and not really a rabbit. Instead, it would be Petit's *daemon* of a rabbit, which no doubt he always successfully caught, and in vast quantities. And what other daemons, Carmineau curiously wondered, did Petit possess? A paramour. . . ?

Who would have though it? How splendid! That a dog too might live another life, while back on his cushion Petit's big furred body *seemed* to lie, the simulacrum twitching in sleep. Yet Petit was out *there*. As Jeanne probably was. While he, Maurice Carmineau—

Ah. Monsieur half turned, and saw the phantom shape that now occupied his bed. It was old and grey and it snored softly, poor old man. While he, obviously, *he* stood at the window.

Carmineau glanced down at himself. He was twenty-five years of age, his hair the deep brown of polished wood, his skin smooth. Quite muscular, yet very slim. An attractive young man and see, dear me, already erect.

Because, without the whisper of a lie, he knew what came next. What *always* came next.

It did, too.

The panelled wall had melted. And there he stood as well, the *other* young man. Oh God, so beautiful, in his amethyst silk coat of over a hundred years ago, and his black hair worn unpowdered and long, to tantalize—as it did, oh it *did*—and his shirt undone and—such an abundance. Such eagerness so visible, even though the pale handsome face was grave.

"Why, Maurice. How is you are so selfishly *out* of bed? Well then, dear friend, you'd better come with me to *my* bed, hadn't you? Before I perish of *lack*."

And Maurice left the window and the pre-dawn light, the dog, and his wife, and crossed to his lover, kissing and kissing him, and cupping as he did so the excellent greeting already evidenced, through the purple clothes.

"I missed you, Pierre. Three days and nights since we met."

WRIT OF EXCEPTION

by Madeleine E. Robins

Madeleine Robins is a former fencer, a lifelong Anglophile, a parent, a New Yorker, an administrator, and a student of cake decorating. She is also the author of nine books (including *Point of Honour* and *Petty Treason*), the mother of two daughters, the person who throws the ball for Emily the Amazing Air Dog. She blogs occasionally at deepgenre.com and all the time at madrobins.livejournal.com.

    About this story, Madeleine writes, "When offered the chance to write another swashbuckling tale, I could not resist the opportunity to return to Meviel, a very new world which seems to bring out my fascination with playing with gender roles and expectations. The first line or two of the story come directly from my research on the meaning of family in medieval Europe; if you take the idea that marriage is for the preservation of property, then maybe it doesn't matter who marries who so much as what property they join and protect. Voila: 'Writ of Exception'!"

"Don't be stupid, girl. Marriage is for the consolidation of wealth and property. Romance is for diversion. And love—" Deira do Morbegon's tone was derisive. "Love is for poets."

"Mamma, I know better than to speak of love and marriage in the same breath. But *this*—even if I liked it, what good would it bring? There can be no children—"

"When our families are joined, one of you will get a child from somewhere." Madam do Morbegon shrugged as if children might be bought at the Actenar bazaar. "You may take lovers now and then. Discreetly."

For a moment, Madam do Morbegon appeared to soften; she sat on the unmade bed beside her daughter and took her daughter's hand in her own. "If your brother had not died, *he* would have married her. Evida do Caudon and I have schemed since we were girls to unite our families, even before she married the Cindon. Your father meets with the bishop today to get a Writ of Exception; such marriages are uncommon, I grant you, but—I was at court when Prince Ebuen wed Prince Beqis, and Meviel annexed his principality. When the property is *important* . . ."

Madam do Morbegon reflected for a moment upon the importance of the Caudon holdings. "Ellais, she inherits *all*. You will be Cindiese one day, or at least the consort of a Cindiese. It is an excellent match except in one *little* way." She rose from the bed, pulling her hand from her daughter's. "Now get dressed. You will wish to look well for your betrothed."

It was a command. Madame do Morbegon left before her daughter could protest anew. Ellais heard voices, low, outside her door, and then Lilsa, her body-maid, entered the room, almost invisible behind a pile of dresses.

"Madame says we're to be turned out nice for visiting," she said around the fabric. "I thought the green, or praps—" Lilsa made the error of meeting her charge's eyes. "Is he *very* bad, sweet?"

"You don't know?"

"How could I? Madame set her maid to watch at the door while she talked to you." Lilsa sniffed aggrievedly. "But she did say *betrothed*. Who is it? Is he old? Rich, at least?"

WRIT OF EXCEPTION 263

"Rich," Ellais agreed. "And young. But not *he*. They've betrothed me to Taigna me Caudon."

"*Taigna—*"

Ellais nodded. "Papa is meeting with the bishop about a Writ of Exception for the Marriage. Mamma and the Cindiese have scheduled the wedding in six weeks—just long enough to prepare two sets of bride clothes. The Cindon and Papa are delighted with the settlements. My wishes count for nothing, and Taigna—God alone knows what she makes of this. Mamma has made it plain I have no chance of refusing. Married I will be, to a girl I'm on no better than speaking terms with."

"Praps the bishop will say no to the Writ," Lilsa suggested dubiously.

"I wish I thought so. But it's all money and property; there'll be talk, but Papa is wild to have the Caudon properties in the family, and the Cindon is apparently just as interested in our money; between the two of them, they'll bend the bishop to their will. I'm sure of it."

"Well. What can't be cured must be endured." Lilsa spread the dresses she held upon the bed in a colorful fan. "Madame said you was to be ready to make a call within the hour. I think the green, don't you?"

ೞಚಿ೩೮ಎ೩

House Caudon stood three streets from the Great Hub and the House of Speakers in the Vocarle district. The white stone edifice rose four highly ornamented stories; to Ellais's eye, it resembled a towering wedding cake. She, with her mother one step behind her (*to block all escape*, Ellais thought) was shown to a drawing room by an elderly manservant, and within a minute the Cindiese do Caudon appeared in the doorway, one hand firmly clasped round the wrist of her daughter, Taigna. From the look of things, Ellais reflected, Taigna was no better pleased than she at the engagement.

The older women greeted each other with uncomplicated joy. The girls curtsied dully, neither meeting the other's eye. When the two mothers fell to planning, their daughters were silent, until Madame do Morbegon, lips pursed, broke off a discussion of veils to rap Ellais on the wrist and exhort her to make some conversation with her betrothed.

"For heaven's sake, you ought to be excited! This is the day you've waited for all your life; if you do not wish to be a part of planning it, at least say something to *dear* Taigna."

Madame do Caudon nodded her head, made imposing by a beribboned cap of lace and black lilies that threatened to pitch forward into her lap. "Tainey, my dear, why not take your—take Ellais out to the conservatory and see if you can agree about flowers for your bridal posies. I think they should each carry the same, don't you?" The Cindiese turned back to Deira do Morbegon, and the two mothers were lost in discussion at once. Taigna rose from her chair and led Ellais to the back of the house and the large, draughty conservatory.

Ellais examined a pot of scentless flowers.

"Well." Taigna's voice echoed.

"Well. Are you . . . happy?" Ellais asked.

"*Happy?*" For the first time, Taigna me Caudon met Ellais's gaze straight on. So far from being pleased, she looked furious. "Happy! I have made it perfectly plain to my parents for years that I had no wish to marry, at least not until I had finished my schooling, and perhaps a year or two of study at the University in Hadsilon. Happy to be married at nineteen, without so much as a first degree to my name? Are you mad?"

Ellais gaped. "A first degree? You want to be a scholar?"

"I always have. Papa promised me that I needn't think of marriage until I had at least that, and then your brother dies and suddenly Papa and your father are in a great hurry to marry us off, lest one of *us* die and stall their plans to unite our fortunes forever. Mama is saying I must stop attending classes, that it's not suitable for an affianced woman. Well *I* never wanted to be affianced, and I—"

"You don't mind it's *me*?" Ellais broke in.

Taigna blinked. "Is there something wrong with you?"

Ellais stamped her foot so hard that her dark curls danced around her face. "You don't mind that we are both women?"

Taigna considered. "I suppose you might be rather less . . . intrusive than a man. But Mama says once we're wed I'll have to give up studying, so it hardly matters, does it?"

"If you're Cindiese, oughtn't you to be able to do as you like?" Ellais asked. A flower, pinched between her thumb and forefinger, came off its stem in her hand.

"*When* I'm Cindiese—but Papa may live for *years.* All that time, I'd be falling behind in my work."

Taigna was not Ellais's idea of a scholar; until now, she had assumed that all such were elderly men with braided white beards and heavy black robes, wandering through the corridors of the university with abstracted airs, or scurrying about Meviel to tutor the children of great families. Her own schooling had been intended only to make her literate enough to read romances, of which she had consumed many, and numerate enough to keep a set of household books.

"What can we do?" Ellais asked.

Taigna blinked nearsightedly. "Do?"

Ellais looked about her for a chair, saw a wrought-iron loveseat, and dragged her betrothed to it. When they were seated knee to knee, she leaned forward conspiratorially. "You do *not* wish to marry me."

Taigna shrugged. "I don't want to marry at all. If I must, I suppose you're—"

"*I* don't wish to marry *you!*" Ellais whispered fiercely. "I want to have a regular sort of life, with a man and babies and everything I ever expected. I know better than to expect romance, but at the very least I want the possibility that I might—I might—" Words failed her.

Taigna frowned, her sandy brows drawing together. "What are we to do?"

Neither had an answer for such a question. The two girls sat, knee-to-knee and dark head to light, considering, until a servant came to summon them back to the drawing room. When asked if they had agreed upon flowers for their bridal posies, Ellais suggested freesias at the same moment that Taigna asked for daisies, and the two mothers shook their heads and decreed roses and balm with ivy. Madame do Morbegon swept her daughter away with every assurance of kind wishes, echoed by the Condiese. Ellais parted from her betrothed with a look of despair.

ఇఁఠ

Once the Writ of Exception had been granted and the engagement made public, neither Ellais nor Taigna could escape whispers or speculative nods when they went out. The girls paid formal calls, one upon the other, but their parents seemed determined to keep them from any sort of private conference, and neither girl wanted to commit to writing anything their mothers might take into their heads to read. As the day of the wedding drew near, Ellais me Morbegon spent hours making and rejecting plots to escape.

A fortnight before the wedding, she was invited to a musical evening with her father; Madame do Morbegon had no ear for music and pled a sick headache to stay home. Master zo Morbegon settled his daughter on a straight-backed chair next to Taigna me Caudon and vanished at once into the smoking room with the Cindon. As the rest of the company seemed happy to give both girls a wide berth and examine their relationship from afar, Ellais and Taigna had, for the first time in almost a month, the opportunity to speak as privately as one might against the din of a string quintet.

After courtesies had been exchanged, Ellais asked, "Have you any money?"

Taigna took up her beaded purse. "I have a little, I think—a few—"

"Not *with* you. At home. Have you any money?"

"Oh." Taigna pursed her lips and considered. "Just enough for vails and pin money."

"Have you any jewels you can sell?"

Taigna's eyes opened wide. "Sell? But Mama would find out—"

Ellais shook her head. "Not if we run away."

The cello hit a low, sustained note. "*Run away?*"

Ellais nodded. "I've already sent my maid out with some of my jewelry—I told her I needed it to give presents to the servants before I left home—and I have nearly five hundred *senesti* so far. That might last us, oh, a six-month if we are careful. If you have as much, that's a year we could live before we needed to think of working."

"Working? Where? And what? I don't know how to—"

"You could tutor and I could—" she shrugged. "Sew, or wait at table, or . . . something. Not in Meviel, though. We'll have to go somewhere else."

"But how?"

"I know someone—"

Taigna raised an eyebrow. "A *friend?*"

"Not that sort of friend." Ellais wrinkled her nose. "The stableman's son. He'll hire us a carriage, and we'll go to Coustel, on the coast. And thence to Hadsilon, if you like, so you can study."

For the first time in the weeks of their betrothal, Taigna's brows went up instead of down. "*Study?*"

"It's what you want, isn't it?"

"Well, yes, but what will *you* do?"

"*Not* marry you."

"As good as, if we're traveling together," Taigna said practically.

"We can travel as sisters."

After a few moments' serious thought, Taigna nodded. "There's logic to it. *If* we can travel fast enough to avoid my father's men; he's sure to send someone."

Ellais agreed. "Travel like the wind, and let it bear us across the sea to Hadsilon."

When Master zo Morbegon returned to collect his daughter, he found the betrothed couple sitting quietly, attending to the music. He could be pardoned for believing, looking at the girls' faces, that they grew daily more resigned to their marriage.

***

Four nights before the wedding, Ellais pled exhaustion brought on by the relentless demands of the dressmaker, and went early to bed. When Lilsa had finished fussing over her and left for the night, Ellais left off her die-away manner and hopped from the bed. She dressed in the plainest gown she owned, pulled a satchel from under the bed, and wrapped herself in a woolen cloak she had taken from a peg in the servants' hall. Thus disguised, she went down to the mews.

The stableman's son, true to a promise extracted from him earlier that day at the cost of five *senesti*, had a carriage and pair awaiting her. It was an old carriage with sprung upholstery and an unpleasant smell of cat piss, but it seemed sturdy, and the driver appeared sober. Within the hour, Taigna me Caudon had joined Ellais, and the carriage was rattling west toward the coast.

Taigna spent the first several hours in the throes of motion sickness made worse by the smell of the carriage, but finally fell sleep. Ellais, too excited to doze, went over her plans. They had between them a little more than fifteen hundred *senesti*, and that would not last them forever. Taigna would be a scholar, and earn her way teaching; but what could *she* do? All

Ellais's skills were those of a nicely raised young woman: embroidery and china painting and the recitation of epic poetry. As the carriage thumped along, she realized she didn't even know how to make a bed properly. You tucked the sheets in somehow, but how to make them smooth, as they were in her mother's house?

She fell asleep musing that elopements were easier in novels, and woke to the sound of voices. The carriage had stopped; could they be in Coustel already? A peek from behind the leathern curtain showed her that it was still night. The driver had come down from his seat and was talking with a man whose face was shadowed from the moonlight by a broad hat brim. A few coins changed hands and the driver walked away. The other man began to unhitch the horses from her carriage.

Ellais wanted to leap from the carriage and chase her driver. She had paid him good money, and now someone else was bribing him! And this other man, who was he? Caution kept her silent, which was good, for a moment later another man joined the first and helped unhitch the second horse.

"Whozzit zis time?" the newcomer asked.

"Coupla wommin, Tadde says," the first one answered. "Probly got jewels and gold and—"

"And theys *wommin*," the first one agreed. "Tie 'em horses up and less see what we got."

Ellais looked around her for a weapon but found none. Taigna, asleep on the opposite seat, snored softly. The handle to the door rattled and Ellais acted without plan. She pushed the door outward, knocking the man off balance, and jumped out of the carriage, scolding as she came.

"Put our horses back immediately! What do you think you're doing? If my—my sister and I don't reach Coustel by morning. there will be immense trouble!"

The man stepped back a pace, evidently taken aback by Ellais's excellent impersonation of her mother in the servant's hall. She hoped that he might turn and run, but after a moment he grinned wide and grabbed her wrist to pull her to him.

"'is one got a temper," he called to his mate.

"I certainly have, and if you don't take your hands off me immedi—" Ellais was silenced by a backhanded slap.

"I say 'is one got a temper," he repeated. "Ai, Pol, I say—"

At the same moment that Ellais looked back at the carriage two things happened: Taigna, awake at last, began to scream, and the second highwayman lurched backward across the clearing. The first highwayman released Ellais's wrist. His mate rose unsteadily to his feet and pointed into the shadows. A second later a third man—tall, wearing a hat which shadowed his face in the moonlight—stepped forward. He had a staff in his hands.

Taigna kept screaming.

Ellais's assailant grinned, drew a long knife, and stepped forward to meet the new man. She knew too little about fighting to entirely follow what she saw, but she could say afterward that the new man had blocked the highwayman's blow with one end of his staff before he swung the other end into the man's gut. The highwayman bent double with an "oof." The second highwayman had scarpered off with the carriage horses before his mate hit the ground. Their rescuer paused to deal the first man a knock to the head, then stepped forward to bow to Ellais.

"Good evening." His eyes were dark, his smile polite. "I trust you are unharmed?"

Ellais was disconcerted by such manners here, now. Their rescuer did not sound like a courtier of the Hub, but neither did he sound like a ruffian from the Dedenor. Had she been asked, she would have said he was a gentleman farmer or a prosperous physician.

The man turned toward the carriage where Taigna, blinking, pale, and no longer screaming, peered into the moonlight.

"And down you come." He lifted Taigna down from the carriage and set her beside Ellais. "I do wonder at your parents letting you travel through the countryside at night, all unprotected."

Ellais opened her mouth to spin a story about a family emergency, but at the same moment Taigna vomited.

Their rescuer, looking down at the flow which had spattered his boots, grimaced. "An effective weapon in the short term, perhaps, but ultimately not compelling."

He picked Taigna up, stepped over the mess she had made, and sat her on the side of the road.

"It appears your horses are gone and you are several hours ride from the city—I assume you are come from there? There's a town some five miles that way—" the man gestured ahead on the road, "but perhaps you'd prefer to go back—"

"*No!*" Ellais and Taigna spoke with one voice. Ellais continued, "If we can only reach somewhere where we can hire an *honest* carriage."

"Ah. That might be another ten or twelve miles ahead."

Ellais raised her chin with resolve. "There is a moon. We shall walk."

The man shook his head. "Ten miles in the dark, in city shoes?"

"If we must." Ellais reached her hand to Taigna to help her to her feet. "Come, we'll start walking."

Taigna stopped. "Our boxes!"

Ellais shook her head. "We shall have to send back for them."

"But my books! At least let me bring the most important."

"Books?" their rescuer said. He sounded amused.

"Books!" Ellais was not amused in the least. "Taigna, do you want to carry a bag full of books ten or twelve miles?" But Taigna had already clambered onto the carriage and was unstrapping her satchel.

"Take this!" She tossed a thick tome down to Ellais. "And this one. And—"

The man caught the third book. "*Philosophical Reflections Upon the Virtue of Familial Gems, with Particular Investigation into the History of Luck,*" he read. "Well thumbed, too. It goes against the grain to permit two scholars to walk alone in the middle of the night. Permit me to escort you until you find a place that will hire you a carriage."

"Thank you, sir," Taigna said. "I am Taigna me Caudon, and this is—"

"I am her sister," Ellais said quickly. She glared at Taigna.

The man bowed. "Vaun ha Tesne, honored to make your acquaintance."

The three, each carrying one of Taigna me Caudon's books, started down the road.

Ellais had been too optimistic about her shoes. In less than a mile, the soles of her "walking boots" had developed holes, and there was a growing blister on the inside of her left heel. Taigna began to limp sometime in the second mile. Vaun ha Tesne said nothing. Finally, when they had been walking for over an hour, Ellais sat by the side of the road and unlaced her boots. "Better I walk barefoot."

"There's a shepherd's cot a little way up that path," Vaun ha Tesne said. "You might sleep in the darkest part of the night—see, the moon is setting—and start fresh in the morning."

"We can't," Ellais murmured.

"We *must*," Taigna returned. "Beside, who would think to look for us in a shepherd's cottage? Ellais, my feet *hurt*."

Ellais turned back to their companion. "How is it you know so much about this road and shepherd's cots on it?"

"My family's property is a few miles in that direction. Another thirty or forty feet ahead, past that shrub—aha, there is the cot." Vaun ha Tesne held the lower branches of the shrub to permit the women to pass. "My horse came up lame a mile or two before I found you, so I was already resigned to walking,"

The cot was a small, square stone structure, mossy on the north side, with no sign of recent habitation by shepherd or sheep. Inside, it was unfurnished and chilly, but the reed roof appeared sturdy and there was room to lie on the packed earth. Taigna sat down at once, stretched out on the floor with her books piled at her head, and fell asleep.

"I'll stay out here," Vaun ha Tesne said. "Watch for badgers and highwaymen and such."

Ellais nodded. She had not been sleepy until the possibility of sleep presented itself; now she was exhausted. "Thank you. I'm sorry I have been so suspicious. It's only—"

"Two women traveling alone." Ha Tesne nodded. "Sleep. I'll watch."

Ellais took only a moment to wrap her cloak around her, curl up next to her betrothed, and fall soundly asleep.

ಬ‍ೞ‍ಏ‍ಐ

When she woke, the morning sky was milky white. Ellais stepped out of the cot and almost stumbled over Vaun ha Tesne, who sat with his back against the wall, breathing rhythmically. She noted creeping roses on the side of the cottage—that had not been visible in the moonlight—and a low stone fence on one side of the path.

"So what is it you and your friend are fleeing?" His voice was quiet and gentle. "If you tell me, I might be able to help you."

"I cannot see how," Ellais said. But she turned back to face him.

"At least give me the opportunity to try."

Ellais found herself explaining her betrothal and the plans she had made to escape it. "Taigna only wants to study—she said she might as well marry me as anyone. But I—"

"Your heart is given somewhere else?"

She shook her head. "But it *might* be. Someday. Of course, Mamma keeps telling me that marriage and love have nothing to do with each other."

Vaun ha Tesne nodded thoughtfully. "I suppose so. I know that if I loved a woman I should not let a thing like a legal fiction of marriage stand in my way."

"That's very romantic. But with a husband—if I didn't like him, I might suffer under his dominion, but at least I'd be done with my parents meddling. This marriage will be the worst of everything."

"Which one of you plays the husband?"

Ellais wrinkled her nose. "Plays the husband?"

"In most marriages, one spouse has dominion over the other—if one of you were a man, there would be no question. A woman is passed from her father's dominion to that of her husband. In a case like this, dominion is usually spelt out in the Writ."

"I've seen the Writ," Ellais said slowly. "There's no mention of dominion."

Ha Tesne laughed. "Well, then I imagine it would be up to the two of you to decide who rules the house."

"We could take turns," Ellais said thoughtfully. After a moment, a smile quirked at the corner of her mouth. "Are you sure of this? That if one of us has dominion, that ends the other's parents' right to interfere?"

Ha Tesne nodded. "I studied law for a while, until my father died and I had to come home to manage our farms and property. But the theory should be entirely defensible. I doubt your parents would want to appear before the Magistracy to contest the matter."

"You *should* have been a lawyer," Ellais said firmly.

"As it happens, I like farming. I like knowing the land and the people working it. I'm proud of my home. In fact, if I bring back a carriage for you, you would like to see it? Before you continue your escape, that is."

Ellais had no chance to answer; a cloud of dust plumed beyond the shrubs as if several riders moving at great speed were approaching.

"*Inside*," Vaun ha Tesne said.

A man on foot rounded the shrub, wearing the livery of House Caudon. Ellais ducked into the cot and shook Taigna. "It's your father's men!"

Taigna sat up, blinking. Outside, Ellais heard the approaching man hail Vaun ha Tesne. She turned away from Taigna to peer around the doorsill.

Vaun had risen and was going to meet the Caudon servant. He had his staff in one hand, walking as if with its support. Ellais did not hear the Caudon rider's words, but she heard Vaun greet him as friend and ask how he could help. There was a low murmur from the Caudon rider.

"No, there's only me. My horse was lamed, and I paused here in my walk home."

This time Ellais heard the rider's words: "You'll not mind if I look for myself?"

"Do you not trust me?" Vaun sounded affronted.

"Beg pardon, sir, but it's my job to be certain." The man pushed Vaun aside and started for the cot. Vaun's staff came up, caught him square on the jaw, and the man dropped. In the sudden silence, Vaun returned to the cot.

"Ladies, I think it is time that you decide if you want to continue your elopement or return home. I pledge to assist you either way, but that fellow was not alone, and his friends are doubtless going to come round the path in a moment or—and here they come." Ha Tesne stepped outside again.

Three appeared behind the fence, calling a name, seeking the first Caudon rider. Ellais returned to her post at the door, explaining Vaun ha Tesne's interpretation of the law to Taigna.

One rider spied the fallen body of his companion, cried out, and all three drew swords and made to attack ha Tesne. Ellais, horrified, would have run out the door except for Taigna, who grabbed onto her arm with both hands, reminding her friend that she had no weapon, no skill, and would only cause more trouble.

Vaun ha Tesne had disarmed one rider with a circular swoop of his staff, buffeting the man across the shoulders so that he was knocked to his knees, retching. Another man stepped in, cutting downward at Vaun's shoulder; he barely caught the foible of the blade with the back of his staff, and stepped back to face his attacker. Behind them, Ellais saw the last rider approaching, circling around between Vaun and the cot.

Without thought, Ellais took up the heaviest of Taigna's books, stepped outside, and hit the rider on the side of the head, as hard as she could. He staggered but did not fall, so she hit him again, on the other side of the head. This time, he dropped to his knees. She raised the book again for a third blow.

"Ellais, *stop!*" It was Taigna behind her. "We'll go back! There's no need to hurt anyone—for anyone to be hurt. You, there!" She called to the swordsman who was still harrying their protector. "Stop at once! I am Taigna me Caudon, and I want you to leave that man alone! He thought he was protecting us! We're ready to come back to Meviel—I hope you have a carriage ready, for I cannot walk any further."

"Are you certain?" Ellais and Vaun ha Tesne asked in the same moment.

"Yes. Thank you, sir." Taigna nodded at Vaun. "I am sure, with your counsel, we will do very well. Ellais, are we agreed?"

Ellais nodded. "Although I wish I'd had a staff rather than a book," she murmured. Taigna took the book out of her hands and cuddled it to her chest.

Vaun ha Tesne lowered his staff.

His opponent appeared put out but lowered his own weapon. "You'll come back to Meviel?" he asked.

"We will," Taigna agreed. Ellais nodded.

When the riders had recovered themselves and been dissuaded from fetching Vaun ha Tesne back to the city to be charged with assault, the girls said goodbye to their protector. Ha Tesne bowed over Taigna's hand; "I can see you will make a very fine Cindiese, as well as a scholar."

Then he kissed Ellais's hand. She felt her face go hot.

"I'm sorry not to see your house," she said quietly. "Thank you for your help, Master ha Tesne."

"It was my very great pleasure to help, Mistress me Morbegon."

෴

The marriage of Taigna me Caudon, Cindiese-apparent of House Caudon, to Ellais me Morbegon, was celebrated with enough ceremony and lace to satisfy both their mothers, each of whom wept at the service with relief and joy. The Writ of Exception, illuminated with gold leaf and sealed with the Bishop's Great Seal, was on display for all to see. The Cindon zo Caudon clapped his daughter's new father-in-law on the shoulder and thought of the thousands of *senesti* that were now in his daughter's control, and thereby, of course, his own. Similarly, Master Meil zo Morbegon considered the extensive holdings to which his daughter was now half-heir, and was content. And the brides themselves appeared to have put all reluctance or reservation behind them and to be genuinely pleased with their marriage. At the end of the fete given to celebrate their nuptials, the two women left in their own carriage for the house in the suburbs of the Vocarle district that was part of their dower.

The next morning, Taigna do Caudon-Morbegon returned to her studies. The sight of a married woman of rank wearing the black stole of a first scholar and walking unaccompanied to the university, sent ripples of curiosity and dismay through the best society of Meviel. By mid-afternoon, Madame do Morbegon was demanding entrance to her daughter's house. She found Ellais in a tidy parlor where the chairs had been pushed against the walls, swinging a staff about inexpertly.

"Ellais, stop that at once. You'll break something!"

"Good afternoon, Mamma." Ellais put the staff down and advanced to kiss her mother.

"Ellais! Your—Taigna do Caudon was at the university this morning, and I find you here, doing—whatever you are doing. What *are* you doing?"

From her sleeve Ellais took a kerchief with which she wiped her brow. "Please be seated, Mamma. I am trying to learn something I saw in my travels. And my—" she smiled. "My *wife* is at her studies."

"Well it stops now, do you hear me? This instant!"

Ellais drew her mother to sit beside her upon one of the sophas that lined the room. She spoke gently. "Mamma, do you realize that your authority over me stopped when you wed me to Taigna? If *she* does not object to my drilling in the parlor, why should you?"

Madame do Morbegon's eyes bulged with outrage. "Because it's wrong! Talk is already beginning; they're saying—"

"Mamma, since I no longer intend to move among the courtiers of the Hub, what they say is of no concern to me. And since Taigna intends to be a scholar—without the beard, I think, unless they absolutely require it—gossip matters not to her." Ellais released her mother's hand and stood again. "We made very certain of this before we were wed, Taigna and I. You—and Papa and her parents—wanted this marriage, but it has given us dominion over each other, and taken that control from you. You may disinherit us, of course—but that would only undo all your plans to wed our fortunes. So. Taigna and I, as good married couples do, want each for the other what she wants. Taigna wants to be a scholar, and I think that is excellent. I want—"

What Ellais wanted was not to be spoken, for Lilsa appeared in the door, begged her mistress's pardon, and announced a visitor.

"Master Vaun ha Tesne, miss—mistress. Says he knows you from the road?"

"Here? In Meviel?"

"In Meviel, and in your parlor, if you will permit me."

Madame do Morbegon beheld a tall, fair-haired man in the doorway, dressed for riding in the country rather than calls in Town. When she looked at her daughter to see how Ellais regarded this unmannerly stranger, she was surprised to see her blushing. "Ellais, who is this?"

The stranger bowed deeply. "Vaun ha Tesne, at your service, madam. By your resemblance to your beautiful daughter, I take it that you are Madame do Morbegon?" The man touched his hand to his heart in salute, then turned back to Ellais. "I hope you do not mind the intrusion. I wanted to felicitate you upon your marriage."

Ellais turned to her mother. "This gentleman . . . helped us in the woods, Mamma. You owe him your thanks. " She smiled Vaun. "As do I, sir."

"Do you? I came to renew my invitation to see my house. You and your bride, of course."

"My bride will be much engaged with her studies for some time." Ellais felt curiously out of breath. "I, however, am hardly engaged at all."

"If she can endure your absence—"

"I should like to come. Perhaps, sir, you could teach me to use a staff as you do."

"That might take some time," Vaun ha Tesne said soberly.

"I have nothing but time, sir. And a good deal to learn."

This was too much for Deira do Morbegon. She grabbed her daughter by the hand and pulled her from the room. "Have you lost your mind?" she whispered. "A visit to the estate of an unmarried man, when you are just barely wed yourself?"

"Well, I've little else to do, Mama. Taigna will be at her studies, and I would like very much to see how Master ha Tesne manages his property, since I will one day have the management of the Caudon properties, as you have reminded me often enough."

"Ellais, you're married!"

"I am yes, Mamma," Ellais said firmly. "But that's no problem; you often told me that marriage is not an impediment to love."

Ellais do Morbegon-Caudon kissed her mother's cheek in dismissal, then returned to the parlor and her waiting guest.

About the Editor

Deborah J. Ross has been writing science fiction and fantasy professionally since 1982. In addition to teaching writing and leading writer's workshops, she served as Secretary of Science Fiction and Fantasy Writers of America. Under her former name, Deborah Wheeler, she published two science fiction novels, *Jaydium* (DAW, 1993) and *Northlight* (DAW 1995) and approximately fifty short stories in *Asimov's, Fantasy and Science Fiction, Sisters of the Night, Star Wars: Tales From Jabba's Palace, Realms of Fantasy,* and almost all of the *Sword & Sorceress* anthologies.

    Recent projects include continuing the Darkover series created by the late Marion Zimmer Bradley: *The Fall of Neskaya* (DAW 2001), *Zandru's Forge* (DAW 2003), *A Flame in Hali* (DAW 2004), *The Alton Gift* (DAW 2007), *Hastur Lord* (forthcoming), and an original fantasy series, *The Seven-Petaled Shield*. In 2008, she made her editorial debut with the first *Lace and Blade*.

    Deborah lives in a redwood forest in Central California with her husband, fellow writer Dave Trowbridge, and an assortment of animals.

Books in beautiful packages...

Norilana Books
Classics

www.norilana.com

Publishing some of the best, rare, and precious classics of world literature in trade hardcover and paperback editions.

Delight Your Imagination...
with original anthologies from
Norilana Books!

Norilana Books
www.norilana.com

**Baroque, lush, erotic, occult.
Or a stodgy decadent antique...
Strange new fantasy in the vein of
Mervyn Peake's *Gormenghast*...**

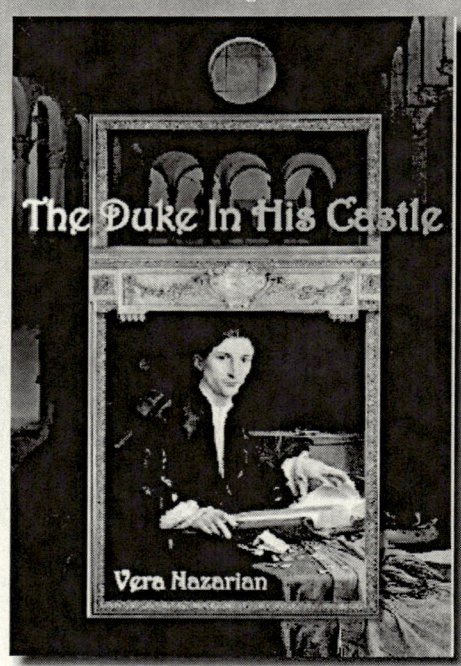

"Nazarian has created a work of great power, one that is lyrical, magical, mysterious and enthralling... a fairy tale for the thinking reader."
—**Colleen Cahill,** *SFRefu*

"Vera Nazarian's superb novella *The Duke in His Castle* uses the form of a classic fairy tale or fable to explore the psychology of good, evil, ennui, and despair in terms that are anything but black and white.... a sequence of moving, disturbing, sensual dialogs and encounters that change the very concept of power, from the acts of gods or great mages to something more subtle that may lie within human grasp."
—**Faren Miller,** *Locus*

"*The Duke in His Castle* is philosophy couched in a fairy tale couched in a murder mystery tinged with children's games. It's a kaleidoscope of thought and emotion, the howling winds of despair, and the sometimes soft, sometimes fierce flow of life. Not only is it quickly absorbing and a quick read, but it sits up and begs for repeat visits..."
—***The Green Man Review***

The Duke In His Castle
a literary fantasy novella by
Nebula Award-nominated author
and award-winning artist
Vera Nazarian

Illustrated by the author.

ISBN-13: 978-1-934648-42-1
ISBN-10: 1-934648-42-6

Norilana Books
www.norilana.com

"I would recommend *The Duke in His Castle* to new fantasy readers to give them a sense of the originality that is still possible in the post-Tolkien era, and to those sunken into fantasy-apathy as a way to break out, like Rossian from their prison."
—**Georges T. Dodds,** *SF Site*

Coming soon from Norilana Books...

TaLeKa

A New Dedicated Imprint

Showcasing the Works of **Tanith Lee**
and the Art of **John Kaiine**...

www.tanithlee.com

First title from the *Tales of the Flat Earth*

Night's Master by **Tanith Lee**
September 1, 2009

www.norilana.com/norilana-taleka.htm

Where can you find jewels of language from **Catherynne M. Valente, Mike Allen, and JoSelle Vanderhooft**?

Curiosities
the imprint of poetry and unclassifiable delights...

Norilana Books
www.norilana.com

Discover **Modean Moon** and her award-winning novels set in "Pitchlyn County."

Modean Moon is the critically acclaimed author of works of quality women's fiction, regionally flavored and with a thrilling hint of the supernatural.

Her novels have won numerous awards, including the prestigious Romance Writers of America's RITA, OKRWA's National Readers Choice, and Oklahoma Writers' Federation's Teepee Award, as well as being finalists or nominees for the Holt Medallion and Romantic Times Magazine's Reviewers' Choice Award.

Norilana Books
www.norilana.com

Printed in the United States
138095LV00003B/28/P